Readers love *David, Renewed*
by DIANA COPLAND

"In *David, Renewed*, Diana Copland has delivered a classic, well-crafted romance in which not only the main characters are appealing, but the supporting crew are wonderful as well."
—All About Romance

"I would highly recommend this book to anyone who loves MM romance!"
—Gay Book Reviews

"*David, Renewed* gets a rare 5-stars rating from me— literally could not put this book down."
—Alpha Book Club

"If you like hurt/comfort stories of characters dealing with real life issues within a small town setting and a feel good HEA, give *David, Renewed* a try."
—Joyfully Jay

"Sexy and very sweet… the story was fun to read and I can't wait to see what other stories that are out there."
—MM Good Book Reviews

By DIANA COPLAND

DELTA RESTORATIONS
David, Renewed
Michael, Reinvented

Published by DREAMSPINNER PRESS
www.dreamspinnerpress.com

DIANA COPLAND

Michael, Reinvented

Published by
DREAMSPINNER PRESS

5032 Capital Circle SW, Suite 2, PMB# 279, Tallahassee, FL 32305-7886 USA
www.dreamspinnerpress.com

Michael, Reinvented
© 2017 Diana Copland.

Cover Art
© 2017 Anne Cain.
annecain.art@gmail.com
Cover content is for illustrative purposes only and any person depicted on the cover is a model.

ISBN: 978-1-63533-640-5
Digital ISBN: 978-1-63533-641-2
Library of Congress Control Number: 2017901551
Published May 2017
v. 1.0

Printed in the United States of America
∞
This paper meets the requirements of
ANSI/NISO Z39.48-1992 (Permanence of Paper).

For Betsy, because there is no way I could do it without her.

ACKNOWLEDGMENTS

To SARITZA Alicia Hernandez for your steadfast belief, to Becky Condit for loving all my silly, wonderful, funny men, and to the real Dr. Gail Shumway for your generosity and expertise. You wonderful ladies have every bit of my love and admiration and thanks.

CHAPTER ONE

MICHAEL CRANE flipped up the collar of his coat as he walked briskly down the sidewalk, black leather boots clicking on the concrete, Justin Timberlake's "Can't Stop the Feeling" flowing into his ears. He liked the song, and it provided a steady bass beat that helped him keep up his pace as he walked through the crowded downtown corridor. The high-rise building housing his employer, A.F. Interiors, was six blocks from his apartment, and usually getting there was a painless process. Not today. The cold cut through his coat, the wind lifting the front of his medium brown hair and slipping under the coils of the heavy dark blue scarf around his neck. His cheeks even ached from the cold.

Berms of icy sludge lined the busy thoroughfare, blackened by dirt and exhaust, and heavy dark clouds hanging low over the city carried the promise of more snow. February might be the beginning of spring in some places, but in the inland Pacific Northwest, the temperatures were still in the low twenties. Michael's breath rushed out in a puff of condensation, and he huddled deeper into the short gray peacoat, picking up his pace. Starbucks was only half a block away.

When he pulled open the glass door, coffee-scented air rushed out to him, warmth brushing his cold cheeks. He sighed gratefully, taking his place in the short line, pulling his black gloves from his long pale hands and shoving them into his coat pockets. Red cardboard hearts hanging from the ceiling on monofilament strands twirled slowly in the movement of the heated air. Michael eyed them with disgust, moving forward when the woman in front of him stepped closer to the register. He was four back, and he checked his watch. It was eight forty. He still had time.

When Michael looked up, the young man steaming milk gave him a flirtatious smile. He was very cute, with dark curls and big brown eyes. He gave Michael a nod and urged him closer with a flick of his head.

"Michael, isn't it?" he asked when Michael reached the counter. "Flat white, right?"

Michael wasn't surprised he knew the order; he got the same thing every morning. He also wasn't particularly surprised the barista had called him up to the counter. He'd checked Michael out head to toe the first day he'd worked there nearly six months before and had been cruising him ever since.

"Yes." Michael gestured toward the irritated people who had been in line in front of him. "But shouldn't I—"

"What're friends for?" The come-hither smile was back, and Michael decided to ignore the irked stares burning into his back. He'd take his perks where he could get them.

Five minutes later the barista handed him the white paper cup. Michael had seen him scribbling furiously on the side for several seconds with a black marker. He'd written "I'm Carlos" and a phone number. Under that he'd drawn a heart with "Be My Valentine" inside it. Michael managed, just barely, not to roll his eyes.

"Thanks." He gave the man a weak smile, dropping a dollar into the tip jar before leaving the store.

It was only February 7, and he was already over Valentine's Day. He hated the stupid holiday. A friend called it "Singles Awareness Day," and Michael laughed even as he agreed. He was single by choice, but to have hearts and flowers crammed down his throat every February 14 irritated the hell out of him. He sipped his coffee as he wove in and out of the active foot traffic, already knowing the cup with the note was going into the trash can in his office as soon as he got there.

His cell phone buzzed in his jacket pocket. Taking it out, he thumbed to his text screen.

Good morning baby, the message read. *How are you this beautiful morning?*

Michael huffed, pausing next to a building, and set his coffee on a window ledge.

I am not your baby, he replied. *What do you want?*

I can't just send my cutie a good morning text?

Michael's lips curled up at the corners. He couldn't help it; the man was maddening and endearing at the same time. He was just glad Gil couldn't see his smile.

Gilbert—What. Do. You. Want.

2

He could almost imagine Gil sitting in his truck, that snarky smile in place while he tried to compose a witty comeback.

Fine, don't let me flirt with you.

Michael snorted. *We've discussed the whole "flirting" thing.*

You discussed it, Gil shot back. *I didn't agree.*

I will stop talking to you.

There was a pause.

Fine. Please tell David I need those color chips for the Watersons' today if I'm supposed to start painting the exterior next week.

Why don't YOU tell David, Michael shot back. *You have his number.*

I think his phone must be off, because he isn't responding. I'm guessing he and Jackson are fucking like bunnies. Besides, you are his assistant, aren't you? Aren't you supposed to take his messages?

Michael scowled at the small screen. This was why Gil drove him nuts.

Leave him a voice mail, Michael typed back. His fingers were beginning to ache in the cold; his gloves were still in his pocket. *My hands are cold, and we've had this conversation before.*

Gil's response popped up almost immediately.

But if I leave him a voice mail I don't get to give you grief, now do I?

Michael huffed another irritated sigh. *Piss off, Chandler. I have better things to do and you're going to make me late.*

I'm breaking you down, Michael Crane. Admit it. It won't be long before you're putty in my hands.

Michael thumbed off his phone in exasperation without responding, shoved it into his pocket, and yanked his gloves out. He pulled them on and retrieved his coffee before resuming his commute down the sidewalk. His temper was simmering. The man infuriated him, poking at him on an almost daily basis. And Michael honestly wasn't sure what to do about it.

He'd met Gilbert Chandler the day his best friend, David, bought an entire houseful of beautiful mission-style furniture from him. Gil's dad had been diagnosed with Alzheimer's. They'd moved him into assisted living, leaving Gil to sort out the details of his life. One of those details was the furniture, and David brought Michael along as "muscle" on moving day. That had been a joke; Gil's friends were all built like CrossFit Junkies, and Michael, at five ten and a hundred and fifty pounds soaking wet, certainly wasn't comparable. But for some reason, Gil, six foot four and roped with muscle, Mr. Clean bald head gleaming in the sunlight, deep blue eyes shining and dimples popping by his mouth, had decided he wanted Michael.

He didn't just want a casual hookup, either, which Michael might have been amenable to. Who wouldn't want to climb all those muscles, feel those big arms close around him? He'd admit he wasn't immune to the idea. But Gil didn't want a one-night stand; he was looking for happily ever after, and Michael didn't believe in it. Not anymore. He pushed through the heavy door into the building and sent a jaunty smile to the receptionist, saluting her with his coffee cup.

"Michael," she called, gesturing for him to come over. He changed direction through the crowd, waiting for several people to pass, before arriving at the marble desk. He leaned his elbow on it.

"What's up, Kylie?"

The pert blonde Michael had befriended on her first day six months before turned in her swivel chair, picking up a long slender white box from the counter behind her before turning back.

"It's Monday." She gave him a wry grin.

Michael sighed inwardly. "Yes. Yes, it is." He took the box, which was still chilled, and thanked her before he turned away.

The box was surprisingly heavy, and even though the lid was taped closed, he could smell the soft, sweet fragrance of Hawaiian ginger. Michael shook his head as he entered the elevator and quietly asked a woman in front of him to push the button for the second floor.

David had a tall cylindrical black vase on the file cabinet in his office. He traditionally kept curly willow in it, the twisted spirals reaching toward the high ceiling. Once he'd casually mentioned to his boyfriend Jackson that he loved red ginger and thought it would be beautiful in that vase, but it was a little pricey to keep fresh. After that conversation, three red ginger blossoms on long, sturdy stalks with heavy, waxy spear-shaped leaves arrived every Monday morning. There was never a card, but there didn't need to be. Michael left the elevator, empty coffee cup dangling from his fingers and the long florist box under his arm.

A.F. Interiors took up the entire second floor, and he nodded politely at the woman on the front desk, Candy, as he passed. He refrained from speaking with her; Candy was a dreadful gossip, and everything he said to her seemed to spread through the rest of the staff like wildfire.

David and Michael's offices were at the back of the floor. He detoured around examples of office furniture in several wood tones and past hotel beds and chairs. A.F. Interiors specialized in hotel décor and design for office spaces. Michael walked between walls of carpet samples and racks hung with different styles of bedding. He loathed almost everything they used, but it wasn't his job to love it; it was his job to help David make it look as good as possible. Sometimes it was a challenge, and sometimes, with the right client, David would let Michael steer them to his favorite midcentury modern. Those jobs were rare unless they got a request for a Mad Men setup, but when they did, Michael was in heaven.

He passed other employees on the floor, some at drawing tables, others on the phone. Most nodded or waved, but there were a couple who studiously ignored him. Debra in textile acquisition hated him and called him a "bitchy queen" behind his back. Neil in sales emphatically turned his back as Michael passed, and Michael fought a smile. Neil had asked him out, and Michael had archly informed him he didn't date where he worked. (He told David it was more like he didn't shit where he ate, particularly when the main course was so unappetizing. David had howled for a full minute.) His refusal hadn't been particularly well received. He should probably make more of an effort, but he didn't really care if people at A.F.I. liked him or not. He was there to do a job, and his job was to help David. Full stop.

He'd meant what he said about not dating where he worked too. A few weeks before, after Christmas, David and Jackson took an idea of Michael's and ran with it, starting Delta Restoration, Renovation, and Design. So far the fledgling company had only done a few jobs on turn-of-the-century homes, but Gilbert Chandler and his crew had been involved in every job. Michael, as David's assistant, dealt with the contractors who worked for them. He knew it was a lame excuse for turning Gil down repeatedly, but it was the best he had. They could not date because they worked together; that was his standard line. The truth was he turned Gil down because the man scared him to death. The idea of letting Gil past his self-constructed protective barriers was not an option.

Michael took out his keys and unlocked David's office. They hadn't been as careful before Trevor, David's ex, made a nuisance of himself by breaking in and rifling through David's desk, but now Michael was much more vigilant. He checked the locks at least twice every night before he left the building. No one would break in to that office again if he had anything to do with it.

He flipped the lights on as he passed, and set the floral box on the desk. Pausing, he held the empty coffee cup above his head and lined up his shot. With elaborate care, he launched the cup into the empty trash can.

"He shoots—he scores!" He punched the air once. "Or he doesn't, depending on who's offering."

Last week's red ginger blooms were drooping and turning black around the petals, looking very sad. Michael took the heavy vase down and dealt with the old flowers and water in the nearby janitor's closet. He was putting the new flowers in the vase when his best friend sailed through the door wearing a black knee-length overcoat, a subtle plaid scarf looped around his throat. His blond hair was mussed, green eyes bright, fair cheeks and the tip of his nose pink from the cold.

"Good morning!" David smiled brightly, dropping his messenger bag in a chair next to his desk and unwinding his scarf. "You don't have to do that, you know." His smile turned soft as he stared at the long-stemmed red blooms. "I don't expect you to arrange my flowers."

"I don't mind." Michael slipped the last dark red blossom into the vase. "Gives me something to do when you're late." He gave David a pointed look.

"Oh, come on." David slipped out of his coat and hung it on the coatrack by the door. He was wearing dark slacks and a bright teal sweater beneath it, and Michael approved of the slender cut and the splash of color. "I'm not that late."

Michael moved the vase to the file cabinet, then tossed the clippings into the empty box amid the tissue paper. "Late enough that I was getting texts from our resident Neanderthal because he couldn't get you on the phone. Thanks so much for that, by the way."

"Michael," David scolded. "You should be nicer to Gil. He really likes you."

"I don't care if he likes me." Michael wrinkled his nose.

David sighed. "You know I love you, but you can be such a bitch."

Michael smiled. "Thank you. Anyway, he says he needs the color chips for the Watersons'."

"Which is true." David circled around behind his desk as Michael moved the box, standing it up on end beside the office door. "Jackson is taking them by on his way to see Paul O'Donnell."

"Good. Call your painter and tell him that, would you please?"

"You don't want to do that for me?"

David was teasing, but Michael gave him a withering look. David laughed as he held up his hands, the corners of his green eyes crinkling.

"Fine, I'll do it. But you are my assistant."

"Not for Delta, I'm not," Michael said. "Mind you, I'll be happy to come onboard once you're paying me, but in the meantime, make your own damned calls." He moved David's messenger bag and took its place, sitting in the chair and draping his long leg over the arm.

David took his cell phone out of the pocket of his slacks and punched in the number.

Five months before, David had met his boyfriend Jackson when he bought a hundred-year-old house in dire need of repairs. Jackson was a handyman, David hired him, and while he'd been working on David's house, they'd fallen in love. Now they were nauseating. The upside was David was very happy. The downside was he wanted to pair off the world, including Michael, no matter how many times he insisted he wasn't interested. He had good reasons for being stubbornly single, reasons his best friend was well aware of.

"Hey, Gil." David leaned back in his swivel chair. "Good. How're you? Excellent. Jackson is bringing you the color chips so you can order the paint, and we've gotten the approval from the homeowners' association. So no one will hassle you once you're on the job. Put all the paint on the business account, okay?" He paused, his eyes resting on Michael. "He's right here—do you want to talk to him?"

Michael glared. "I will poison your coffee."

"No, that's okay." David's eyes sparkled. "He doesn't scare me."

Michael crossed his arms. "I should. I know all of your dirt."

David just continued to smile. It was much harder to get a rise out of him now that he was domesticated. Sometimes Michael missed the old David, the one who would tell him to fuck off when he got irritated. Now everything was sunshine and bunnies. It was disgusting.

"Okay, Gil. Let me know how much that scaffolding is going to run. I'll see you later."

David hung up, then started going through the messages neatly stacked on the corner of his desk. Michael stared at him pointedly, and David did a pretty good job of ignoring him, only laughing when Michael stretched out his long leg and kicked his elbow.

"Ow." He rubbed the spot, completely unable to manufacture a frown.

"Do not make me hurt you."

David huffed, but the smile remained. "He said you need to work on your people skills." He chuckled when Michael glared.

"Me? He could start by not sexually harassing me every time he talks to me."

"He doesn't do that."

"He calls me 'handsome' and 'cutie.'"

"Good Lord, the fiend." David's tone was dry. "You don't like an attractive man telling you that you're cute?"

Michael crossed his arms over his chest, lifting his chin. "I've told him not to repeatedly, David. The man can't take a hint."

"It might be that you send some pretty mixed signals." David leaned back in his chair, eyeing him.

Michael's mouth dropped open. "I do not."

"Michael. When Jackson and I had everyone for dinner last week, you sat next to Gil and giggled at all of his jokes."

Michael waved a hand. "They were funny. And I was drinking."

"How about the night we all went out to the club? That night you actually ended up sitting on his lap."

"Again, I was drinking. You can't blame me for what I do after a couple of cocktails." Michael would die before admitting to anyone that just sitting on that thick thigh had made him hard every time he'd thought about it for a week. And if what he'd felt against his hips was any indication, he wasn't the only one.

"I'm not blaming you for anything. But is it possible that what you're doing when you're relaxed after a couple of drinks is what you actually want?"

"Not with Gilbert." Michael made a face. "You know he isn't my type at all."

"I also know you've been pretty much fascinated with all of those muscles since you first saw him."

Michael grimaced. "The muscles, maybe. But not that thick head." He picked at a perfectly manicured thumbnail so David wouldn't see any regret in his eyes. He liked Gil, more than he wanted to. But he hated David trying to manage him.

"Gil isn't stupid and you know it."

Michael could feel David's scolding look without glancing up. "Why are you pushing this?"

"Michael, I'm not pushing anything." David paused, and Michael finally looked up to find his expression tentative but kind. Michael instantly dreaded what that expression meant. "And Gil isn't Evan."

Michael stiffened in anger. He could scarcely believe David had gone there.

"And now you're pissed at me, and I don't suppose I blame you. I certainly wouldn't want Trevor thrown at me."

Trevor was David's scuzzball ex, the one who'd stalked him and then broken into his house. It was only due to David's good heart that the man wasn't in prison. It was also only due to David's good heart that Michael didn't tell him to mind his own goddamned business.

"I love you," David went on. "And I hate to see you miss out on something that might be wonderful because of something that happened when you were in college."

Michael straightened in the chair. "If you're thinking Gilbert Chandler is that something wonderful, you're wrong. And I don't want to talk about this anymore." He stood up. "I'm going to shipping to see if those samples came in for today's meeting with the restaurant chain." He turned and started for the door.

"Michael."

He stopped at his best friend's tone, looking at him over his shoulder. "Don't be mad."

That was so David. He hated confrontation, especially with people he cared about. Michael's irritation faded.

"I'm not mad," Michael answered almost truthfully. "I just don't want to dwell on it. Okay?"

David seemed to make a conscious effort to let it go. "That stuff we ordered from Dallas should be here too."

"I'll check." He grabbed the florist box and headed out the door.

Everyone had arrived at work now, and the floor buzzed with conversation. Michael was stopped several times on his way to the elevator.

"Michael, what thread count were the sheets for the high-end hotel?"

"Michael, what color upholstery was supposed to go on the couch in the lobby?"

"Michael, what kind of candy should we put in the depression era glass turkeys for the restaurant tables?"

"I don't know," he answered to that one. The chain was owned by a talk show asshole, and all eighteen locations were reopening the next week. "Use red, white, and blue M&M's. The checkerboard tablecloths are red-and-white gingham, so they should be happy." He'd pretty much begged David not to make him work with the client, but David seemed to be entertained by Michael's agony during every conference call with the owner. He was prone to say things like "it's all about mom, baseball, and apple pie. Old-fashioned values. A place a family can eat together without worrying that their kids being kids are going to offend some stuck-up hipster with his iPhone."

David had covered his laugh while Michael glared at the speakerphone.

He stepped onto the freight elevator, pulled the door closed, and pushed the button for the basement. The old elevator made a clunking sound, then began to descend. Michael tossed the florist box in the corner and leaned against the wall.

He was still stinging from David's mention of Evan. There had been something of an unwritten rule between them from the beginning, that he wouldn't rag on David about how big an asshole his ex was—something he managed with limited success—and David wouldn't bring up the biggest mistake of Michael's life. Michael still had nightmares of walking into an empty apartment, dents in the carpeting left by the missing furniture the only indication he hadn't hallucinated two years of his life. Everything was gone but his clothes and a few framed pictures, tossed in a corner like garbage.

Michael blinked, straightening when he felt a vibration in his jacket pocket. He took his phone out and looked down at the screen, eyebrows rising.

"Hello?" he said tentatively.

"Michael. Hey."

It was no wonder David had fallen in love with Jackson Henry. He had a deep, smooth voice like dark chocolate and was practically sex on legs. He also rarely, if ever, called Michael.

"Hi, Jackson. Um… why are you calling me?"

Jackson laughed, and the sound went straight down to his dick, even knowing the man was taken. By his best friend, no less.

"You don't screw around, do you?"

"Not that you're asking, but not with my best friend's boyfriend, no."

Jackson's laugh mellowed into a deep chuckle. "No, I'm not asking. I just meant you get straight to the point."

"I find it saves time." The elevator jolted to a stop at the basement and he yanked the cage doors open. "What can I do for you?"

"I was wondering if you could meet me for lunch."

Michael paused as he bent to pick up the florist's box, straightening without it. "Why?"

"There's something I could really use your help with. And I need you to not say anything to David."

Michael frowned, instantly suspicious. "I'm not sure how comfortable I am with that, Jackson."

"Even if I promise that it's for a really good reason?"

Michael pursed his lips thoughtfully. "Where?"

A rush of relieved breath came through the line. "Thanks, Michael. How about Aspens in the mall?"

Michael huffed. "Only if you're buying."

Aspens billed itself as a "martini bar," and was just pretentious enough to be well out of his price range.

"I'm buying. What time is good for you?"

"I take lunch at one, but I usually go with David. I'm going to have to make something up, and I don't like lying to him."

"You're a good friend, Michael."

"If I was that good a friend, I'd tell you no. But now I'm curious."

Jackson chuckled again, sounding nervous, which had Michael interested. Jackson was a very nice man, but not one Michael would describe as animated. Tall, dark, handsome, and serious, that was Jackson.

"So, see you at one? I really appreciate it."

"Oh, stop"—Michael bent and snatched the box from the floor—"before you make me regret this. I'll be there."

He hung up before he could question his decision any further.

THE SUN, anemic as it was, broke through the cloud cover briefly. It was an unusual enough occurrence in February to make Michael glad he was out taking a walk instead of sitting in David's office with a bagel and a Diet Coke from the vending machines. He hadn't liked telling David he had an optometrist appointment, but he'd been complaining about his glasses enough lately to make it believable. When he entered through the main doors of the mall, he was startled to find Jackson standing in the huge lobby, waiting for him.

"Thanks for coming." Jackson offered his hand. Michael gave it a wry look and Jackson retracted it with a sheepish smile. He looked edgy, and Michael frowned.

"What's the matter? Are you all right?"

"Yeah, yeah, I'm fine." Jackson rubbed his hands on the denim covering his hips. He was wearing nicer clothes than Michael usually saw him in, too, and Michael's concern ratcheted up a notch.

"Jackson, what's going on?"

"Can we hold that until we're in the restaurant?"

Michael stared into the sky-blue eyes, noting the flush on the high cheekbones, the nervous way he kept biting and releasing his lower lip.

"I guess so," he reluctantly conceded, following Jackson onto the escalator.

Aspens was on the third floor of the towering mall entrance. Bronzed branches and dark leather marked the decor, which gave it the feel of an exclusive gentlemen's club. It also looked out over the city, which lost some of its midwinter dinginess that far above the ground. A hostess dressed all in black showed them to a booth with a city view, offering them menus before she departed.

"The pizza is actually pretty good here." Jackson fiddled with the cloth napkin.

"I'm sure it's delightful." Michael leaned forward, his elbows on the tabletop. "What the hell, Jackson?"

Jackson looked up at him, momentarily surprised, then blew out a breath, more nervous than a sigh. He stared at Michael's intractable expression, then fumbled for something in the pocket of his short leather jacket. When he placed the small, velvet-covered box in the center of the table, Michael stared at it.

"What?"

"Open it," Jackson prodded. He was back to chewing on his lower lip, and Michael huffed. He snatched the box up from the table and flipped it open, then stopped and stared.

Nestled on the cushy black satin interior were two rings, a mingling of yellow and rose-toned gold twisted in an artful vine design. The etching caught the light, making them gleam warmly. One was quite a bit larger than the other, and Michael lifted his gaze to Jackson's large hands.

"Oh, Jackson," he said, his voice soft.

"Do you think he'll like them?"

Michael stared down at the matching rings again, his heart so full he was afraid for a moment he might tear up, and that would never do. He snapped the lid closed and pushed the box back toward Jackson.

"Are you kidding? He'll be doing backflips and driving us all crazy with the story of your proposal for months." Jackson reached for the box a bit tentatively, and Michael instantly regretted his glib tone. Sometimes he could really be so obnoxious. He caught Jackson's hand before he could retrieve the box, felt how cold it was, and realized how nervous the taciturn man was. Jackson looked up into Michael's face.

"They're beautiful, Jackson. Truly. He'll be thrilled."

Jackson exhaled, gave Michael a tentative smile. "Yeah?"

"Yes."

Jackson pocketed the ring box as a waitress came to the table. Michael ordered a burger without looking at the menu; everyone had a burger.

As she walked away, he returned his attention to Jackson. "So, are you proposing tonight?"

Jackson took a drink from the glass of water the waitress had delivered, then shook his head. "That's something I could use your help with too."

Michael stared at him, having a feeling Jackson was going to suggest something sappy and obnoxiously romantic, and he was going to be forced to go along because he loved his friend.

He wasn't wrong.

CHAPTER TWO

IT WAS ridiculously cold, and Michael tightened the gray scarf around his throat as he locked his car in front of David's house. He wished it were May. Actually, he just wished it were any time other than this, and that he was anywhere else on the planet. On any other day of the year.

A thin layer of snow in the yard crunched beneath his boots as he made his way toward the porch. He hunched into his jacket and glanced over his shoulder. He loved David; he even loved David's house. In the daylight. After dark he always had the skin-crawly feeling that someone sat out there, watching him. It was five thirty and the sun had set, and the temperature had dropped. He climbed the front steps quickly, pausing to stomp the snow from his boots. He wanted to be home with a container of soup from the market near his apartment, spending the evening in his sweats, watching movies with things that blew up. Preferably anything remotely Valentine's-Day related.

God, Jackson was going to owe him.

The doorbell echoed through the house, accompanied by the sound of a dog barking. David opened the heavy front door, giving Michael an anemic smile. Michael was tempted to smack him, but he managed to refrain. Instead, he bent and smiled at the little black-and-tan corgi who danced around his feet.

"Hello, princess," he greeted, sinking his hands into her thick, soft fur. The dog rolled to her back, short legs in the air, and he rubbed her belly. "How's my girl?"

"Skittish. She's been whining at the door for the last hour. She's also pouting." David gestured for her. "In, Scooter." The corgi went into the house, looking at Michael over her shoulder. David opened the door wider for Michael to enter, and he considered David's face as he passed.

"She isn't the only one who's pouting," Michael observed. David sighed as he closed the door behind him.

"You know, I get that he had to go out of town to deal with some leftover business from his dad's estate. But did it have to be this weekend?"

15

Michael gave him a flat look. "David, you have a boyfriend. The fact that he isn't with you on Valentine's Day is not exactly tragic."

"Oh, I know. I'm just feeling sorry for myself." David grabbed his black wool overcoat from the antique rack on the wall.

"Not that one."

David looked at Michael with incomprehension.

"Not that coat. Wear the gray wool military cut."

David apparently didn't feel the need for restraint and rolled his eyes, returning the first coat to pull down the one Michael suggested. "What difference does it make? It's not like I have to dress up for you."

"Nice." Michael gave him a sardonic look. "Asshole. And it does make a difference. We're going to eat at a nice place, and I won't be seen with someone who cares so little for his appearance that he'd wear an old-man overcoat with that sweater and jeans. And take off that ugly scarf."

David glared at him. "Are you just unusually bitchy tonight, or is it the fact that you think Valentine's Day is really stupid?"

"Both." There were several scarves on the coatrack, and Michael flipped through them, finally taking down a green-and-gray plaid to hold up next to David's face. "This one is better."

"Thank you so much, Tim Gunn. I didn't realize I was on *Project Runway*."

"If you were, you'd get voted off the first week. You can't sew, remember?"

There had been a disastrous weekend with an expensive length of broadcloth and a borrowed sewing machine. Michael ended up ordering curtains from Wayfair.

David stuck his tongue out at him, wrapping the scarf around his throat before donning the short jacket. He looked very nice, but Michael wasn't going to tell him so.

"So, where are we going, anyway?" David asked, following Michael out the door after he bent to give Scooter one last scratch behind her ear.

"Lyra. Which is why I care how you look. I can't be seen with a mess."

Lyra was a small, trendy restaurant in a newly revitalized area of town. There were tea shops and florists and antique stores, and one of the newer, classier gay bars just around the corner. They'd talked about trying it for months but for some reason always ended up somewhere else. David's despondent expression lightened slightly.

"My car or yours?" he asked, locking the door.

"Mine." Michael shot him a look as they walked down the stairs. "Unless you're offering that cute little Mercedes."

David shook his head with a slight smile. "Not mine to offer. And it's parked in my mother's garage. Stopping there would add an hour to our evening."

That was true. Michael was very fond of David's mom, but she was chatty. Besides, the Mercedes in question belonged to Jackson's mother, who had moved in with David's mom a few months before. They'd been friends for years, and it was a sensible decision for both of them. David's mom, Beverley, was newly widowed after taking care of her husband during a long bout with cancer, and Shirley, Jackson's mom, had been diagnosed with MS. Jackson had been living with his mom and trying to care for her while building a business. The moms, without consulting their sons, merely made a decision that was beneficial for everyone.

"So why is Scooter pouting?" Michael hit the fob on his key ring to unlock the car doors. He crossed behind the trunk.

"She hates it when her daddy isn't home." David opened the door and slid into the bucket seat.

Michael got in and locked the doors. "You missing your daddy too, honey?" He gave David a lopsided grin.

"Oh, shut up," David huffed as he pulled on his seat belt. It was dark in the car, but Michael would bet he was blushing. It didn't take much to make David blush.

Michael drove carefully through the neighborhood streets. It hadn't snowed in the last week, but it was brutally cold and the streets were icy and treacherous, even with studded tires on his car. He breathed a silent sigh of relief when they merged onto a cleared main thoroughfare.

"So, why Lyra?" David asked. "Wasn't it hard to get a reservation for tonight?"

"They had a cancellation. And you've talked about trying it for months. I can't be the boyfriend. I don't have the shoulders. But I can at least take you someplace nice."

David reached over and patted Michael's thigh. "Thank you. You can be very sweet when you want to be."

Michael gave him a quick, dour look. "If you say that ever again, I will rip out your tongue."

David's teeth flashed in the dim lights from the dash. "Okay, tough guy. I'll keep it to myself."

The parking lot attached to Lyra was packed, so Michael found a place along the curb several blocks down. They walked shoulder to shoulder, passing a wine bar and a florist still open and doing a bustling business. Michael refrained from making a snarky comment on the hearts and flowers that seemed to be everywhere.

"You know, I was sort of surprised," David began, staring at the huge bouquet of roses a man carried out of the florist shop.

"You're surprised—by what?" David pressed his lips together. Intrigued, Michael elbowed him gently. "Talk to me."

David sighed, pushing at his pale bangs when the icy breeze stirred them. "I was sort of surprised Jackson didn't do anything," he admitted.

"Wait." Michael caught his arm above the elbow. David looked over at him. "No card, no candy, nothing?"

David shook his head miserably. "He's not really demonstrative that way," he said quickly, as if fearing he'd been overly critical of the man he loved. "I mean, this is the guy who fixed my garage door opener when the window was smashed on my car, so I could park in a secure place. He's more likely to do something around the house. And he does send the ginger every Monday, so I really don't have any reason to complain."

"Uh-huh." Michael shook his head as they resumed their walk down the sidewalk. "And it's your first Valentine's Day, and he's out of town. I think I'm going to have to have a chat with Mr. Henry, remind him of the finer arts of dating."

"Oh, please don't." David sounded alarmed. "He already does so much. I don't want him to feel bad. And honestly, I get the feeling Valentine's Day just might not be his thing. He didn't mention it at all, and…."

"Relax, David." Michael gave him a wry look. "I can certainly relate to Valentine's Day not being a person's 'thing.' I won't say anything to him," he added near David's ear. "This time. He misses your birthday and all bets are off."

David caught his hand and squeezed it. "He wouldn't."

"Uh-huh." Michael looked around curiously.

Lyra didn't look like a restaurant from the street. It was located in an old, square brownstone that opened directly onto the sidewalk, and the exterior kept a low profile, with a few minor decorative elements near the second-story roofline.

When the buildings had been constructed on the busy street near the turn of the nineteenth century, businesses operated on the main floor, with residential apartments above. A simple sign swung in the light breeze above the door to Lyra, the name written in gold. Window boxes hung at each window down the length of the building. In spring they would no doubt be lovely but were now full of dead plant tendrils and a dusting of snow.

Michael opened the door for David, and once they were inside, he took in the mismatched antique furniture and the stained glass above the bar, the candles on the tables and the rosebuds in vases. Someone very skilled had put together an eclectic, unique interior, and Michael realized why the first word everyone used was *charming*. It was. There was also the mouthwatering scent of something delicious in the air. Several people milled around the small entryway, and Michael gestured toward the hostess stand with a jerk of his chin. David nodded, leaning against the wall by the door.

Michael approached the hostess, glancing back to make sure David hadn't followed him.

"My name is Michael Crane," he said, his voice low. "I believe there's a reservation?"

She searched the book in front of her, then gave him a bright smile. "Oh yes." She looked at David, her smile ripening. "If you'll follow me?"

Michael turned to David, gesturing him forward through the crowd. David made slow progress, apologizing to everyone he nudged aside.

"Today, Snyder." Michael rolled his eyes.

"I'm coming."

"So's Christmas. Lord, you don't need to apologize to them all."

"It makes me a nice person." David huffed when he reached his side. "Something you could use a little work on."

"I don't need to be nice." Michael gave him a wry look, and they followed the young woman through the main dining room into another, smaller room behind it. There were only five tables, but there was also a gas fireplace with an ornate mantel, and a crystal chandelier hanging from an ornamental medallion in the ceiling. The only Valentine's decorations were the rosebuds in the small vases, which Michael appreciated. Candles flickered on the tables, and the flames were reflected in the large windows. The hostess showed them to a table just to the left of the fireplace, and Michael slipped out of his jacket and hung it on his chair before he sat down.

"This is beautiful." David looked around with an expert's eye. He was the most gifted interior designer Michael had ever met; he would know.

"Thank you," the girl replied, handing them menus. "The owner will be glad to know you like it. Your wine list is on the table, and your server should be with you shortly."

David slipped out of his coat, sitting as Michael scooped up the wine list. He wasn't going to order any—he knew what was on the evening's agenda—but it couldn't hurt to look.

"This was really nice of you, Michael," David said.

Michael glanced up from the wine list. "I wasn't looking forward to spending the evening by myself any more than you were. And they have a really fine wine list."

"Oh? Can I see?"

Michael handed him the leather-covered folder and watched as his friend studied the list. David knew far more about wine than Michael did, and he made an appreciative noise as he read. The restaurant featured all Washington State wines, many of them on the *Seattle Times* food critics' list.

"I've heard the Wild Goose Riesling is really good."

"I'll take your word for it."

"They have microbrews." David turned a page. "I know you like the Firebox IPA."

"That's true, I do."

"I think that sounds good too." David set the folder back on the table, glancing around. "As soon as I can catch the eye of a server, I'll order us each one. Where are they?" A line formed between his brows.

"It's busy tonight." Michael leaned back in his chair. "They'll get to us."

David's lips twisted. "I hope they didn't put us back here and forget about us."

"I'm sure they won't." Michael fought a smile. David's irritation was starting to amuse him, and he didn't know how much longer David would buy into his calm demeanor; usually slow service was Michael's pet peeve.

Two very nicely dressed women were shown into the room by the hostess, and even though he was expecting them, it took Michael a moment to recognize them. Beverley had chosen a lovely green-and-gold dress with a dark blue coat, and Shirley was wearing her hair in a new style since he'd seen her last. Michael bit back a smile at the look on David's face.

"Mom?"

Beverley turned and looked at him, and Michael thought he'd have to compliment her on her acting chops later. She looked genuinely surprised.

"Why, David." She paused to hug him. "What are you doing here?"

David gestured toward Michael. "Michael knew Jackson was out of town, and so he invited me out."

"Well, aren't you a sweet thing!" Beverley held her arms out to Michael, and he walked into them, hugging her.

"Well done, Mom," he whispered, and she leaned back and looked up at him, an impish twinkle in her eye.

David was hugging Shirley. "I feel so bad about this," she was saying. "It's my fault that he had to go over to Seattle."

"No, it wasn't." David shook his head, smoothing his hand down her arm. "It's just something that needed to be done. I don't want you to worry about it."

"Well, it's nice your friend wasn't already busy." Shirley gave Michael a sweet smile.

"Oh, that's me." Michael couldn't help a smidge of sarcasm. "The friend who isn't busy on Valentine's Day."

Beverley gave him a mildly scolding look.

"What are you doing here?" David looked between Shirley and his mother.

"We have tickets for *Wicked*, remember? We thought we'd get a bite to eat first instead of waiting until almost midnight." Beverley gave her son a bright smile. "You know every restaurant in this town closes down at ten."

"Would you like to join us?" David glanced at their two-person table. "I'm sure we could get a larger table."

But all the tables in the room were two-seaters. He turned to the hostess.

"We could probably set something up for you," she said regretfully, playing her part as well. "But it would have to be out in the main dining room, and you'd have to wait. This room is usually reserved for couples, particularly today."

"Sweetheart, it's okay. Don't worry about it. We'll just sit over here and throw olives at you." Beverley winked at him.

David gave her a wry look, but a laugh lingered on his lips. The hostess seated the ladies on the other side of the fireplace, and Michael caught her before she could leave the room.

"We haven't even seen a server yet."

"Oh, I'm so sorry. If you'd like something to drink I can get it for you, and I'll send your waiter right back."

"Thank you," David said. "We'd like two Fireboxes, please."

She smiled at him. "Coming right up."

"Finally," he muttered when she'd walked away. "The food may be great here, but the service leaves something to be desired."

"It's Valentine's Day, David. Cut them a break."

David arched a brow. "This from you? The original cranky customer?"

Even Michael thought he was probably laying his relaxed attitude on a little thick. He was grateful when the waiter arrived.

He was a very nice-looking young guy, but instead of two tall glasses of pale beer, he was carrying a tray holding a bottle of champagne in a silver ice bucket and two crystal champagne flutes. He set it on the table and turned to go.

"No, wait." David was clearly flustered. "We didn't order this."

"No?" The waiter looked at his ticket. "This says it's for table 27, and this is table 27…." He frowned, looking charmingly confused. He wasn't Michael's type, with his reddish hair and freckles, but he was very cute. "Let me go see if I can sort this out."

David huffed in aggravation. "Oh, for God's sakes. We aren't paying for a bottle of champagne. We should just go somewhere else."

"This is getting pretty ridiculous," Michael agreed. "But about the only place we could get into at this point would be McDonald's. You might as well relax, David. It's this, or PB and J at your place."

David sighed, sitting back in his chair. "I can't believe the reviews this place has gotten."

Michael shrugged.

The hostess appeared again, and this time she had three men with her. Michael stiffened slightly at the sight of them, even though he'd known exactly who'd be coming tonight.

When David spotted them, he sat bolt upright, his mouth slightly open. "Wait…." His eyes narrowed. "What—?"

"Well, look who we have here!" Gilbert Chandler, all six-foot-four, broad-shouldered, head-shaved inches of him, came through the door first. He smiled, and a dimple popped beside a mouth full of straight white teeth. He came to their table, reached out, and patted David on his shoulder. Michael was glad he was sitting down, because much to his chagrin, the damned man made his cock twitch and his knees weak.

David was frowning at Gil; he hadn't seen Vernon Dwyer and Emanuel Martinez yet. Vernon, with his shoulder-length silvery gray hair pulled back in a sleek ponytail, wore perfectly pressed Levi's and a sports coat. Breathtakingly beautiful Manny Martinez followed Vernon, his head ducked, a shy smile on his face. His dark curls gleamed in the soft light, his slender but strong physique set off perfectly in tailored slacks and a short black suede jacket. The scar that bisected his brow and followed the line of his cheekbone wasn't as angry as it had been, growing less noticeable on his handsome face.

"Hi." David looked from Gil, Vernon, and Manny, three of the men he and Jackson had begun their business with, to the two ladies across the room, a frown of confusion deepening. He finally whipped his head around and glared at Michael.

"Michael. What's going on?"

"Yeah, Michael." Gil arched a thick brown brow at him, the smartass smile firmly in place. Michael wanted to kick him. "What is going on?"

"Oh, stuff it, you—" Michael bit back "asshole" in deference to the moms seated nearby.

"I don't understand." David looked from his friends to his mother and back again. "Why are you all here?"

"Dinner," Vernon said dryly. "You know, food? They do serve that here, right?"

"Be nice, you old cow," Gil scolded. "Restaurant manners, remember?"

Vern curled his lip. "Bite me, Gilbert."

"I'm so confused." David looked back to Michael, who shrugged.

Fortunately, David didn't have to be confused for long.

The hostess made a swift exit just as a waiter came through the door holding the most ridiculous, obscenely large arrangement of flowers Michael had ever seen. It was made up of roses, lilies, and red ginger blooms, and was so huge it obscured the man from the waist up. "Delivery for David

Snyder?" The voice was intentionally lowered, and Michael saw Gil hide a smile behind his hand.

"What? That's… me." David frowned, still trying to figure out what was going on.

"It's a good thing he's pretty," Vern grumbled.

"Vernon." Gil shot him a look. "Knock it off. This is important."

Gil, Vern, and Manny stepped out of the way to let the man set the flower arrangement on the table between Michael and David. Michael had to pull back or get batted in the face by a huge lily, and he pushed the offending flowers to the back of the table.

David jolted, nearly knocking the arrangement over when his lover was revealed from behind the colorful cover.

"Jackson?" David seemed to finally realize that the inner circle of people he cared about was gathered in the room, it wasn't an accident, and he didn't know why. "This is making me nervous."

"Don't be nervous." Jackson caught one of David's hands. He was wearing unrelieved black from head to toe, just like the other waiters. Black shoes, black slacks, black shirt. On some men it didn't work at all, but on Jackson Henry? Michael couldn't think of a thing that wouldn't look good on Jackson Henry. His hair was tousled, he needed a shave, and he looked perfect. His free hand went into the pocket of his slacks. "I tried to figure out a way—" He pulled out the gray velvet box. "—to do this without it being cheesy."

"Missed that off-ramp, boy," Vern grumbled. This time it was Manny who shushed him.

Jackson held David's gaze, speaking just to him. "I thought of taking you out to our spot by the river and doing this there, just you and me. Then I realized that while I might prefer that, you wouldn't. And this is never going to be about just me, babe. Not ever again."

Jackson knelt gracefully on the hardwood floor. One of the moms gasped and the other sniffled, but Michael couldn't have looked away from the couple across from him if he tried. His hand lifted reflexively to press over his heart as he watched. Jackson fumbled for a moment with the jeweler's box, then opened the lid, and Michael studied David's face when he saw the rings. His expressive eyes widened, then filled with tears as Jackson took out one of the artfully etched bands.

Jackson gave David an almost shy smile. "I love you, David. And I don't want to go through life without you. Will you go through it with me? Will you marry me?"

The little group of friends and family held its collective breath. In fact, even though the noise of the outer restaurant filtered through the door, the room seemed as if it was in a bubble, holding the world at bay while they all waited for David's response.

David had covered his mouth while Jackson proposed. Tears that had welled now traced down his cheeks, and when he moved his hand, his lower lip trembled. Finally, he nodded and solemnly helped Jackson slide the ring on. Then he curled his hand around Jackson's neck.

"Yes," David managed, finally moving. He slid to his knees in front of Jackson and threw his arms around his neck. "Yes. Oh my God, yes."

There was cheering and bubbling talk and laughter. Some waitstaff and a few customers had crowded into the doorway and joined in with applause, smiling. Jackson wrapped his arms around David's slender frame and hugged him, then leaned back enough to smile into his fiancé's eyes, wiping at his tears with his thumbs.

Michael couldn't look away from David's face, from the awe in his expression. They'd all been raised with the idea that marriage was not an option, not for them. That the best they'd ever be able to do was find someone they loved and call that person *partner*, *lover*. Michael had never imagined seeing a man propose to another man in person, and yet here it was. He was unable to stop tears or prevent them from slipping down his face.

That was when he felt someone watching him, and he tore his gaze from the couple now kissing where they knelt on the floor to one of the three men standing just behind them.

Gilbert Chandler's hazel eyes were also suspiciously bright as he stared at him, and he gave Michael a slow smile.

"Gotcha," he mouthed.

Michael scowled and flipped him off. Gil's lopsided grin deepened, and Michael looked away, focusing on one bright red rose in the riotous arrangement as he dashed at the tears on his cheeks.

CHAPTER THREE

MICHAEL PULLED his car to a stop, parking as close to the snow berm as he dared while still leaving room to open his door. Fortunately he was thin and could fit in the small space; even as he left the vehicle's warm interior and straightened, traffic zoomed by inches from his car. The enormous house where he was scheduled to meet David and Jackson loomed above the wide, busy one-way street heading into downtown. He was relieved that even while parallel parking on the "wrong" side of the street was a bitch, at least he didn't have to play Russian roulette with speeders while he navigated across two lanes of traffic. He'd only have to climb over the dirty, icy pile of snow the plows had left when they cleared the streets.

He grabbed his messenger bag, then cursed under his breath as he scaled the slippery three-foot pile of ice. A wide driveway cut in down the hill about fifty yards from where he stood, but he could see himself slipping and sliding on black ice and landing on his ass in front of rush-hour traffic. The winter had felt so long; he couldn't wait for the temperatures to rise and some of the filthy snow piled all over town to melt. Going out after dark, when the temperatures plummeted, exacerbated everything.

Even with the parking negatives, when David told him where they were going for the bid, Michael grew excited about this possible job. Of course, David was pretty much excited about everything and had been since Jackson's proposal two weeks before. Michael could give him a pass. Jackson was gorgeous, they were mad for one another, and he supposed a wedding was the natural outcome for couples like them. What wasn't welcome or easily forgiven was the seed of longing watching Jackson propose had planted in Michael's chest. He prided himself on his disinterest in the whole "happily ever after" pile of crap, believing it was impossible for a gay man to ever truly find his other half. Then he watched Jackson get down on one knee and ask David to marry him. He saw someone get his Prince Charming, and a longing unlike anything he'd ever felt rocked him to his core. He didn't like it.

Once he was over the berm—skidding the last two feet until he could steady himself in the softer snow on the lawn—Michael finally straightened, looking up at the house they were going to tour.

Of course, he was aware of the Patrick O'Banyon Mansion. It was like the Mercer Hotel, the turn-of-the-century jewel the same man had built downtown. You didn't live in the area and not know the story of the mining millionaire who was considered one of the founding fathers. Brash and egotistical, Irish immigrant Paddy O'Banyon had owned a silver mine in Northern Idaho and had his mansion built on the hill in eastern Washington in 1894 so his Boston-born bride would have other stylish people to socialize with. At the turn of the twentieth century, most of the local well-heeled crowd had made their fortune through mining or railroads or both. Michael hadn't grown up locally, but even he knew the story of the people who'd built downtown. Some of the families had even stayed. Old money was currently being used by a new generation on remodeling buildings of similar age in the downtown corridor. But this house was the crown jewel, situated on the hill, visible for miles. Michael had heard the stories about the house, even though he'd never been inside. It was on the National Registry of Historic Homes and had been a bridal destination until the last few years, when the owners were no longer able to afford the upkeep. It had changed hands recently, but whoever purchased it was keeping a low profile.

Some said it was haunted. As Michael stared up at the Tudor beams and slate that decorated the front of the old house, he could believe it. A cross between an English country manor and a Craftsman, the house had a great stone arch above the fifteen stairs leading to a porch that wrapped around the entirety of the twelve-thousand-square-foot house. There was even a place on the side where the balustrade was interrupted so carriages could unload their passengers directly onto the porch. It was a testament to the era when the house was built, and Michael was surprised it had never been remodeled. In fact, the whole structure seemed an anachronism, an old-fashioned house in a modern world. It needed paint where it peeled from the heavy beams. The dusting of snow added a bit of charm to the roofs and chimneys and windowsills, but the slate rock that formed the foundation looked dingy, gray, ugly.

What Michael saw in front of him would be an enormous job, even if it was just the exterior. But David had told him they were there to see the first two floors. This was a job that might, as David suggested, make it so they could actually get Delta Restoration, Renovation, and Design up and rolling. There were seven of them at the first meeting, all who had conditionally joined the business. They were doing smaller jobs, and their sign, the delta triangle with elegant black script, was currently in the front yards of three vintage homes on the hill. But something like this? All of them would be able to pull a paycheck. Michael didn't care if the ghosts were playing Parcheesi in the parlor; he was in.

He walked across the snowy lawn, paused on the walkway to stomp the snow from his boots, then hurried up the stairs. His feet were freezing, but they had been all day. He was about ten minutes late for the meeting and hoped he hadn't missed too much. Pausing before the enormous door, Michael studied the leaded glass window above it as he rang the bell. The half-circle window was in the shape of a peacock, and Michael admired the detail as the door swung open. To his surprise, David stood on the other side.

"Well, hello. Are you playing Lord of the Manor?"

David grinned. "I could with this place, couldn't I? No, I knew it was you, and our client got tied up with a phone call."

"Sorry I'm late." Michael stepped over the threshold, immediately admiring the hardwood floors. They were darkened with age but still beautiful. "I got tied up in traffic."

"I figured. So, what do you think?" David closed the huge door behind them.

Michael looked around the enormous entryway. To the left, a solid wooden staircase climbed along the wall to a landing, then turned and followed the back wall to a second floor. The balcony, bordered by the wooden balustrade, curled around the entirety of the cavernous space. It was hard to make out the ceiling far above; Michael could see there was a mural, but it was dark outside, so there wasn't any light coming through the stained glass windows on the wide landing. Michael thought it might be a peacock painted there, its ornamental feathers spreading around the edges. The sconces in the entry looked dingy, and a dark chandelier hung from the center of a plaster medallion that appeared to be missing sections. It was all beautiful but reminded Michael of an aging beauty queen, still lovely but beginning to show her mileage. "Peacocks, huh?"

"Apparently." David looked around. "But isn't the woodwork glorious?"

Michael turned to reply to David's comment but paused when he heard voices. Jackson came through a large doorway from the next room, and just behind him, tablet in hand, was Gil Chandler. Michael stiffened and turned his back. "Why is he here?"

"Who?"

"Who?" Michael gave his friend a dark look. "Who do you think? I knew Jackson would be here. I didn't know his cohort would be."

"We need him here, Michael. The walls are damaged in pretty much every room, and Gil's our wall and paint guy. You know that."

"I guess I didn't realize he was part of the bidding process." He shoved his hands into his pockets and hunched his shoulders.

"Please play nice. We need to look professional. This job could translate into tens of thousands of dollars, and the publicity alone would be priceless. You know what people in this town think of this place." He lowered his voice further. "Can't you imagine our sign on the lawn, how much attention it would get? We could really use this one, Michael. It would do more than just pay the bills—it could set us all up."

Michael sighed. "I'll be good." He hoped he could manage it.

"Well, hello, Mr. Crane. Aren't you looking fetching this evening."

Michael stiffened, but he bit back the snarky retort on the tip of his tongue before he turned. Gil was standing behind him, his large face wreathed in a teasing smile. He wore khakis, a green shirt, and a slightly darker green jacket. The color did wonderful things for his hazel eyes, and Michael took a deep breath. "Mr. Chandler. Allow me to return the compliment."

Gil pressed a hand over his heart in mock surprise. "Be still my heart. The man just gave me a compliment. Is the sky falling?" He looked toward the ceiling as if expecting it to land on him. Michael opened his mouth to retort and saw Jackson elbow Gil in the ribs. Gil grimaced and was rubbing the spot when another voice echoed in the empty room.

"Mr. Snyder?"

An attractive man entered through a side door, his step light on the wooden floors. He was perhaps fifty, with short, dark brown hair, a slightly receding hairline, and an elegantly silvering goatee. Slender and graceful even in the casual jeans and sweater he wore, the red of his top was exactly the same shade as his Nike running shoes. Something of a shoe whore himself, Michael had been looking at those for months. Now that he'd seen them on this classy man's feet—well, it was only a matter of time. The potential client offered his hand to David, and Michael noticed the slender gold band on his ring finger.

"Mr. Lawrence." David gave him a small smile.

"Richard, please. I'm sorry about the delay. And I'm sorry my husband wasn't able to be here." He looked from face to face as David introduced everyone. When he shook Michael's hand, Richard's was warm, the skin soft.

"No worries," Jackson assured him. "We were just looking around a bit. I hope that's all right."

"It's fine." Richard pressed his palms together. "You can see the potential, yes?"

"Absolutely."

"Shall we take the tour?"

Michael took his tablet out of his messenger bag and pulled its stylus free, trying to pay close attention as Richard gestured around where they were standing. Gil at his back was a spicy-scented distraction. Michael didn't know what cologne he wore, but whatever it was made his mouth water. He shifted a few steps away.

"This, as you see, is the foyer."

Michael looked around the huge room, incredulous. "This is a foyer?" It was bigger than his entire apartment.

"Oh yes." Richard gave him an amused glance. "Back in the day, guests would enter through the side doors, there." He pointed toward a huge set of double doors. "Depending on what was on the agenda for the evening, they would either go through into the green parlor to wait for dinner to be announced, or they would move on into the ballroom. Some evenings they would set chairs up in this space for musicales. You can see the spots on the hardwood where a piano sat for nearly a hundred years." He gave Michael a smile when he bent to see that, yes, there were three indentations on the floor where the piano legs must've sat. "There will be another instrument in that spot when we finish the renovations. The ballroom is through this way."

He led them around the corner. "Good Lord," Michael muttered.

Richard's smile widened. "It seems a bit over the top for a private home, doesn't it?"

"Not if they planned an indoor skating rink." Michael looked around the massive space, suitably impressed. Richard chuckled. It was a warm, pleasant sound.

"No, but they did a lot of business in this house during grand events. Railroad expansions were discussed here, and mining revenue. The men who frequented this home back in the day were the Warren Buffetts and Bill Gateses of their time. At least for this part of the country."

Michael looked at it through new eyes.

The ballroom was at least fifty by a hundred and fifty feet, floor-to-ceiling windows with dark velvet drapes along one side, mirrors on the other. Four crystal-and-brass chandeliers hung from the ceiling at intervals, like giant metal-and-glass flowers blooming from elaborate plaster medallions.

"Those are stunning." David's awe showed on his face. Michael agreed. He'd never seen anything like them. They were almost steampunk in their use of metal, the shapes organic and yet mechanical.

"Aren't they? We're excited to see what they look like when they're clean."

Fireplaces centered the walls at either end of the large room, with black marble facings and mantels. Fine plasterwork decorated the walls, like the swooping swags of fondant on a wedding cake. Whole sections of the designs were missing, lending what was once no doubt a stunning room a sad, neglected air. An ugly Pepto-Bismol pink covered the walls, and the brass on the wall sconces was tarnished. Gil walked past, looking intently at the wall. It afforded Michael a chance to study him without getting caught.

Usually Gil wore worn, paint-splattered jeans and long-sleeved ribbed shirts, a dark apron covering him from barrel chest to stocky thighs. Even with Gil so completely covered, it was impossible for Michael to ignore the tapered waist to hips, the thick biceps, the broad shoulders. Dressed as he was now, Gil's muscular physique was even more obvious. He reached up to touch the wall, long, tapered fingers spread on the plaster. He had such big hands. Michael jerked his gaze away, feeling an unpleasant quivering in his midsection.

"Lath and plaster?" Gil asked.

"Throughout." Richard walked to Gil's side, studying the finish. "The color is awful, of course."

Gil shrugged. "That's easy to fix. You do want to keep this treatment, don't you?"

"Where we can, absolutely. I'm big on preserving as much as possible."

"Good." Gil wrote quickly on his tablet. "So are we, and we can do it. It might mean removing some of the damaged plaster, but in this era they knew what they were doing underneath. There won't be termites, so it should still be solid. As long as there's no mold."

"God forbid," Richard said meaningfully.

"Word." Gil sent Richard a smile, that dimple popping next to his mouth, and Michael felt something uncomfortably akin to jealousy. He didn't like it a bit.

Gil continued to scribble notes, his smooth head gleaming slightly in the soft light. Michael hated that he wanted him, had pretty much always wanted him. Michael felt the electrical hum of it from his head to a stirring at the base of his spine, one that was directly connected to his cock. It twitched unhelpfully. He forced himself to take a step back and look away. For whatever fucked-up reason the universe had for anything it did, Gil Chandler appealed to Michael on a purely physical level. But just because he wanted to climb the man like a tree didn't mean he'd ever act on it. He forced himself to turn back to the ongoing conversation.

"Our thought," Richard was saying, "is to use the ballroom and the grounds out back as a wedding venue during the season from April through July, while leaving the rest of the house open to the public as a restaurant. We can divide the space with these." Richard pulled out pocket doors between the main entry and the ballroom, and Michael thought Jackson was going to have an orgasm of sheer joy.

"Oh my God." He reached out to touch the dark wood. "Are all of the doors throughout the house original?" He stroked his fingers over the dark wood with a lover's caress, following the carved detail of vines and flowers. If he were David, Michael thought he might be jealous of the old doors.

"As far as we know." Richard watched him, smiling faintly. "They aren't all this elaborate."

Jackson looked like a kid who'd found the best toy ever under his Christmas tree.

As they continued through the downstairs, Michael could start to see why Richard and his husband had bought the old house. He also felt Gil's eyes following him almost as often as his followed Gil. He was trying to ignore him, but it was difficult. At one point there was a fleeting touch on the back of his neck. He glared over his shoulder, only to find Gil carefully studying the surface of a wall, a picture of innocence. Michael turned away with a huff.

They wandered through the rest of the downstairs rooms. An enormous kitchen that needed to be completely gutted for Richard's husband, Lyle, occupied a back corner of the house. Lyle was a Michelin Star chef who would be running their restaurant and catering. It looked as if the appliances had been replaced during the last thirty years, but the tiles were all original. On the floor they were small hexagons, white and black, and around the wide upper crown molding, there were bigger tiles in pale rose, featuring geometric patterns.

Michael had been notating each of the areas that needed repairs on his tablet, and before they ever climbed to the upper floors, the list was impressively long. He could see this job taking months. He could also see it being very lucrative for Delta, which was really exciting. He was the one who'd had the original idea for them to form a business of primarily gay men. Now he felt a vested interest in its success. It wouldn't hurt his personal bottom line either. His dream was for him and David to be able to leave A.F.I. and not look back.

Richard led them to the main staircase that ascended to the landing. "There's some minor damage to the wood." He gestured toward some nicks in the railing. "We want to preserve as much as we can."

"Of course." Jackson's hand had followed the wood from the ground floor, over the elaborate newel post at the landing, and now he bent to study the expertly turned balusters. "I know someone who can reproduce these, if necessary."

"That would be wonderful. I know there aren't many of those kinds of artisans left. Then there are these." He gestured up at the stained glass windows, and Michael gasped softly, climbing closer to study them. It was impossible to see more than hints of the colors in the dark, but the images were clear. Here the peacock motif had been realized in all its glory; the two tall windows depicted proud male peacocks, beautifully arched throats and angled heads almost forming a heart, full feathered tails overlapping at the bottom. Behind the birds was a low white railing, and beyond that the delicate shapes of sailboats floated on a still lake.

"This looks like something Louis C. Tiffany did." Michael bent at the waist, studying the bottom of the windows carefully. He was searching for a small rectangular shape with the distinctive signature…. When he found it, his hand shot out, touching the hundred-year-old window delicately. "Oh my God. These are Tiffany."

"We have the paperwork from when they were ordered," Richard said. "Again, O'Banyon wanted only the best for his bride."

"These are worth a fortune." David studied them closer.

"There is some damage." Richard pointed to a couple of cracks and a place where someone had used duct tape to cover a missing piece in one corner. Michael had a strong desire to smack whoever had done it in the mouth.

"We know someone who can repair them, probably without taking them down." David turned to Michael. "Make a note to call Elizabeth."

Michael nodded, straightening. When he did, he felt a strong body standing close all along his back. He knew without turning who it was.

He glared over his shoulder, not at all surprised to find Gil looking down at him.

"Oh, sorry." Gil took a step back, a slow smile spreading, dimples popping. "Was I in your way?"

"Oh no, not at all." Michael elbowed him subtly in the side as he passed. Gil grunted softly, but his smile stayed in place.

When the five of them arrived on the second floor, Michael looked up at the mural on the ceiling and saw that yes, it was indeed a peacock painted there. A smirking peacock. He angled his head slightly, frowning. Why in the world would a peacock be smirking?

"Someone attempted to repair that at some point," Gil said from beside him. Michael looked over to find Gil studying the mural. "They didn't do a very good job of it."

Richard laughed. "They did a horrible job of it. Have you ever seen a more condescending bird?" He pointed to a far corner. "There was water damage about a decade ago right there; a pipe burst. They brought in a well-known muralist to execute the repairs once that section of the wall was replaced. I don't know what happened. Fortunately, when we were going through the attics, we found the original artist's renderings."

Gil's expression brightened. "Really? I'd love to see those."

"Are you the muralist? Mr. Snyder told me he knew an excellent one."

Michael's head jerked around, and he looked at Gil in surprise. A ruddy flush spread on Gil's neck above his collar.

"I haven't really had the time to do much mural work lately, but I have before."

"He's being too modest," David said. "He's amazing. He did the murals in the new wing of the children's hospital downtown."

"All of them?" Richard asked. Michael studied Gil, startled. He looked uncomfortable, as if unaccustomed to being the center of everyone's attention. "We were there when the new wing was dedicated. The murals are really beautiful, Mr. Chandler."

"Thank you." Gil fidgeted, his face filled with hot color.

Michael gave David a pointed look. How could David know Gil was an artist but not have told him? Surely this should have come up. In Michael's mind, Gil painted houses. Beautifully, but—the idea he didn't even know this about Gil made Michael feel off-center. He didn't like it.

As they continued through what had been bedrooms on the second floor, Richard explained his and his husband's vision for the rest of the house. There would be private dining and meeting rooms, a special room for brides and bridesmaids to dress, even a large room set aside for a staff breakroom. At one time the house had fifteen bedrooms and nine bathrooms, and he had plans for them all.

They were in a room at the corner of the house. Dim and suffering from a heavy, musty smell, the room still had elements of charm. A window seat tucked in against a wall of windows was like an invitation to curl up there with a good book and a cup of tea. A fireplace with a spectacular white marble mantel only needed a crackling fire. "Of course, the paint is ghastly," Richard said. He was right, it was. Dark red and mottled, it looked like blood. "But if you look here in the closet—" He opened the door, pointing to the interior wall. David stepped close and Michael looked over his shoulder. Wallpaper on the interior walls was faded and tattered, but remnants of its former beauty remained. The background was gray, with what looked like a satiny stripe. A repeating floral bouquet of red roses and pale green leaves climbed between every other stripe. "We found a book of wallpaper samples in the attic. I don't know if anyone even makes something like this any longer—"

"Actually, they do." David stepped closer, reached up to grab the rusted metal chain, pulled it, and flooded the inside of the closet with light. "We've worked with a supplier out of Philadelphia that reproduces old patterns specifically for vintage restorations. It isn't glued like modern paper—"

"Which means installation is…." Gil grimaced.

"A pain in the ass?" Richard had a twinkle in his brown eyes.

Gil grinned, the dimple popping next to his mouth. Michael felt a wholly unwelcome pull in the center of his chest at the sight of it. It was why he was uncomfortable being around Gil. Most men fell into two categories for Michael: men he'd screw and those he wouldn't. He'd given up on anything more than that a long time ago. He could certainly see himself sleeping with Gil, but the idea of doing it made his palms sweat and his mouth go dry with the fear there might be more to it. Why couldn't the man be ugly, or short, or scrawny? That would have made things so much simpler.

"Yeah, it's a pain in the ass," Gil agreed, still talking about wallpaper. "The glue stinks and it's backbreaking. Getting it on the wall can be time-consuming, and lining it up…." He shook his head. "But the old papers are thick, sometimes hand embossed. You can't beat the quality. If you want vintage wallpaper, we can get it on the walls."

Richard gave him a satisfied nod.

"Eventually we'd like to convert the attic into an apartment, so we could live on-site," he explained ninety minutes later. They'd all taken seats on folding chairs around the lone round table in the ballroom. It was dwarfed by the room's sheer size, and their voices echoed. "We have an alarm system, but we're talking about an enormous investment here; we'd like to be on-site to protect it."

"I can certainly understand that." Jackson looked at David, and they shared one of those long, drawn-out, silent exchanges Michael saw so often. Half the time they didn't even speak. They communicated with their eyes. He'd never had that level of understanding with anyone. Even when he'd thought he was in love the one disastrous time, there had never been that. He tried not to resent it.

Jackson turned back to Richard. "We should be able to have a bid for you by Monday, Mr. Lawrence. I don't know who else you're talking to, but—"

Richard raised his hand, silencing Jackson gently. "You really must use my first name, please. If we're going to be working together, I can't have you calling me Mr. Lawrence. I'm older than all of you, and that makes me feel like my father." He leveled a kind, steady look on Jackson. "We aren't entertaining other bids. I've checked out your business. Your company is new, but everyone you've worked with so far raves about your professionalism and your finished product. It takes a special touch to work on an old building, honoring the way it was made instead of wanting to change it." He paused, looking around the table at the tableau of startled faces. "Lyle and I stumbled on this purchase at the right time. The family who owned the house just wanted to be out from under the running expenses. We were very fortunate in our choice of real estate agent, and we paid far less for the place than it's worth. We knew even before we closed that we were going to hire your company. Our budget is—generous. I don't think you'll have a problem staying within it. So—" He smiled, offering his hand to Jackson. "Welcome aboard. This should be a fascinating experience."

They all stared at him in stunned silence. Finally David spoke.

"Seriously?"

"Very seriously."

David turned a shocked look on Jackson. Michael feared for a moment he was going to cry. Instead David let out a sound that would embarrass the hell out of him later and threw his arms around Jackson's neck.

Michael sputtered, unable to stop his laughter. Within moments they were all laughing. Jackson wrapped his arms around David, squeezing him with an indulgent smile. Richard offered his hand to each of them. "When can you start?"

"We have two small jobs to finish up"—Jackson glanced at the men around the table—"and we'll want to confer as we write up the bid, just so you know what we're thinking in terms of cost and time frame. But I think—a week from Monday?"

"Excellent!"

Once they were done talking, Richard showed them to the door, saying he'd await their estimate. They managed to get down the stairs onto the driveway before they lost their composure completely.

"Oh my God, David," Michael laughed. "You squealed like a little girl."

David bit his lower lip. Michael couldn't see it in the dark, but he knew his friend's face and ears were bright red. David brought his hands to his cheeks.

"Oh Lord, I did, didn't I?"

Jackson encircled his waist from behind, pressing a kiss to his neck.

"You were excited. It's okay."

David melted back into Jackson, his body and horrified expression softening. Michael looked away. He loved them, but sometimes their displays of affection were almost painful to watch.

Gil laughed, wrapping Michael up in his huge arms and lifting him easily from his feet.

"Oh, put me down." Michael pushed against Gil's chest. The temptation to cuddle into the big body was too strong, the feel of the muscled stomach where Michael's cock pressed too arousing. Desire rammed into him like a truck, and he knew if he didn't get down, and soon, he was going to be fully hard, which was just a bit more illuminating than he wanted to be at the moment.

"Put me down." He smacked Gil's large bicep and wriggled in his arms.

"Aw, join the celebration, Michael," Gil teased. "This means Jackson and David can put you on the payroll. That's worth a celebratory hug, don't you think?"

"I can join the celebration without being manhandled, thank you."

"You're so fucking prickly." Gil laughed and let him drop onto his feet, but for a moment Michael thought he saw hurt in the hazel eyes. He turned to David and Jackson, convincing himself he'd been mistaken.

"This is going to be a huge job. Are we going to be able to do it and still keep our jobs at A.F.I.?"

David looked thoughtful. "It's really mostly on Jackson and his guys, at least at first. It will be a couple of months before we're even relevant."

Michael scowled at him. "Speak for yourself, big boy."

The look David shot him was tolerant. "You know what I mean, Michael. God only knows what they're going to find when they start pulling plaster and rewiring. That kitchen alone is a major undertaking. We can start looking at wallpaper samples, fabric for drapes. Pricing the refinishing on the floors. Finding someone qualified to clean those chandeliers will take a major search."

"But aren't they cool?" Michael smiled as they started walking down the driveway.

"They are very cool. I've never seen anything like them."

They paused to chat for another few moments at the end of the driveway, but it was cold. As Jackson and David began to say good night, Michael caught hold of David's sleeve.

"Can I have a moment of your time before you take off?"

David gave him a concerned look, his brow furrowed. "O-kay."

They separated, Jackson and Gil turning to look back at the front of the house, talking softly as Michael and David walked a short distance away.

"How is it," Michael asked, leaning in to speak in David's ear, "that I had no idea Gil painted murals?"

David leaned back to look at him, one brow raised. "I don't know." A corner of his mouth quirked upward. "Maybe I didn't think you'd care. But you do, don't you?" His expression evolved into a slow, slightly mocking smile. "Now isn't that interesting."

Michael felt his face heat and was glad it was dark. He did not blush. Not over Gilbert Chandler. "Oh, bite me, David."

David chuckled, and Michael turned to make a purposeful exit. He started for his car, but he should have taken more care; he hadn't gone five steps before he skidded sideways on the icy asphalt. His arms windmilled for a moment before he found his balance.

"Care for some help there, darlin'?" Gil called, laughter in his voice. Michael flipped him off without turning.

"I am not your darlin'," he muttered, but it was during a break in traffic and his voice carried.

"No? How about sweetheart? Baby boy?"

Michael made a gagging sound, and Gil's booming laughter followed him all the way to his car. He grabbed the hood, skidding again, but he wasn't about to look back. He slipped and slid around his car, finally grabbing the door handle, and used his keychain fob to unlock the little Subaru.

"Oh, well done!" Gil applauded, and Michael was quite sure he'd never loathed anyone more in his life. He yanked the door open and nearly slid under the car before he managed to throw himself into the seat. Gil's mocking laughter carried to him. Michael was fuming as he started the car and pulled away from the curb, his studded tires spinning before they caught. He refused to even look at the men still standing in the wide driveway. Except he couldn't help but see the tallest of the three smiling in his peripheral vision. Damn him.

Michael headed down the hill, his hands white-knuckled on the steering wheel. He didn't understand why Gil riled him more than any man he'd ever met. David's theory involved sexual tension.

Michael was sure David was out of his damned mind.

As he drove toward downtown, his irritation faded, and he saw the lights of the Sacred Heart Medical Center on the hill to his right. Without consciously planning ahead of time, he turned, taking the road that led between the hospital and the doctors' building.

If there's no parking, I'll just go home, he thought. But there was a parking place where there was never any parking, and he pulled into it, letting his car idle. He stared through the tall glass doors of the hospital, wondering what the hell he was doing. After a moment he exhaled a rough breath, turned off the car, and snatched the keys from the ignition. If he was going to do this, he needed to get out of the bloody car.

He crossed the street, hands jammed in his pockets and shoulders hunched, almost turning back to his car more than once. The wind had come up and was tearing at his carefully combed faux hawk, pitching the long strands down over the frames of his glasses. He pushed at them in irritation as he entered the lobby, sighing in relief as the warm air brushed his chilled face. A directory hung on the wall next to a vacant reception desk, and Michael studied it even though he had no idea what he was looking for.

Pediatric Endocrinology and Diabetes, Pediatric Gastroenterology, Pediatric Hematology and Oncology. Michael shuddered, but it wasn't from the cold. The idea of a little kid dealing with any of those illnesses was awful. Thinking about their parents was even worse.

"Can I help you?"

Michael jumped in surprise and turned, his hands clutching his arms.

A very attractive woman with dark hair stood behind him. She had bangs and large green eyes, and the badge pinned to her blue jacket read Louise Pewsey, Administration.

"I—" Michael glanced back at the directory. "I was actually looking for…." He shook his head. "This is going to sound very odd, I think, but I'm looking for a series of wall murals? The artist's name is—"

"Big Gil?" She smiled at Michael's startled expression. "They're on the fourth floor; hematology and oncology. They really are very special. Unfortunately, there are limited visiting hours on that floor for anyone other than families of the patients."

"Oh." Michael was surprised by how disappointed he was.

Louise seemed to see it, too, and she held up her hand with a slight smile. "Hold on." Crossing behind the desk, she leaned over to take something out of a drawer, then scooted it across the counter to him. It was a volunteer's badge.

"It's really kind of late for volunteers to be on the floor, but if anyone asks, just tell them I know you're there."

Michael took the badge and clipped it to the front of his jacket. "Thank you. I appreciate it."

Louise studied him. "Do you know Gil?"

He gave her a weak, sheepish smile. "Not as well as I thought, apparently."

Her answering smile was kind. "Take the elevator to the fourth floor, then walk across the sky bridge. You can't miss them."

"Thanks."

Michael gave her another small smile of appreciation, then went to the bank of elevators. One opened on his pressing the button, and he stepped onto the empty car, pressing another button for the fourth floor. As the elevator ascended, he chewed on his thumbnail.

What was he doing there? He didn't have an answer. He just needed to see, as if seeing Gil's work could help him decipher the puzzle that was the man. He pushed away the thought that he shouldn't care. When the elevator doors opened, he saw a nurses' station directly in front of him. Phones were ringing, and nurses in bright scrubs answered and bustled about with charts and medication. Skirting the busy desk, he followed a hall to the left. A low buzz of conversation came from the rooms up and down the hall, and the lights were still high. It was dinnertime, he realized, smelling something surprisingly edible. It masked the medicinal smell that usually accompanied a hospital. Not far down the hall, there was a woman walking with a child. The boy—he thought it was a boy; what little hair was on his head looked soft, barely more than stubble—had a wheeled IV pole beside him. The woman gave Michael a slight smile as he passed them, and he thought it looked tired and careworn. Oncology, he suddenly remembered. Cancer. The sight of the child's vulnerable, soft little head would probably stay with him forever.

Just past a set of doors he saw a burst of color on the wall, and he quickened his steps.

And caught his breath.

A beautifully executed mural spanned the wall, depicting a wooden mantel and fireplace, evergreen garland with bright red berries draped above a set of elaborate Christmas stockings. In one sock a small stuffed toy rabbit nestled, brown with lighter spots, shining black button eyes, and an embroidery-stitched grin. He was a lovely toy. Next to him was painted *The Velveteen Rabbit by Margery Williams*. Michael caught his breath. *The Velveteen Rabbit* was one thing he had shared with his busy, socialite mother. She was never too busy for the Velveteen Rabbit.

"He was fat and bunchy," Gil had painted in even, steady-handed script, "as a rabbit should be."

Michael walked along the walls, absently smiling at anyone he passed, studying the whimsical paintings, reading the remembered story of the little toy rabbit who was bullied by the other toys, who all thought themselves very grand when compared to a bunny stuffed with sawdust. The boats and cars and fire engines, which were faithfully rendered, were sure they were "real." Even the jointed lion who thought himself "connected to the government" was certain of it, making the rabbit feel insignificant.

When Michael arrived at the painting of a worn and tatty rocking horse, he stopped. The beloved toy was so beautifully painted. His skin was threadbare, and his mane and tail, which had probably been very splendid, were now sad things, down to a few stray hairs. Michael's hand drifted up to touch his own lips, reading the words he'd always loved.

"…by the time you are Real, most of your hair has been loved off, and your eyes drop out and you get loose in the joints and very shabby. But these things don't matter at all, because once you are Real you can't be ugly…."

Michael blinked quickly, forcing tears back. He moved on to the next illustration, and the next. They were all beautiful, telling the story of the little rabbit, so faithful, the constant companion of the little boy until scarlet fever separated them forever. The words echoed in Michael's head, only he was hearing his mother's voice, the way it softened on the words, the way her fingers felt in his hair. By the time he arrived at the last panel, he was feeling brittle. But there was no mistaking it; Gil was an artist of true talent, and his hand with the well-loved story was gentle, delicate, perfect for the place and for the audience. Michael studied the piece in front of him, the rendering of the little rabbit made real, and he could see his soft fur, almost thought his little nose should twitch as he sat in the thicket, bright eyes looking out at Michael. It was exquisite.

Down in the corner, almost lost in the long green grass, was some writing, and Michael bent to read it.

"For Stevie Manyon, who was always real, from Big Gil."

Michael straightened, frowning.

When he was back in his car, Michael searched the name Stevie Manyon in his phone. Almost instantly an article popped up.

"Courageous Five-Year-Old Loses Battle with Leukemia." Michael groaned softly but read the entire article, his heart sinking further with each word.

"He was buried with his toy rabbit," Stevie's mother said. "*The Velveteen Rabbit* was his favorite story. Now they're both real."

Michael let his head fall back against the headrest, tears slipping down his cheeks. Finally, irritated, he tossed the phone into the passenger seat and dashed at the tears on his face.

Starting his car, he took a deep breath before he put it in gear and pulled out of the parking place.

"Damn you, Gilbert Chandler," he muttered. "Why couldn't you be a jerk?"

CHAPTER FOUR

"I REALLY appreciate this." David grabbed rolled socks from the open drawer of his dresser and put them in a small carry-on bag. Michael lay on the bed beside him, his hands behind his head.

"No worries." Michael brought one hand down to sink his fingers in Scooter's dark fur. "Princess and I will have a good time, here all by ourselves. Won't we, sweetheart?" She licked the inside of his wrist, then laid her head on his hip.

David looked up at him, fair hair falling into his eyes. He pushed it back impatiently.

"Why don't you go mousse that mess?" Michael asked. "It won't stay out of your face that way."

David went bright red to the tips of his ears. He mumbled something, and Michael angled his head. "What was that?"

David huffed. "I don't want to take the time to shower first when we get there, all right?"

"First before…?"

David gave him an incredulous look.

"Oh!" Michael laughed. "First before *that*. And seriously? This is why I'm single. No man is worth leaving the house without doing my hair first."

David smirked, adding another shirt to his bag. "You just haven't had the right man yet. By the way, you could have someone over if you wanted," he offered, trying to sound casual.

Michael scowled at him.

Clearly it had been a mistake to tell David he'd gone by the hospital to see Gil's murals. He hadn't seen the man himself in the week and a half since, and he was relieved. Michael wasn't sure how he'd respond to him now, and the thought made him nervous. David was just exacerbating the situation every chance he got.

"I don't understand you." David shook his head and folded a pair of slacks. "You go to the trouble to see his work at Sacred Heart, but you won't call him. Even to tell him how beautiful you think they are."

"He doesn't need my opinion." Michael rubbed his thumb gently down between Scooter's closed eyes. "I'm sure everyone has already told him how wonderful he is."

David shot him an irritated look. "There's no crime in liking him, Michael." He took another shirt from a hanger and folded it neatly. "And I think your opinion would matter to him more than just about anyone else's."

Michael snorted. He doubted it. "How long of a trip are you packing for, David? Because right now you could be gone a week without wearing anything twice."

"Oh, shut up." David placed the shirt in the bag, then looked up at Michael, his hands going to his narrow hips. "You know how much I love you, right?"

Michael's lips twisted. "That usually precedes something I don't want to hear."

"And this probably qualifies. I'm going to say it anyway." He held up his hand when Michael opened his mouth. "Let me say this."

Michael huffed out an irritated sigh but lay back and closed his mouth.

"It's been what? Five years since Evan? And you haven't seen anyone?"

Michael felt his jaw harden.

David's face softened. "Don't do that. I'm really trying to help."

"I don't need help." He sounded harsh and he didn't care. "I'm fine. And I have seen people."

David scowled. "Hooking up isn't seeing someone."

Michael shrugged one shoulder. "It works. I get laid, and I don't…."

He stopped, suddenly awkward, afraid he was about to reveal an aspect of his character he didn't want even his best friend to know.

David sat on the edge of the bed. "And you don't what?"

Michael curled his fingers in Scooter's fur. "Leave it alone, David. I'm all right. I might feel like being in a relationship at some point, someday. But I don't want it now. And I won't want Gilbert."

The front door opened and closed in the other room, and Scooter jumped up and ran down a small set of stairs at the foot of the bed Jackson had built for that purpose. "Babe, where are you?" Jackson called.

"Bedroom," David answered, his gaze still on Michael. He looked so sad that Michael reached out and patted his hip, attempting a smile.

"I'm fine. Stop worrying and go away to get laid by your lovely boyfriend."

David sighed, but he straightened, looking into his bag. "Fiancé," he said absently. "What am I missing?" He looked around the bedroom.

"Black jock strap?" Michael offered. He'd given the skimpy black underwear to David as a joke on his birthday the year before. David stuck his tongue out at Michael, but then reached into the open drawer, grabbed the aforementioned item, and stuffed it under his shirts in the carry-on. Michael smirked.

"You about ready?" Jackson came to the bedroom door, Scooter dancing around his feet.

David grabbed a pair of jeans from a hanger and laid them over the top of everything in his bag, then closed and zipped it shut. "This one is ready. I just need to grab my shaving stuff from the bathroom."

Jackson came to him, slipped his arm around David's waist, and kissed him gently. "You don't need to shave. I like you scruffy." His voice was soft and smooth as twenty-five-year-old scotch, making Michael's cock twitch. Which was wrong on so many levels, Michael didn't even want to think about it. Jackson's large tan hand lifted, his fingers slipping through David's blond hair. "I love your hair all soft like this."

"I know." Jackson cupped David's cheek, and he leaned into the touch.

Michael leaned around David, looking up at Jackson. "You do realize I'm right here, right?"

Jackson glanced over at him. "Oh, hey, Michael." He looked back into David's face. "Hey to you too."

David's whole body seemed to go soft, relaxing into Jackson. Michael couldn't see his face, but knew he was smiling at him. "Hey," David murmured, humming softly when Jackson leaned in to kiss him again.

Michael rolled off the far side of the bed and stalked around the foot. "When you two are done, I'll be in the living room. Come on, Scootsy."

Usually the pet name drove David crazy, but he was too wrapped up in Jackson to notice. Michael closed the door behind him a bit harder than was strictly necessary and went into the front room, flopping back on the leather couch after he lifted Scooter up next to him.

He didn't begrudge David and Jackson their weekend away; work began on the O'Banyon mansion on Monday, and they'd all be tied up for a while after that. He and David wouldn't be as busy as the construction guys at first, but there would be plenty for them to do: going through catalogs, taking meetings with Richard and Lyle over fabric and paint samples.

Ordering in the antique wallpaper Richard wanted would have to happen soon if they were going to get it in time for installation. David had already priced it, but there was so much more they'd need too. Paint, drapery fabric, windows. Michael was tempted to pull out his tablet and make more notes, then decided against it. If Jackson and David could take the weekend off, he could too.

He looked over to find Scooter watching him, her head cocked to one side. "So, what'll we do, princess? Read? Play video games? Watch TV?"

She hopped away across the cushions, and Michael had no idea what she was doing until she returned with the remote for the television in her mouth. He laughed.

"Oh, you are entirely too smart for your own good." He took the remote from her, grimacing, and rubbed his palm on his jeans. "Blech, corgi spit." She immediately licked his wrist, and he laughed again. "Okay, I get it. It's medicinal." She sat and looked at him, tongue lolling and eyes bright.

"So, what'll it be? *Ghost Adventures? Dead Files?*" The little dog curled up next to him on the sofa, her head on his thigh. "I get it—you don't care." He turned the TV on and flipped through the channels, then stopped on a rerun of *American Ninja Warrior*. At least the men were pretty. He took off his shoes and propped his stockinged feet carefully on the glass-covered coffee table. Looking at the elegantly carved top of the low piece reminded him that it had once belonged to Gil's father, and he scowled at it.

It was a few minutes before Jackson appeared, carrying David's bag. His hair was tousled.

"It's very rude to give your boyfriend a blow job while you have someone sitting in your living room."

Jackson gave him a cheeky smile and a wink before he walked out through the front door. Moments later David entered the room, carrying a small dark bag that matched his luggage. His face and neck were blotchy, and Michael laughed.

"Good Lord, how did you ever get away with anything when you were a kid?" David looked at Michael, frowning slightly. "You have 'my boyfriend just blew me' all over your face."

David grimaced, his ear tips turning bright red. "Shut up." He set his bag by the front door, then reached to take down a heavy jacket hanging on the coatrack.

"We should be back by two on Sunday." He pushed his hands into the sleeves and shrugged into it. "There are emergency numbers in a list on the fridge. I'm not sure how good cell reception will be at the cabin, but I left the number for the main office. If you need us, someone can run down with a message." David started to close his coat, but his hands were trembling and he was buttoning it lopsided.

"Oh, just turn off your phones." Michael pushed to his feet and crossed to his friend, pushing his hands away to realign the buttonholes. He closed the jacket, then squeezed David's arm. "I'm a big boy. And if anything happens, I can dial 911 with the best of them."

David surprised Michael by pulling him into a fierce hug. "I so want you to be happy," he whispered against Michael's ear.

It startled Michael, the emotion in his friend's voice bringing a lump to his throat. He coughed to clear it.

"I'm not unhappy." He pulled back, forcing a smile. "And you're entirely too wound up for a man who just had an orgasm."

"Oh God!" David smacked him lightly on the upper arm as the front door opened. "It's not all about fucking and blow jobs, you know."

Jackson stepped in, reaching for David's bag. "It isn't?" he said. "Damn. There's no TV in those cabins. Whatever shall we do?"

David gave him a wry look. "I packed Yahtzee. Go warm up the truck."

"Yes, sir!" He gave David a jaunty salute, then winked at Michael. "I love it when he gets all domineering."

Jackson grinned at the exasperated look on David's face and walked out through the open door. David and Michael followed him onto the porch. Scooter ran past them into the front yard, pouncing on any scrap of snow that didn't already have her paw prints in it.

"Scooter, stop," David called. She looked at him, then lifted her front paws and brought them down in another patch of snow. Michael laughed.

"Obstinate little brat." David huffed. "She'll be soaked."

"Don't worry about it. I'll dry her off."

David looked around the dark yard, wrapping his arms around his waist. "I'm not sure how comfortable I am leaving you here alone."

Michael slipped his arm around David's shoulders, pulling him in. He understood David's concern. David's ex, Trevor, had broken into the house in the first few weeks he owned it. He'd tried to hurt Jackson and had injured the neighbor's corgi, Bootsy, who David was pet-sitting.

"David," Michael began.

"You can't tell me you've never felt it, Michael. I know better."

Michael looked into David's face, prepared to lie and tell him he was imagining things. But then he saw the flat line his friend's full lips were pressed into, the flinty, brittle expression around his eyes.

"Don't you think that's carryover from what Trevor did?"

David looked out over the yard. A sigh moved his shoulders. "Maybe that's all it is. I know the night he sat out here in the dark, spying on me while I talked to my neighbor, did more damage than I thought."

Michael felt a faint shudder move through the slender body next to him, and he squeezed David's upper arm.

"I know." Michael intentionally gentled his voice. "And yeah, okay; I've gotten the creeps out here at night too. But Trevor likes his freedom entirely too much to violate his probation by coming anywhere near you now."

David turned back to Michael, his expression startled.

"Oh, I don't think it's still Trevor. I felt like I was being watched even before he turned up on my porch. But I don't think it's him. Not anymore."

Consternation wrinkled Michael's brow, but by the time he'd thought up a response, Jackson was standing at the foot of the porch steps, looking up at them.

"You ready, babe?"

David grabbed Michael's hand, squeezing almost too hard. "Promise me you'll be careful. Don't come outside by yourself after dark. If you have to, bring Scooter with you. If you hear anything, call 911, call Gil. Just—be safe. Please."

Michael swallowed, forcing his voice to remain casual. "You worry too much. I'll be fine. I have the alarm system and the dog. And if all else fails, your mother lives just down the street. Beverley would scare the shit out of any prowler." He gave David a teasing hip check. "Now go take your man away for the weekend and have fun."

Jackson looked up at David expectantly. "Come on, sweetheart," he said. "If you want to get there before midnight, we need to go."

"Okay, okay. Scooter!" David called the little dog, and she bounded up the steps to sit at his feet. He crouched down and sank his fingers into her fur, scratching behind both large black ears. "You be a good girl. Take care of Michael."

"That's right, Scooter," Michael quipped. "You take care of Michael, because God knows it couldn't be the other way around."

"Shut up." David stood up, kissed Michael's cheek, then hurried down the steps to Jackson.

"You know," Jackson complained wryly, catching David's hand, "the amount you two kiss each other, I'm almost jealous."

"Relax, handsome," Michael drawled. "I've never had your honey's tongue in my mouth."

David turned back, giving Michael a stern look. "I'd just as soon you didn't announce that from my porch, thank you."

Michael grinned. "What? The neighbors don't know you're a big old 'mo?"

David glared, but Jackson laughed and pulled on his hand, propelling him toward the driveway.

"Remember what I said about coming outside. Jackson is convinced we've got raccoons messing with the cans, but I'd just as soon neither you or Scooter came face-to-face with them either. They can have rabies."

"I'll be good, Mom." Michael waved him off. "For God's sakes, go the hell away."

He watched them climb into the cab of Jackson's large silver pickup, waving as they backed out of the driveway. Scooter followed them as far as the sidewalk, and Michael called her back.

"Come on, sweetheart." He opened the front door and stood aside, letting her go in before him. "Just you and me tonight. We'll have a quiet evening watching boring movies and eating crap." He glanced around the dark, quiet street before he closed the door behind him. "Let's get you dried off, then I can raid the kitchen." He led the happy dog into the bathroom.

There was a walk-in pantry in the large kitchen, and Michael pulled on the chain that lit the bare lightbulb in the ceiling. On the shelves to the left, he immediately saw the dog treats.

"Ah-ha!" Michael opened the bag and took out what looked like a cross between jerky and a slice of bacon. Scooter barked once, happily, as if to say "give it to me already," and Michael laughed, holding it out. She went up onto her back legs and took it, then promptly trotted away toward the living room.

Michael searched the rest of the shelves. There was quinoa and brown rice, jarred sun-dried tomatoes, and cans of gourmet olives. "Good God, what are you feeding the man, David? He can't be surviving on quinoa." He turned, and on the other shelves hit pay dirt. Three bags of chips, salsa, and jars of spinach dip. "Now, here's my kind of food." There were also a couple of bags of cookies and microwave popcorn. "Excellent!" He grabbed the box of kettle corn.

After putting the envelope inside the microwave, Michael closed the door and set the timer. It began to hum, and he went to the old Philco refrigerator. If David ever bought a new one, Michael had called dibs on this one. He loved it, loved the "loaf of bread" shape and the heavy chrome handle and accents. Inside he found Coke and Diet Coke lined up in neat rows next to milk and a bottle of apple juice, and Michael grabbed a diet pop with a smile. "Thank you, David." He popped the top, enjoyed the resulting hiss, then went back into the living room. The smell of the popping corn filled the house.

Scooter was happily gnawing on her bacon strip in her little bed, and Michael leaned over the back of the couch for the remote. Searching the channels, he found Guy Ritchie's *Sherlock Holmes* and made a small sound of satisfaction. When his popcorn was done, he vaulted over the back of the sofa and settled in. Within minutes he was lost in the movie. The eye candy in the film was excellent. There was no one sexier than Robert Downey Jr. as he played the brilliant Holmes, and Jude Law was hot as hell in Dr. Watson's turn-of-the-century clothes. The steampunk vibe appealed to Michael's design sense, and the bromance was fun.

He was thoroughly engrossed in the movie when a sound in the driveway pulled his attention. It wasn't loud, but it was loud enough that it yanked him out of the film. He muted the television and turned his head, waiting. Scooter, who had been snoozing in her little bed, lifted her head as well, ears perked. Michael waited, but he didn't hear it again, and he went back to the movie, absently figuring it was probably a neighborhood cat.

The next noise he heard outside was no longer furtive. In fact, it was loud enough that he jumped, his head whipping around. A metallic clang and a muffled thud came from the garage area near the trash cans. Michael's heart leapt into his throat even as he recalled David mentioning the raccoons. Scooter stood up and took a few tentative steps, looking toward the windows, her head angled first one way, then the other.

If there were raccoons in the cans, the only way to deal with it was to scare them off. Irritated, nerves jangling, Michael slipped into his tennis shoes, grabbed his jacket, and at the last minute picked up the fireplace poker, David's warning about rabies ringing in his ears. He didn't want to get any closer to their mouths than he had to. With his luck, he could see having to endure a series of rabies shots because of some damned raccoon. It wasn't going to happen if he could help it.

He worked the code on the security pad next to the door, then grabbed Scooter's leash and clipped it to her collar. David had said he didn't want Scooter going out, but Michael doubted he could keep her inside once he opened the door if she wasn't wearing her leash. The last thing he needed was to have to chase her down the street in the middle of the night while she hunted raccoons. When she was securely attached, he opened the door.

She was surprisingly strong for such a little dog. She yanked him down the steps and around the side of the house.

"Easy, princess," he said, half laughing. Huge trees above cast mottled shadows over the driveway, coating the trash bins in an added layer of darkness. It wasn't so dim that Michael couldn't see the white garage door, though.

Or the figure standing in front of it.

Michael jerked to a stop, yanking on Scooter's leash. So it wasn't raccoons. The man in front of the garage was dressed completely in black, and he was spray-painting dark letters on the white paint of the door.

"What the hell are you doing?" Michael blurted. The man whirled, and for a suspended moment, they stared at one another. The vandal was wearing a black ski mask, making him look like a shadow in the darkness. He threw the can of spray paint aside, sending it rolling into the bushes as he picked up something else from next to the trash can and lifted it over his head. The weak moonlight glinted off the spade of a shovel, and Michael instinctively took a step back.

White noise roared in his ears. The guy was going to come after him with the shovel, and with a jolt of raw clarity, Michael knew it could kill him. He went cold to the soles of his shoes, frozen in place. Then Scooter planted herself between Michael and the man, barking furiously, as if she could somehow protect him. He sensed the attention shift to the little dog, and Michael's fear went instantly from himself to her.

Michael was finally able to move. He scooped Scooter up in his arms and dashed for the open front door. He moved faster than he ever had in his life, pounding up the stairs and across the porch. Heavy footfalls, shaking the porch boards, followed close, and Michael hit the door just ahead of the man behind him. He rushed through and tried to push it closed, but a heavy, gloved hand slammed into the wood, preventing it. There was a suspended moment of horror as Michael and the man locked eyes. Nearly black pupils were revealed by the holes in his mask, a small liver-colored mark on his right eyelid. A burst of adrenaline surged through Michael, and he used his weight, such as it was, to push the thick door closed. Once it was shut, he threw the dead bolt.

Breathing hard, eyes stinging with tears, he cradled Scooter in his arms while she continued to bark, her whole little body trembling. Michael backed away from the door as heavy blows rattled it in its frame.

He couldn't believe what was happening, even as his heart beat so hard the reverberations rattled his chest and went all the way into his throat. He remembered David telling him Trevor had worn a ski mask, but those hadn't been Trevor's eyes locked with his. He'd never seen anything as devoid of humanity, as full of loathing. The pounding stopped for a moment and Michael went still, waiting. Then a huge bang made him duck, shielding his face in Scooter's fur and turning her away from the noise. When he peered up, the man was glaring at him through the large living room window.

Michael backed into the dining room, slipped around the corner, and pressed his back to the wall as the pounding on the front door began again. He leaned against the wall and slid slowly to the floor, clutching Scooter to his chest. Every time the front door rattled, her barking intensified. She was doing her job, trying to protect her home, but he was afraid to let her go.

"Shush, baby, shush," he muttered against her head, but she just barked and barked, and Michael shuddered, feeling trapped and terrified and very alone. Then something in his hip pocket vibrated, and he hauled in a grateful gasp. Oh God, his phone.

He held on to Scooter with one hand as he yanked the phone free of the tight denim with the other. When he saw who was calling, more tears filled his eyes. He pushed the button with his hand, but it was shaking so hard he wasn't sure at first he'd connected.

"Gil?" he gasped.

"Hey, handsome." Gil's voice was in his ear and Michael felt his composure begin to fragment. "Jesus, what's wrong with the dog?"

"Gil. Oh God, Gil. I heard something outside and thought it was raccoons trying to get into the trash cans, but it wasn't raccoons. There was a guy out there, and he was spray-painting something on the garage doors. I asked him what the hell he thought he was doing, and he picked up a shovel and he chased me onto the porch, and I almost couldn't get the door closed and locked, but I finally did. Now he's pounding on the door!" He was babbling so fast he didn't know if Gil even understood him, but he couldn't help it. The man, that man who wanted to hurt him, was still trying to get in the house.

As if to prove his point, it sounded as if the vandal outside threw his body at the front door, and Michael heard Gil inhale sharply.

"Michael, listen to me, baby. Can you hear me?"

"Yes."

"Hang up the phone and call 911. Do it now. Yell that you're calling the cops. You hear me, Michael?"

"Yes, I hear you."

"Good. Do it now. I'll be there as fast as I can."

Gil hung up, and Michael followed his instructions. With wildly shaking hands, still gripping Scooter to his chest, he managed to dial 911.

"I'm calling the police," he yelled as loudly as he could, as near hysterical as he'd ever been in his life. "You'd better get the hell out of here. I'm dialing 911, and then this place is going to be crawling with cops!"

"911, what is your emergency?" a pleasant woman's voice asked.

Michael hauled in a shuddering breath. "I'm house-sitting for a friend, and someone is trying to break in."

"Right now?"

"Yes, he's trying to get in. Please send someone quickly. Please."

"Give me the address, sir."

Michael rattled off the address, cradling Scooter the whole time. She'd stopped barking, and Michael could only hope his threats had scared the bastard away. The dog tucked her head beneath his chin, shuddering against his chest, her sides heaving. He ran his hand over her fur, petting her, soothing her. "It's okay, sweetheart," he murmured as he heard the woman on the phone giving the address out over the police radio. "You did good."

"Sir, what's your name?"

"Michael. Michael Crane."

"And it's not your home?"

"No. I'm house-sitting for a friend."

"Are you in immediate danger?"

Michael leaned around the edge of the wall, looking toward the front door. The house now seemed almost ominously silent.

"I don't know. I yelled at him I was calling 911. I don't hear him now. It might have scared him off."

"I'll stay on the phone with you until the officers arrive."

"Thank you so much."

"Of course."

A loud crash came from outside, and Michael's car alarm went off. He grimaced. "Shit, I think he just hit my car."

"Hit it with another vehicle?" she asked, sounding completely calm.

"I don't know. Maybe he hit it with the shovel. The alarm is blaring."

"Shovel?"

"He threatened me with a shovel before I was able to lock him outside."

"Oh dear. Well, I can hear your alarm. Go ahead and just let it sound off. It might work to frighten him away."

Scooter began to whimper softly, and Michael tightened his hold around her. "It's okay, baby."

"Is the animal with you injured?"

"No, I think she's just scared. Shit, I'm scared."

He heard a soft chuckle come through the phone. "Well, you're doing very well."

"I think it's a win that I didn't piss my pants, pardon my language."

"I think I'd be trying out some Depends myself, given the situation."

Michael relaxed enough to chuckle weakly.

He heard vehicles jerking to an abrupt halt out front, and he leaned around the wall to look. Red and blue lights cast shadows on the walls.

"The police are here."

"Just stay with me until they knock, okay?"

"Okay."

It only took a few moments for them to reach the door.

55

"They're here." Michael pushed to his feet, still holding Scooter in his arms. She was starting to get heavy, but he couldn't seem to convince his arms to put her down.

"Can you see the officers through a peephole?"

A uniformed officer looked in through the large window, raising his hand. "I can see one through the window."

"Do you feel safe now?"

Michael could see at least one more uniformed officer standing on the porch, studying him as he approached. "I'm okay now. Thank you."

"You're welcome, Michael. You did good too."

He wasn't so sure about that, but it was nice of her to say so. He shoved the phone back into his pocket, then juggled Scooter as he unlocked and opened the front door.

"Sir, you called about a prowler?"

Michael nodded, suddenly weak-kneed with relief. He leaned, shaking, against the doorframe.

"Are you all right, sir?"

Michael looked up at him. Tall and square-jawed, the officer studied him with keen blue eyes. His nameplate read Slater.

"I don't know," Michael answered honestly.

"Do you need to sit down?"

"Might be a good idea."

When Slater went to take Michael's arm, his hand covered in a black leather glove, Scooter snarled at him.

"Oh no, girl, no." Michael tried to gentle her with a stroke down her spine. "He's a good guy."

"Well, thank you for that." Slater gave him a wry smile. The officer behind him stepped forward. He was shorter, with a friendly expression. His name was Preston.

"Can I take her?" he asked.

"She's scared. I'm afraid she might bite you."

"Naw, I'm good with dogs." Preston stepped around his fellow officer, reaching out. "Easy, girl. Aren't you a pretty little thing? I love corgis."

Michael was surprised when Scooter let the police officer take her.

"Can I put her in the other room?"

"Um, yeah. Just through there." He pointed to the hall door. As Officer Preston walked across the room with Scooter, Michael turned back to the imposing man in front of him.

"Are you injured?" Slater asked.

"No. Just rattled."

"I think you should sit down anyway."

"Okay."

Michael crossed to the sofa and sat, rubbing at his forehead with trembling fingers. His body felt like one large raw nerve.

Two more officers came to the open door, and Slater turned.

"There's vandalism," one of them said. "Spray paint on the garage door and a shovel through a windshield, but no suspect."

Michael thought of the last crash he'd heard, the one that had triggered the alarm. He groaned. Shit. His car.

"Do you have keys to the Subaru handy, sir?" Slater asked. "It would be good if we could cut that alarm. We've already got neighbors sticking their heads out, and your assailant is lurking somewhere."

"Oh, right." Michael dug his keys out of his pocket and handed them over. Moments after the other officer disappeared, the alarm abruptly cut off.

The remaining policeman touched Slater's shoulder. "I think we need to call Mitchell in hate crimes."

"Secure the scene first, then call it in."

The man nodded and left the house. Preston came back after closing Scooter in the hallway. She whined pitifully, and Michael looked over his shoulder at the door.

"She's okay," Preston assured him.

Michael pushed his glasses up on his nose. His hands were still shaking.

A raised voice came from out front and his head lifted, his heart urging him to his feet. Without pausing to think, he moved across the room.

"Sir?" Slater said. "Sir, we need your statement."

"I'll be right back," Michael muttered. He left the house, then ran across the porch and down the steps, searching the faces gathered at a line of yellow tape that had been strung from tree to tree.

"Michael!"

Michael heard the shout, and turned in time to see a large, shadowy figure lift the tape and straighten on the other side. Before Gil could approach, an officer was there, one hand outstretched and the other on his gun.

"Stop right there."

Michael's heart stuttered and his gut clenched. "No!" he shouted, approaching. "He's here for me. He's with me! Please." The officer looked at him. "Please!"

There was a weighted silence.

"Let him through."

Michael looked over his shoulder to see Slater standing on the porch.

"Michael." Michael turned back and Gil was there, an arm's length away, his voice rough as he reached out.

The next thing he knew he was in Gil's arms, pressing his face into the massive chest, clutching the wall of muscle. Gil surrounded him, holding him, his chin on the top of his head. The scent of him, the feel of him, provided Michael the ability to take his first full breath since he'd seen the prowler. Gil's warmth went into Michael's muscles and tendons and his knees gave up the ghost. Gil caught him before he could collapse.

"Baby, are you all right?" he murmured, and Michael's throat thickened. He wanted to answer, he really did, but he couldn't. Instead, he shook his head as Gil held him upright.

"Are you hurt? Do you need a doctor?"

"No," he finally managed. "No, I'm not hurt."

"Gentlemen." Slater had apparently approached, because he sounded close. Michael glanced over and found him standing right beside them. "Mr. Crane, do you need medical assistance?"

"Are you going to be able to walk?" Gil asked.

That was the question that brought Michael up short. What was he going to do? Let Gil carry him, like he was some sort of damsel in distress? Michael took a deep breath, forcing strength back into his knees. He'd never been so scared, but he'd never been weak either. He swallowed, straightening away from Gil's body.

"I'm okay." He looked over into Slater's face. "I'm okay."

"Shall we take this in the house, then?"

Michael nodded, following him when they started back inside. He'd never tell a living soul how grateful he was for Gil's hand on his lower back. Particularly when he saw the blade of the shovel driven into the windshield of his Impreza, the wooden handle sticking straight out.

"Jesus," Gil muttered.

Michael turned his face away, mounting the steps with as much dignity as he could. He stopped abruptly, staring.

Someone had sprayed an upside-down triangle on the soft gray siding, clearly in reference to their company logo, with a swastika over it. At his elbow, Gil made a disgusted sound.

"That's so ugly." Michael shook his head. "Who would do that?"

Large hands closed over his biceps and he felt Gil along his back. "We'll paint it out as soon as the cops say it's okay."

Michael turned his face away as they entered the house.

After Gil introduced himself to Officers Slater and Preston and presented his ID voluntarily, Michael sat on the couch while Slater took his statement. While they talked, Gil went into the hallway to comfort the unhappy Scooter, then into the kitchen. A few minutes later, he approached Michael with a mug in his hand. He handed it to him, and the scent of chamomile lifted to his nose. He inhaled gratefully, wrapping cold palms around the hot mug. He gave Gil a grateful look as he sat beside him.

"So you have no idea who this might have been?" Slater went on.

Michael paused. "No. David had some trouble with his ex in the beginning, but that's been over for a while."

Slater flipped back through his notes. "Mr. Snyder is the owner?"

"David, yes."

A man cleared his throat and they all looked up.

Michael recognized Detective Dennis Mitchell standing in the doorway. He'd met him when he went to court with David for Trevor's sentencing. He came into the house, and Michael thought even if he hadn't known he was a cop, he'd still have figured it out. He was the stereotypical aging, balding detective in a bad brown suit. He looked like someone right out of central casting.

"Detective Mitchell." Michael stood and offered his hand.

"Michael, right?"

"Yes, sir."

Mitchell turned to Gil. "I don't believe we've met."

Gil stood, and he towered over everyone in the room. Mitchell's sparse brows shot up. "Gil Chandler." He shook Mitchell's hand.

"Sounds like you've had a busy night." Mitchell dropped his hands into the pockets of his baggy slacks, his arms holding back the sides of his jacket. "Care to start at the beginning and catch me up?"

Michael took a deep breath and did as Mitchell asked. The detective listened patiently, asked pertinent questions, but mostly he just let Michael talk. At one point, when Scooter's whining became particularly loud and pitiful, Michael asked if they could please let her out. When they opened the door to the hall, Scooter streaked through and went straight to Michael, going up onto her back feet to put her front paws on his knees.

"Aw, baby girl." Gil bent and picked her up, setting her in Michael's lap. "He's okay, see?"

She licked Michael's chin and neck, pressing her muzzle against his face. It was the first time since Gil arrived that he felt tears threaten.

"Is she injured?" Mitchell asked gently.

Michael shook his head, took a moment, and then cleared his throat. "She protected me."

"I'm not surprised." Mitchell leaned forward to rub her head. "Corgis are a very protective breed." He glanced toward the front door. "A couple of my forensics guys have been processing the scene outside and on the porch, but if you're done with your statement, I think you should probably take a look."

Michael grabbed Scooter's leash, then clipped it to her collar. He wasn't leaving her behind. He followed the officers out through the front door, Gil close enough behind him he could feel his body heat. Mitchell paused and studied the graffiti just outside the door, while Michael pointedly turned his face away, his stomach turning at the thought of it.

"I'm afraid it gets worse," Mitchell said apologetically. They went down the steps and paused in front of Michael's damaged Subaru. "I think you might have interrupted him, because he didn't write anything on the car. Just jammed the shovel through the windshield. But…." He turned with a gesture.

Michael turned to the garage door, and he felt cold slip down his spine, clear to his toes.

DIE FAGGOTS.

The letters were four feet tall and ragged. Floodlights lit the driveway now, so there was no mistaking the ugly message.

"Well, that's direct." Michael tried to sound casual. It didn't work.

"How soon can we get rid of it?"

Gil's voice was so raw that for a moment Michael wasn't certain it was him. He turned and looked up, startled by the rage he saw on the usually gentle man's face. Over the months that he'd known Gil, he'd seen a lot of different emotions on his face. He'd never seen rage before.

"We need to take some pictures, and we should probably speak to the owner."

"I'll call Jackson," Michael and Gil said in unison, then looked at each other.

"Seriously," Gil went on. "Can't we do this without discussing it with David?"

"He's already so jumpy," Michael added, speaking to Mitchell. "You know what dealing with Trevor did to him, what handling the break-in has been like."

Mitchell rocked back onto his heels, his hands still in his pockets, his lips pursed thoughtfully. "If we're able to determine who did this, the property damage is yours, Michael, and Mr. Snyder's. You should both be able to receive recompense."

"I have insurance on the car," Michael said. "Fortunately David and Jackson have friends who paint houses, and I'll buy the damned paint if I have to."

"The hell you will," Gil growled.

"I'm just saying we're all willing to take care of it. I want you to find as much evidence against whoever did this as possible. But I don't want Jackson and David coming home to this after the first chance they've had to get away in months. And I don't want David to know I was here by myself and someone tried to terrorize me. He was already afraid something like this could happen."

Mitchell frowned. "Has there been another incident?"

Michael shook his head. "No, I don't think so. He says he still feels like someone is watching the place, but I don't know how much of that is left over from Trevor. I just know he's been afraid."

Mitchell studied him for several seconds, then turned to the officers around him. "Let's make sure we get everything, including photos, tonight."

"There's also a can of spray paint under the bushes, over there." Michael pointed. "He threw it."

"Make sure to get that. Oh, and brush both the can and that shovel handle for prints."

"There won't be any," Michael said. "He was wearing gloves."

Mitchell studied him. "You knew Trevor Blankenship, right?"

Michael grimaced. "Unfortunately."

"Could this have been him?"

Michael wanted, so very much, to say yes, it could have been Trevor. The guy had been wearing a ski mask too, after all. And Michael loathed Trevor. In David's agreement with his ex, made at sentencing, the district attorney stipulated that Trevor was supposed to stay at least five hundred feet from David and his house, or the deal between them would be null and he would be heading off to serve five-to-twenty.

The guy wearing the ski mask had been taller than Trevor by at least four or five inches. He'd also had a bulkier build, and his eyes, the eyes Michael still shuddered to remember, were a completely different color than Trevor's.

"No." Michael sighed. "Much as I'd like for it to be, it wasn't Trevor. But whoever he was—" Michael shuddered. "—whoever he is, he's really pissed off."

"At who?" Gil turned to stare at the garage. "At David and Jackson, or at all of us?"

"I'm not sure there's any way to know."

There was a pensive silence; then Gil pulled his phone out of the pocket of his cargo pants. "I'll see if I can get ahold of Jackson, find out if it's okay if we paint tomorrow. Do you need to talk to them, Detective?"

Mitchell nodded. "But one day next week is soon enough."

Gil paced a few feet away.

"Detective," Michael said. "Do you think these attacks are the same person?"

"Which attacks, Michael?" he asked mildly.

"Jackson's truck, David's car, now this."

"Blankenship did maintain that he'd never damaged David's car." He looked thoughtful. "I honestly don't know. We have a certain amount of hate crime here, but these are more serious, with a higher amount of property damage. And where your group of friends is concerned, if there is a common denominator, they seem to be escalating. I mean, you did say you thought this man would hurt you if he'd had the opportunity."

Michael remembered again running, certain that shovel was about to cleave his head in two, the face so close to his, the rage. He swallowed heavily.

"He would have, yes."

"Well, you don't have to worry about that tonight, because he isn't getting anywhere near you." Gil held the phone out to Detective Mitchell. "This is Jackson. He's going to give you his permission for us to paint over the graffiti." The detective took the phone.

"Is he on the mortgage?" Mitchell asked Gil.

After the detective took the phone and walked away a few paces, Michael looked up into Gil's face. "When did David put Jackson on the deed?"

"When they got engaged," Gil answered. "And I meant what I said. You won't be staying alone tonight. You can either stay here or come home with me, but you will not be staying alone."

"Gilbert," Michael complained.

"No, dammit." Gil advanced on him, his square jaw hard and his gaze flinty. "There's such a thing as being heroic, and there's being a damned fool. This guy might not want anything more than to spray paint on the house and chase you with a shovel. What will keep me awake nights, Michael, for a long damned time, is what he could have done to you with that shovel if he'd caught you."

Gil's voice rang on the cold night air, and Michael shuddered. He didn't want to think about it, because he knew. He'd have hit him in the head, and God only knew what he'd have done to Scooter. She sat and leaned against his leg, and Michael scooped her up, burying his hands in her fur, pressing his face behind her head. He couldn't think about it; he couldn't.

"So pick, Michael. Here or at my house, but you aren't staying alone right now."

He sighed into Scooter's fur, and she wiggled around to lick his face. He set her back on her feet.

"Here," he answered finally. "I told David I'd keep an eye on things. I may have done a piss-poor job of it so far, but I won't give up."

"You didn't do a piss-poor job at anything," Gil growled. "I need to get my phone back from Mitchell so I can call Vern and get some guys here in the morning. If it doesn't rain and if we all hit it, we can have this done by Sunday morning, and it'll look as good as new." He paused, searching the driveway for Mitchell among the other police officers. "I'll be right back."

Michael watched him walk away, all six-foot-four muscled inches of him, and knew he would feel safer with him in the house. There was something reassuring about Gil that went beyond his size. There was also a sense of the inescapable, as if all the time he'd spent keeping his distance from Gil had just delayed the inevitable.

Tomorrow, Michael thought. Tomorrow, when he didn't feel so raw, he'd remind himself of all the reasons he'd had for staying away. Tonight he was just glad Gil was there.

CHAPTER FIVE

THE POLICE were in the driveway for what felt like hours. They turned off the strobing red and blue lights, and after a while the patrol cars left, but the detectives and the crime scene people were there for a long time. Gil tried to interest Michael in his popcorn, in maybe making dinner, but Michael had no appetite and couldn't seem to tear himself away from the windows overlooking the driveway. He watched the cops do their meticulous work, digging a trash bag from beneath the bushes, an empty can of spray paint from beside the trash cans. Every few moments he'd look back to the garage doors, and he'd read the ugly message.

DIE FAGGOTS.

Who thought like that? Were there actually people who wished someone dead, just because they were different? He knew about homophobia; he wasn't an idiot. And he'd survived high school, which hadn't been easy. He'd looked gay in sixth grade, apparently, although if that meant clean and fastidious about how he dressed, well then, so be it. By high school, the kids he'd gone to private school with had been divided into categories: jocks, nerds, geeks, and apparently queers. He'd even admit he was as guilty of stereotyping as the next person. But had he ever wished anyone dead? Not even Trevor. He'd hated him, but he didn't wish him dead.

But someone did, badly enough to spray-paint it all over his best friend's garage. Michael exhaled heavily and wrapped his arms around himself, shuddering, wondering if he'd ever be warm again.

"I wonder how long they're going to be?" Gil murmured at Michael's shoulder, looking out at the police, who didn't seem anywhere near done if sheer numbers had anything to do with it. When they'd started there'd been three, but now there were at least a dozen. Mitchell had told them there was a new task force in the city, appointed by the mayor, to investigate all hate crime incidents. He'd put special emphasis on it and alerted the police department that he expected all hate crimes to be thoroughly investigated and taken seriously. Michael supposed they should be grateful, but now all he wanted was the floodlights gone from his friend's driveway and the crime scene tape out of the front yard.

"I don't know," he replied in answer to Gil. "I can't imagine the neighbors are real excited about all of this."

"I think the neighbors are in bed. It's nearly 1:00 a.m." Gil leaned against the window frame. "I am sort of surprised David and Jackson's moms haven't been down here."

"The bedrooms and den where they watch TV are in the back of the house. They wouldn't see any of it."

"That's probably a good thing." One side of Gil's mouth curled up. "Can you imagine Beverley and those cops?"

Michael laughed, feeling a weight lift in his chest. The thought of David's helicopter mom and Detective Mitchell in the same room was pretty hilarious.

There was a soft knock on the front door, and they exchanged a quizzical look before Michael went to answer it. Detective Mitchell stood under the porch light, his balding head shining slightly. "We're wrapping up out here."

"Can we paint over that crap?" Gil had come to stand behind Michael's shoulder.

Mitchell gave him a wry smile. "That's fine." He gave Michael a polite nod. "I'll be in touch next week. Sooner if we catch anything on this guy."

"Thank you." Michael was surprised by how much he meant it. "I don't think I'll ever take the police for granted again."

Mitchell grinned, a surprisingly youthful expression on his careworn face. "People always like us better when they need us. Talk to you soon."

Michael watched him go, then closed and locked the door.

As the bolt slid home, it dawned on him that he and Gil were actually completely alone for the first time. His heart began to pound a slow, steady rhythm in his ears, and he pressed his palms to the oak door, sliding them out from the center. He was so tired his skin vibrated, but Gil was right behind him. He sagged and took a deep breath. Would Gil expect something from him, some sort of gratitude? Michael was grateful, but he couldn't even think about it, not tonight.

"I'm not going to hit on you."

Michael went still, his shoulders stiffening.

"Come on, Michael, this isn't the time. I can see how raw you are. I'm not stupid."

Michael turned slowly, his hands nervously tracing the wood grain of the door, then linking, white-knuckled, at his waist when he looked up into Gil's face. "I didn't...."

Gil shook his head, expressive hazel eyes rolling. "You did, and I think I sort of resent it. Yeah, I tease you, and I hit on you because frankly, and I don't know what it is about your snarky ass, but I really like you. Jesus, what kind of guy do you think I am? You've had a hell of a rough night, and all I want to do right now is provide you with some reassurance so you can relax and go to sleep." Guilt made Michael's stomach roll. "You think I can't see you're so wired you're shaking?"

"I'm not." Michael thrust his hands behind his back, fingers locking above his butt. He wanted to be strong, but tremors spread into his shoulders and he couldn't seem to stop them.

"The hell." Gil propped his hands on his sturdy square hips. "Michael, seriously, take the princess and go curl up in the bed. You're dead on your feet, and frankly, I need a couple of hours before my guys get here."

Michael stared at him, feeling like a jerk. "Gil, I...."

Gil shook his head. "It's all right. Just... go to sleep, okay?"

Michael's hands were sweaty and his grip slid apart. He rubbed his palms on his tight jeans. "Yeah, okay. Do you need blankets or anything?"

Gil grabbed a chenille throw off the back of the rocking chair. "This is good."

Michael knew it would only cover Gil from his waist to his ankles, but Gil had already turned away, flicking off the television and the lamp on the end table next to the sofa, dismissing him without another word.

Oddly bereft, Michael paused long enough to lower the shades on the windows, then called softly for Scooter. Her nails clicked on the hardwood floor as she approached him, and he turned toward the door to the hall.

"Michael?"

He stopped, pivoted, peering into the dark. "Yes?"

"If you need me, don't forget I'm out here, okay?"

Michael allowed himself a slight smile because he knew Gil couldn't see it. "I won't. And thanks, Gil. Really."

"You're welcome."

Michael turned and headed into the darkened hallway, Scooter on his heels. He closed the door at his back and lifted her up onto the bed, then found the remote on the nightstand and flicked on the TV. Climbing onto the soft bed, he pulled the thick duvet up and over his shoulder.

"Come here, baby." He patted the bed so Scooter would lie next to him. The memory of Gil's voice hit hard, of the deep voice saying "Michael, listen to me, baby." He shivered, then considered turning off the light next to him on the nightstand, but decided he really wasn't ready to lie in the dark, even with his mountain of a protector in the next room.

As he curled his arms around Scooter, he realized that his fallback attitude was snarky as hell—even he would cop to that—and he was lucky Gil still liked him.

THE LOW hum of some kind of equipment and men's voices woke Michael the next morning. He blinked, looking around, realizing that instead of his own narrow Murphy bed, he was in David and Jackson's bedroom, lying on their queen-size bed, still fully clothed. He hadn't even taken his glasses off.

He had no memory of what had happened after he'd gotten on the bed; one moment he was holding Scooter, watching television with the sound down low so it didn't disturb Gil, the next he was waking, the television off and Scooter gone.

He sat up, peering toward the windows and wondering what time it was. The sky was overcast, which wasn't unusual for March; the sun wouldn't really make its return in any appreciable way before May.

Michael scooted off the side of the bed just as someone passed in front of the bedroom window, and he reared back, nearly landing on his butt when his stockinged feet slipped on the hardwood floor. He grabbed the footboard, putting his butt back on the bed.

"Oh for fuck's sakes, get it together, Michael," he grumbled, feeling for his phone in his pocket. He fished it out, noting it was down to less than 10 percent battery life and it was six forty-five in the morning.

Six forty-five? Who the hell was hanging around outside of David and Jackson's house at—

Cold fear chilled him as memories of the night before raced to the forefront of his mind. He padded over to the window and peeked around the edge of the frame.

"You're so stupid," he muttered when he saw men working in the driveway. He reached up to run his hands through his hair. He grimaced when he encountered dried hair gel.

Gil had said he wanted to catch a couple of hours' sleep before his "guys" arrived. It had never occurred to Michael they'd arrive before seven. But they were out there, a compressor providing the mechanical hum Michael now recognized. Gil and Vernon were mixing paint, and he figured Manny was somewhere too. Unwilling to be seen with his hair a chunky mess, Michael went to the bathroom and turned on the light.

"Oh God." He looked like last week's garbage. His hair was every bit the mess he'd expected, thick with gel and hanging over bloodshot eyes. His jaw was shadowed dark with stubble. He couldn't do anything about the beard. He rarely shaved on the weekend unless he was going out, and hadn't brought his shaving stuff with him. But he could wash his face and attempt to get a brush through the mess on his head.

His shaving kit was on the back of the toilet, and he zipped it open and pulled out a bottle of Visine and a hairbrush. His eyes stung and teared when he put in the drops, and he closed them until the burning passed. Getting the brush through his chunky hair wasn't as easy. It snagged on the gel and pulled, and he was cursing by the time it was brushed straight back from his face, revealing his widow's peak. He also realized he was still wearing the clothes he'd worn the night before. By the time he was done helping outside, he was going to desperately need a shower. Being terrified out of his mind and then sleeping in his clothes had left him with a definite funk he hoped no one else would notice. His boots were still by the sofa, and he stepped into them, wondering about Scooter for the first time. He knew Gil would take care of her, but remembering the little dog made him wonder about other things. When Gil came into the bedroom to get her, had he looked down at Michael as he slept? Michael felt hot at the horrifying thought that he might have been drooling, or God forbid, snoring. Snagging his jacket from the coatrack, he opened the front door.

The cold hit him the moment he stepped out through the door, his breath a mist of condensation before his face. He paused on the porch; the ugly graffiti that had marred the front of the house had been painted over. It was a blotch of white, but that was an improvement to what had been there. He went down the steps, seeing Gil's truck parked out front, along with Vern's restored '66 Mustang and Manny's Dodge Charger. His Subaru was still in the driveway. Someone had pulled the shovel out of the windshield and covered the hole with plastic.

As he walked around the corner of the house, there was a happy bark, and relief flowed through him when he spotted Scooter lying in the driveway. She was on a long lead attached to the front of his car, and she bounded over to him, going up to dance on her back feet.

"There you are," he said, ruffling the fur behind her ears.

"And there you are."

Michael looked up at the sound of Gil's voice. The big man stood halfway up a ladder, taping around a window. Relief flooded Michael when Gil smiled down at him. A small part of him had been afraid Gil would be weird this morning, that Michael's reaction the night before would cause things between them to be weird. He was so glad to be wrong.

"Feeling rested?"

"It's seven o'clock on a Saturday morning. Who the hell feels rested at this hour?" The comment lacked his usual bite, but it was the best he could do. Gil seemed to appreciate the effort, because his smile widened to include those lethal dimples.

"What's the matter, your highness?"

Michael turned to see Vern approaching, a roll of blue tape in his hand. He paused in front of Michael, one gray brow raised. "You okay there, little boy?" Vern asked, affection in his faded blue eyes. "Gil told us about your night, and we saw the evidence. I'd like to kick whoever did that square in the balls."

Warmed by the irascible man's obvious concern, Michael gave him a small smile. "Get in line, old man."

Vernon winked at him. "Attaboy."

"You planning to do any work today, Vernon?" Gil asked. "Those windows won't tape themselves."

"Fuck off, Gilbert," he said mildly, giving Michael another subtle wink as he walked away.

"Did you get some rest?"

Michael turned to look at Gil, who was coming down the ladder. "Until the compressor kicked on, yeah."

Gil looked apologetic. "There's a primer that's specifically for covering spray paint. We had to get it on so it could dry. It's damp today."

"It's fine. I'm rested. Are you?"

Gil nodded, but Michael thought he looked tired.

"We usually start at six, so I actually got an extra hour."

"Good Lord, there's another good reason to stay in the interiors business. We work civilized hours."

"Oh, la di da." Gil nudged him in the side. His expression softened. "Seriously, are you okay? You were pretty out of it when I came to let Scooter out."

Michael shrugged. "I've had better nights, but I'll survive." He looked around at Vern taping off windows and Manny spraying white paint over the ugly words on the garage door. They were buried under the white primer, but Michael wondered if he'd ever stop seeing them. He turned back, studying Vernon taping plastic over the windows. "Wait, are you painting the whole house?"

"It's as good an excuse as any. David's been bitching about the colors as long as I've known him."

It was true. David liked the burgundy trim, but the two-toned gray wasn't his favorite, and he'd discussed changing the exterior later in the spring. It was just that Michael had no idea what he wanted in place of the current scheme, and David was so picky…. "I didn't think you could paint a house when it's this cold."

"Depends on the paint. You buy the right paint, you can do an exterior when it's thirty degrees. We haven't hit the freezing point at night in weeks, and there's supposed to be a break in the weather for the next few days, so we're good."

"I didn't know that." Michael looked back at Manny and the beigey, shortbread-cookie color going on the door. It was so… beige. "Um—"

"*Um* what?" Gil angled his head, a knowing smile curving his lips. He'd noticed Michael looking at the garage door. "You think I can't get the colors right?"

"No, no, I don't think that at all," Michael said quickly, even though he sort of did. "It's just, well… you know how David is."

"I do." Gil's lips quirked in amusement.

"And he's weird about the house."

"He is." Again, Gil gave another casual, relaxed nod. "Do you want to see the colors before we go any further?"

"If you'd like to show me." Michael thought his answer was innocuous enough, but Gil rolled his eyes.

"How very politically correct of you, Mr. Crane. Come here." Gil walked toward a makeshift table created by a piece of wood on top of the trash cans. There were three cans of paint on the shelf, and three five-gallon cans on the ground nearby. They'd been opened, and someone had painted three stripes of color on the surface of the plywood.

Michael stepped close, studying them with interest. The soft beigey-brown color, like fresh-baked biscuits, was painted alongside a mossy cypress green and a deep rich burgundy, like the color of pomegranate seeds. He bit his lip. They were beautiful. The limestone component of the rock foundation leaned heavily toward beige, which went well with the biscuit and cypress colors, and the burgundy would be a lively, lush counterpoint.

"Well...." Michael intentionally let his tone drag out, feeling the tension in the bigger man's body. "If he doesn't love it, I'm going to start questioning his career decision."

Gil's face lit with quiet pleasure, the green in his eyes more pronounced than the gray for the moment. That would change, Michael knew. He'd noticed the mercurial shift of the colors in Gil's eyes based on what he wore or his mood. They sort of fascinated Michael, but he tried not to stare.

"The biscuit color is for the big sections, the green is for the square pillars and the horizontal wood framing the windows and the porch, and the burgundy is for the smaller trim."

Michael could see it in his mind, and it would be stunning with the huge trees, the evergreen plants around the foundation, and the flowers that would bloom when the weather warmed.

"I talked to Jackson again this morning."

Michael looked up from the paint colors. "Did he tell David?"

Gil shook his head. "He thinks it will be easier once they're home."

"He's probably right."

"He asked about you."

Michael felt his face heat under Gil's steady regard. "I'm all right."

"That's what I told him. You handled it like a champ."

For some reason Gil's quiet assurance warmed Michael. He straightened.

"How can I help?"

Gil looked mildly surprised. "Seriously?"

"Yeah. What, you think I'm not capable?"

Gil eased into a smile. "Michael, I think you're capable of anything you want to do."

Michael glanced away, flustered. "That's good to know. So, put me to work."

Gil picked up an inch-wide roll of blue masking tape and held it out to him. "Start on the porch, taping down the free side of the plastic on all the windows. The guys are going to start on the back of the house, spraying the beige. We'll start cutting in with the cypress on the framework as soon as the second coat is on and set."

"Okay."

Michael did as Gil instructed, and within minutes he was engrossed in trying to keep the tape straight on the window frames. As his hands worked, his thoughts returned to the night before. He knew, without a doubt, that if Gil hadn't been in the living room, he wouldn't have slept a wink. Knowing he was out there, lying on the couch, had helped him relax enough to close his eyes. He'd also wondered more than once what his reception would be if he'd asked Gil to come join him on the bed. Just to sleep, of course, but the way Gil was so determined that seduction wasn't on his agenda kept Michael silent. He'd never admit it, but it bruised his ego a bit.

Gil getting the guys to the house early, even if they did disturb his sleep, was a huge plus now that Michael realized the scope of work they had left to do. The last thing he wanted David to see were the horrible words on the garage door. He was the closest thing Michael had to family, at least family he spoke to, and he'd do anything he could to prevent him having to face that ugliness. It would be bad enough for him to hear about it, but there was no way they could keep the vandalism from David. Jackson already knew. That had to suck; he took his lover away for a quiet weekend only to have someone scrawl hate all over their house.

Michael finished taping the windows on the porch, then covered the thick oak door with another sheet of plastic. The burnished door with inset iron studs was original to the house, and David was so proud of it. Michael took extra care to make sure every inch of it was securely masked. The generator hummed, the compressor clicking on and off as the spray gun was used to apply paint on the side of the house. The sound was almost soothing, and he worked a long time in the midst of the white noise. Then Gil stepped into his line of sight, gesturing toward the lawn. Michael turned to see Beverley Snyder and Shirley Henry approaching up the walkway.

"Oh hell," he muttered. Beverley waved, a gesture Michael returned with trepidation. He loved David's mom, and he liked what he knew of Jackson's, but he didn't have a lot of experience with the kind of relationship the mothers and sons shared. For the most part, he'd been raised by a series of nannies and only saw his socialite mother between parties or fundraisers. He wiped his suddenly damp palms on the seat of his jeans and took the porch steps down to meet them, wondering what he could say to explain all the activity on their sons' house.

"Good morning."

"Hello, Michael." Beverley smiled, catching his hands and pulling him into a hug. He let her scent surround him. He loved the smell of her perfume and the feel of her soft cheek. His own mother had had so much plastic surgery her cheek felt tight when she deigned to hug him at all. Usually when he saw his mother, there were lots of air kisses involved. "I didn't know David planned to have the house painted."

"He was going to do it in the spring, but Gil thought it might be a nice surprise for when he and Jackson get back from the lake."

"I'm quite sure it will be." She released his hands and slipped hers into the pockets of her camel-colored winter coat. "So this has nothing to do with the graffiti?"

Michael blinked. "Um...." Rarely was he caught completely off guard. He'd assumed the moms had been in the back of Bev's home, in the den, and blissfully unaware of the police crawling all over David's house. "We sort of hoped you didn't know."

"We didn't until this morning," she explained. "My next-door neighbor dropped in, wondering if David knew who sprayed graffiti all over his house and why that would require two police cars. She was certain I'd know all the details, being as I'm his mother."

Michael felt his face heat. "I didn't want to upset you."

She patted his arm. "I know, and I appreciate you trying to protect us. I really do. But Michael, honey, are you all right? Weren't you here by yourself?"

"I'm okay," he assured her softly. "Scooter was with me."

"Not that I doubt she'd try to protect you, but…." She caught his hand. She was wearing soft leather gloves, and she squeezed his fingers. "You're sure you're all right?"

She looked so worried that it caught at Michael's heart. He didn't think his own mother had ever looked at him with that combination of love and concern. "I'm okay, Bev. I promise."

"Did you see who did this?" Shirley asked.

He shook his head. "Not really. And they got away before the police got here."

"You do plan to tell our boys, don't you?" Bev studied the white patch on the wall on the porch.

"Jackson already knows. Gil called him to get permission to paint the house. The colors are really nice," he offered, his voice trailing off. He knew it sounded lame, like a weak offering. Frankly he wouldn't have blamed them if they were irritated at all of them. They were too smart to be kept in the dark.

But Shirley smiled. "You helped pick them, didn't you?"

"Actually, I didn't. Gil did. Would you like to see?"

They were enthusiastic about the idea, and Michael led them over to the makeshift table to show them the color selection.

"Oh, that's lovely." Beverley's eyes were shining. "David is going to be so happy."

"I thought so too."

They had to speak loudly to be heard over the compressor, and Beverley waved at Gil, who was currently up a ladder, spraying the biscuit color onto the side of the house, under the eaves. He gave her a quick smile and wave, then went back to work. Michael was going to give him hell about his evasion tactics.

"How late do you think you boys will work?" Shirley smiled at Manny as he passed her on the driveway. He gave her a quick, sweet smile but kept walking. Michael would have a few choice words for him too. Vernon was nowhere to be seen, the coward.

"Oh, I imagine we'll stop when it gets dark." He led them back around to the front and kissed both women on the cheek before they left him with cheery waves. Michael watched them go, then went around the side of the house. He was fuming.

Gil was still on the ladder, and Michael smacked the support strut. Gil grabbed the top when it shuddered, giving him an alarmed look.

"What the fuck, Michael?"

Michael gave him a saccharine-sweet smile and his extended middle finger.

"Aren't you cute?" Gil said.

"Aren't you a big chickenshit, hiding up there from the moms."

"Hey, work to do." He gave Michael one of his shit-eating grins, and Michael smacked the side of the ladder again.

"Asshole," he called up, but that smile, dimples denting each cheek, made it hard for Michael to stay mad at Gil. He went back to work.

CHAPTER SIX

BY FOUR thirty the sun was setting and David's house had two colors nearly completed, leaving only edges to clean up and the meticulous trim work to be done. The spray gun and the brushes were clean and stored in the garage, and Gil was putting the lids on cans of paint while Michael weighed down the drop cloths on the driveway with cinder blocks.

"What in the name of sweet Jesus's pet duck is this?"

Michael and Gil both turned toward Vernon, then saw the small crowd of people walking toward them across the front yard. Beverley and Shirley were in the lead, and behind them were people Michael thought he recognized as David and Jackson's neighbors. At least Michael recognized the lady who lived next door, the one with the white cat he nearly ran over twice a week. The group might have been alarming if they weren't holding covered casseroles instead of pitchforks and torches. Michael straightened, then went to meet them, his boots crunching on the layers of dead leaves and icy lawn.

"Hey. What's up?" He looked from face to face. Beverley and Shirley were smiling. The people behind them wore expressions ranging from determined to tentative.

"Well, we know you boys have been working all day, and we doubted you've stopped for a decent meal. So—" She held up the casserole in her hands. "—we brought dinner."

"We wanted to say something else too." The person who spoke was decades younger than David's and Jackson's mothers. She had a cute dark bob that brushed her chin, a plastic shopping bag in one hand, and the leash of a sturdy tan corgi in the other.

"Boots!" Michael went down on one knee to greet the dog, who showed his pleasure at seeing Michael again by licking his chin.

"Michael."

He looked up into the face of Bootsy's owner. He remembered Jordyn, and the man holding the toddler at her elbow was her husband. "We saw what happened last night, and we just want you to know that—it isn't okay with us. Not at all."

"Seconded," her husband added, his gaze level on Michael. Michael slowly straightened.

"Thank you." He looked from face to face. "I know David would be happy to hear that."

"We don't just mean it for David, although he and Jackson are good neighbors." Jordyn looked past Michael's shoulder, and he glanced back to see Gil, Vern, and Manny coming toward them, Gil still cleaning paint from his hands with a rag and Manny with his cap pulled down low on his forehead. Michael thought if Bev and Shirley hadn't been leading the group in front of him, his friends could be really intimidating. As it was, they looked as tentative as he felt.

"We want all of you to know," Jordyn went on, apparently the nominated spokesman for the group, "that what happened here last night scared us, but it also made us angry. So we've decided to form a neighborhood watch. Bev and Shirley are around during the day, and Kate and I are stay-at-home moms." A cute woman with long auburn hair and a shy smile wiggled her fingers in greeting. She held the hand of a little girl who was perhaps six, hiding behind her mom, peeking around her hip. "It would benefit all of us. Bev and Shirley are alone in their house, and several of us have kids who play on this street. We want to make sure it's safe. Paul and I have noticed a few people loitering around that we've never seen before, and so have Stan and Angie." A middle-aged couple nodded. Their teenaged son looked awkward but resolute. He dipped his chin in greeting. "We just all wanted—" Her voice wavered and her eyes got suspiciously bright. "We feel bad. We should have said something, or called the police...."

Michael saw the quiver in her lip. He stepped forward and pulled her into a hug. "It's okay," he murmured near her ear.

"No." She dropped Boots's leash and curled her arm around his neck, squeezing hard. "It isn't. But dinner is the least we can do."

"Well, I don't know about anyone else," Vernon announced. He'd bent to greet Boots, who was wiggling in joy at all the attention. "But food sounds pretty damned good to me."

"Language, Vernon. Kids present." Gil stepped forward, offering his huge hand to Jordyn's husband. The man took it, introducing himself as

Paul. That seemed to break the ice. The other neighbors swarmed around them, offering handshakes and tentative hugs. Even Manny tolerated the attention with a shy smile. After a few minutes, Bev led them onto the porch and into the house. Michael dashed over to the driveway just long enough to retrieve Scooter, who had been barking and whining her displeasure at being ignored.

IT WAS one of the most surreal meals Michael had ever eaten. A couple of the husbands seemed to feel awkward, clearly there because their wives made them come. Their wives, in contrast, were enthusiastic about showing their support. This was middle America on display, the sort of people Michael hadn't known growing up, and until that day hadn't had any desire to know. He knew he wasn't a warm and fuzzy person, but these people were all just so—nice.

Once out of the front yard, Jordyn seemed more than happy to let Bev take over, which she did with practiced ease. Plates and silverware were set out, paper towels served as napkins, and food was set on trivets on the dining room table. There was lasagna, a spaghetti and meatball casserole that was surprisingly delicious, a garden salad with vinaigrette, and garlic bread. For dessert, someone had brought apple cobbler, and Kate had made an éclair thing with graham crackers, vanilla pudding, and a chocolate ganache that was one of the best things Michael had ever eaten. There was red wine and a beer called Fat Tire, and over the course of the evening, with the good food and the quality alcohol, everyone relaxed. The husbands laughed at Vernon's jokes, and even Manny managed to smile.

Jordyn and Kate were obviously good friends and were cute as hell. When they found out Michael was an interior designer too, they had a million questions about color combinations and fabrics and treatments. Michael found himself enjoying the conversation more than he thought possible.

He also couldn't help that his attention was drawn repeatedly to Gil.

He seemed to get along with everyone with ease. He talked football and drank beer with the men. He got down and wrestled with the two dogs until they were panting and exhausted—the dogs, not Gil. He sat unselfconsciously on the floor to eat his dinner when it became obvious all the chairs were taken, and he was gentle when a timid little girl joined him, sitting next to him and looking up at him shyly. His voice dropped into a timbre Michael had never heard before, and within a surprisingly short amount of time, Winnie was giggling, blue eyes shining.

Michael watched the interaction between the huge man and the tiny girl and had a sudden recollection of the little boy from the hospital, Stevie Manyon. He surprised himself by wishing he'd known about their special friendship, been there to see it. Been there to hold Gil when the little boy lost his battle with the disease that took his life. These were emotions he'd never felt before in his life.

"So, you and Gil, huh?"

Michael startled and looked over to find Jordyn watching him with a soft smile on her face. Michael scowled. "No."

She gave him a slight smirk. "Really?"

Michael took a drink of beer to buy a couple of seconds. "Really," he finally answered. "We'd kill each other inside a month."

Her smirk deepened. "I hate to tell you this, Michael, but the way you watch him gives you away. You might want to kill one another inside a month, but that doesn't mean you don't want him now."

Michael scoffed. "Girl, you're nuts."

The knowing light in her eyes intensified, but she let the subject drop.

They were finishing dessert, and Michael was so stuffed he could scarcely move, when he sighed and turned to Jordyn. "This was so nice of you all, but I wish David and Jackson were here. It's their house, after all."

"What time are they due back tomorrow?" Jordyn asked.

"Late afternoon, so we're going to be starting early to finish up the trim before they get home," Michael replied.

"Do you need help?" Jordyn asked.

Michael paused thoughtfully, then turned to look at Gil. He and the little girl had their noses together, and the big man's face was filled with delight. Michael's grin was completely involuntary. "Yo, Gilbert, can we interrupt your gigglefest?"

Gil turned his head, then looked back to his partner in crime. "I don't know. What do you say, Winnie? Shall we let them interrupt our 'gigglefest'?"

The way he said it, voice deep and brows raised, made her giggle even more. She put her hand by her mouth to shield it and bent close to his ear, even though her stage whisper was loud enough everyone could hear her.

"I think you should let him," she said, her gaze shifting to Michael and then back. "He looks like Prince Eric."

"From *The Little Mermaid*?" Gil "whispered" back. She nodded emphatically.

Gil looked over at him and pretended to think about it, lips pursed. "Maybe. I'll take it under consideration. So, Michael, now that we are no longer giggling—" Winnie's giggles proved that to be inaccurate. "—what was it you wanted?"

Michael shook his head. "You had to make such a production out of it. Anyway, Jordyn just asked if we needed help finishing the trim tomorrow."

The room quieted and everyone's attention went to Gil, waiting to see what he said.

"I honestly think the more hands we've got, the earlier it's finished."

Jordyn looked over her shoulder at Paul, who was holding their sleepy toddler nodding against his shoulder. "Fine with me. I can paint trim with the best of them."

"If that's the truth," Vern said, looking at him with a lopsided grin, "he may just hire you. God knows Gilbert couldn't paint a straight line with a ruler and tape."

"Be nice, Vernon. I know it's a stretch but try, okay?" Gil gave him a quelling look, but Vern didn't appear to be remotely chastised. "Anyone who would like to help is welcome."

Muted sounds of agreement came from around the room.

"What time do you want us here?" Stan asked. "As long as I'm home in time for the Bulls game, I'm in."

There was a lively discussion about starting time, but they decided eight was early enough. Dinner and dessert were over, and the women wouldn't hear of leaving the mess. The ladies kept their heads together in the kitchen for quite a while, waving away any help from the men, carrying on an intense conversation Michael was quite certain would lead to more food the next day. By the time the neighbors walked out into the night, the house was immaculate, the dishes were done and put away, and there was enough food in the fridge for a small army.

"Nice people." Vernon sat on the ottoman and pulled on his paint-splattered boots. "They didn't have to do all that."

"It was very nice." Gil leaned back in the rocker with his stocking feet on the coffee table. He turned to Manny, who was slipping his shoes on as well. "Think you guys can be here by seven? That way we'll have the trim sanded and taped before they get here."

"Sure." Manny stood up, shaking his jeans legs down over the tops of his boots. "Having them help will cut the time in half."

"As long as we don't have to go behind them, cleaning up a mess."

Michael leaned forward, his fingers deep in Scooter's fur as he scratched her back. "I don't think I'll mind cleaning up a little mess if it creates the kind of good feelings today did. I really like the idea of them all keeping an eye on David and Jackson, you know?"

"After last night, absolutely." Gil became pensive. "I hope the cops are able to catch this creep." There was no need for him to clarify.

"I'd like a piece of the bastard." Vernon snorted. "Going after one of ours with a shovel is not okay."

Michael liked hearing himself referred to as *one of theirs*, but he was still concerned. "I just don't want David to be any more afraid than he already has been. And this won't help."

"No," Gil agreed. "You're right about that. Having the neighbors keeping an eye out is a good thing. Maybe it'll help him feel better."

"Here's hoping." Vernon stood up, digging his truck keys out of his pocket. "See you ladies in the morning." He winked at Gil. "Behave yourself, big boy."

"That was contradictory, Vern." Gil grinned up at him. "I can't be a lady and a big boy in the same sentence."

"Ah, be real, Gilbert. You manage every damned day." Gil gave him the finger, and Vern winked. "Attaboy. You keep denying and denying."

"Hey, Vern." Michael looked at Manny, startled. In the entire six months he'd known Manny, he didn't think he'd ever heard him speak so loudly.

"Yes, Emanuel?" Vern raised a salt-and-pepper brow and waited.

"Where the fuck did you get 'what in the name of Jesus's pet duck'? I mean, did he have a pet duck? And if he did, what did he call it?"

Gil burst out laughing, and Michael snorted. "Moses probably told him about it. He and Vern were good buddies, I hear."

Vern's eyes narrowed on Michael. "Here I've been nice to you all day, Hostess."

"Hostess?" Michael glared at him. "If anyone here was a hostess, it was David's mom." Gil chuckled, and Michael turned to him. "What?"

"He doesn't mean that kind of hostess." Michael frowned at him in incomprehension. "Twink, Michael. Hostess Twinkies?"

Michael scowled at Vern. "Oh, fuck you, you old fart." Gil's laughter got louder.

"Love you, baby boy." Vern winked and tipped an imaginary cap as he went out into the night.

"See you tomorrow, Vern," Gil shouted.

"Not if I see you first."

Manny grinned, pulling his baseball hat on. "I'll be here at seven."

"Thank you, man." Gil stood up and shook his hand. Michael couldn't help but notice the way the muscles across Gil's wide shoulders shifted under the snug cotton. He'd apparently run to his house in the middle of the day and picked up a change of clothes, and the dark T-shirt he wore clung to his musculature in all the right ways. Michael couldn't have ignored it if he tried.

He didn't actually try very hard.

Manny gave Michael a small smile and followed Vern out the door, pulling it closed behind him. Michael locked the door and set the alarm. "Manny is so much better than he was when I first met him."

"Yeah, he is," Gil agreed. "Better every day. This is closer to how Manny used to be, before George."

"I don't really know the story of what happened with that." Michael sat on the couch, pulling his legs up under him. "Other than what I read in the local papers."

Gil sighed, then crossed to sit beside him, leaning forward with his elbows on his knees. "I met Manny maybe… four? Five years ago? The first time I saw him was at the club, after he'd become friends with Jackson. He was hands down the most physically beautiful man I'd ever seen in my life."

"More than Jackson?" Michael shook his head. "I find that kind of hard to believe."

"Oh, don't get me wrong—Jackson was and still is maybe the handsomest man I've seen. But Manny? Manny was beautiful, the way old statues are beautiful. It was his skin and his hair and his eyes; he could stop a room just by walking into it. He'd come into the bar and guys would watch him, unable to believe anything that pretty could be real."

"He's still beautiful." Michael frowned. "He just has the one scar…."

"That shows," Gil replied, leaning back. He rubbed his hand over his jaw, his brow furrowed. "There are others."

"I didn't know."

"Yeah, well, not many people do." Gil blew out a sigh. "The night he met George Wilkerson, we were all in the bar. The thing is, Manny was so pretty that most guys were intimidated by him. Not Wilkerson; he walked right over and started chatting him up, talking about how he had this important job and he made all of this money." Gil scowled. "I thought he was a tool."

"Isn't that what guys do at the bar?"

"Yeah, but not like this. He really did the full-court press, you know? And Manny, who never did understand why guys wouldn't just approach him and say hi, was charmed by him. They moved in together within days of that night."

"So, had Wilkerson been telling the truth? About the job and the money?"

"Oh yeah. That was all true. He was a white-collar guy who worked for a brokerage firm, income into high six figures. There was an over-the-top honeymoon period where he bought Manny lots of stuff and moved him into his big house. Then he started to chip away at his self-esteem."

"Chip away how?"

"He made him feel bad that he was a plumber, said it was beneath him and he was too smart to be dealing, literally, with other people's crap. Manny is hands down the best plumbing guy I've ever met, has amazing instincts about what might be wrong in pipes and how to fix it. I mean, so often Jackson has teased him about being the 'pipe whisperer.' But that wasn't good enough for Wilkerson. He wanted Manny to go back to school, get a degree, be his 'equal.'"

Michael pursed his lips, thinking of his own hard-earned degree. His parents had paid for it, but he was the one who'd made the dean's list four years in a row. "Is that a bad thing?"

"Not at all. It just showed how little he bothered to get to know about Manny."

"How so?"

Gil reached for his beer, even though it had to be warm, and took a drink. He grimaced, then looked at Michael over the lip of the bottle. "This is between you and me, right?"

Michael nodded, he hoped reassuringly. "Of course."

"Okay. Manny doesn't like for a lot of people to know this, but he's dyslexic. So school was kind of a nightmare for him. Plus, he likes what he does, and he didn't want to go back to school. The more Manny said no, the more Wilkerson pushed back. Jackson and I were trying to get him to dump the jerk. Then all of a sudden, Manny just stops hanging out with us or talking to us. The only one he stayed in touch with was Vernon."

"Huh." Michael thought of the grumpy old man. That was a surprise. "I would have thought maybe Jackson."

"Oh, don't get me wrong, Jackson and Manny are good friends. But once things started to get weird at home, it was Vern Manny turned to. And Vern kept trying to tell the rest of us something was off, that we needed to intervene. We tried for a long time, tried to call him just to talk or see if he wanted to hang out, but there was always some excuse. He was tired, he and George had plans. It just got to the point where there's only so much you can do, you know?" Gil sighed, and it sounded like it had the weight of the world behind it. "Well, that's what I thought then. I'm going to tell you something, Michael; if you have a good friend who suddenly starts acting weird, who makes excuses not to hang out, or whose lover seems weirdly possessive, don't ignore it. Jackson and I will never forgive ourselves for not staying closer, doing more."

Michael stared unseeing at the glass on the top of the coffee table. Even though he had tried to tell him what a loser the guy was, David's ex had done such a mind fuck on him he was still recovering. Michael felt guilty every time David got that haunted look on his face.

"Yeah."

"And Vern…." Gil rubbed one of his big hands over his face. "Vernon was convinced everything that happened to Manny was his fault because he hadn't checked in on him more."

Michael had read the clinical description of the crime against Manny in the newspaper, but there had to be more to the story than what they'd reported. "Does Manny know what set Wilkerson off that night?"

Gil sighed. "Honestly? The dry cleaning."

Michael frowned. "What? Seriously?"

"Dead serious. He was pissed off because Manny hadn't picked up his shirts at the dry cleaners. He ragged on him and ragged on him, and finally Manny had just had it and told him to pick up his own fucking dry cleaning. The son of a bitch responded by taking a ball bat to his head."

"God." Michael's heart ached when he saw Gil's eyes fill with tears.

"Somehow the police found the info in Manny's wallet and called Vernon as he was being loaded into the ambulance. I picked up Jackson and we raced to the ER. There were cops fucking everywhere, and at first we couldn't find Vern. When we did, he was—" He closed his eyes and took a deep breath. "That old man has a heart of gold, and it was broken. Once we saw Manny, we understood why. I couldn't believe anyone hurt that bad could still be alive. There wasn't a spot on him that wasn't bruised or broken. And his face…." Gil shook his head. "Let's just say his plastic surgeon is a fucking genius."

"I'm sorry," Michael said, because he was. "I never should have asked."

Gil rubbed his hand over his head. "No, if you're going to be a part of us, you need to know."

The inclusion warmed Michael. He hadn't been included in many groups of friends.

"It's why we live in each other's pockets, why we're so tight now. The paper can tell you about the numbers of surgeries and broken bones, but it can't tell you about Manny's uncle trying to get his mom and dad to come to the hospital, and them saying no because his 'sinful lifestyle' was why he was there. Like he deserved it. I was there when Vern first saw Manny, and there wasn't an inch of unbroken skin on his face. I held the old man while he cried, and it damn near broke my heart. Vern spent almost every night in the ICU with Manny, spending every day with him from ten in the morning until they threw him out at eight at night. Then he'd get up and do it all over again. Jackson and I started staying on weekends so Vern would go home and sleep. He wouldn't take any jobs with me; he said his job was to be there for Manny, because his uncle had to work. So Jackson and I took extra jobs so we could keep both Manny and Vernon afloat. It was touch and go whether Manny would even make it for the first week. Once we knew he wasn't going to die and he didn't have any permanent brain damage, we figured out what to do to help him."

"I'm so sorry," Michael whispered, meaning it. "That's… it's awful. I can't even imagine."

"It was hell." A shadow passed over Gil's handsome face. "Then we get him healed and back upright, which took six months of intensive physical therapy, and the trial starts. That was actually the worst thing, that fucking trial."

"How? Wasn't Wilkerson convicted?"

"Oh yeah. After another six months where his defense attorney tried to make the case that Manny basically asked for it, that he liked to play rough and Wilkerson just got a little carried away."

Outrage filled Michael. "A little carried away? Are you fucking kidding me? All of those broken bones and six months of therapy, and he got a little carried away?"

Gil gave him a wry smile. "Easy, tiger. I'm on your side, remember?"

Michael was still fuming. "It's bullshit."

"You're right; it is bullshit. And it took its toll on Manny. I'm not sure it will ever be over for him. But he is finally getting better."

"I'm glad. He deserves to be happy."

"He does." Gil studied Michael for several seconds, assessing him. "And aren't you a surprise."

"What does that mean?"

"You, talking about Manny deserving to be happy. You aren't nearly the hardass you want people to think you are, are you?"

Michael looked away. "Oh, shut up. I like Manny."

Gil chuckled. "I do too."

Silence settled between them, but tonight it wasn't awkward. Gil rested his head against the back of the couch, lifting his big hands to rub over his head before turning to look at Michael. He gave him a faint smile.

Michael took in the lines around Gil's mouth, the weariness in his eyes. He looked exhausted, and Michael sat forward, preparing to stand.

"You need to get some rest."

Gil shrugged. "I'm okay. It's not even nine o'clock. We can watch a movie or something."

"What time do you usually go to sleep?"

"Depends."

Michael gave him a flinty look. "Don't be stupid. You were up half the night, then got up again at five. The guys will be back at seven. You don't need to entertain me." Michael pushed to his feet. "And tonight you're sleeping in the bed."

Gil frowned. "No, I'm not."

"Gilbert, don't fight with me. We could both use a few hours of sleep, and you have to admit I fit on the sofa better than you do."

"You planning to be my mom now, Michael?" Gil's tone was dry as dust.

"Oh, fuck you, asshole." Michael reached out his hand. "Come on."

One of Gil's brows arched. "You're going to pull me up?"

"You don't think I can?" Michael gestured again in irritation. "Give me your damned hand."

Gil looked amused but took Michael's hand. His skin was warm, his grip firm; the shock on his face was worth the strained muscle across Michael's shoulders when he yanked Gil to his feet. They ended up standing chest to chest, hands linked, and Michael looked up into Gil's widened eyes.

"I'll be goddamned," Gil murmured, looking into Michael's upturned face. He lifted his free hand, hesitating just a moment as if giving Michael a chance to pull away, then cupped his cheek. He stroked his thumb across Michael's cheekbone. "Aren't you just full of surprises?"

Michael's heart slammed into his ribs. "What are you doing?" He wanted to sound stern; at the very least he didn't want to sound so out of breath. But he was breathless. They stared at one another, Gil's thumb moving from his cheekbone to the bridge of his nose. The touch made Michael shiver, and he tried to hide the visceral reaction.

"You have freckles, right here."

"I don't."

"You do." Gil's full lips pulled up in a small smile. "When I was a kid, my mom called freckles on my nose 'angel kisses.' Is that what you have here, Michael Crane? Angel kisses?"

Michael blinked, taken off guard by the gentleness of Gil's touch and tone. "I doubt an angel would bother."

"Oh, I think you sell yourself short." Gil's fingers shifted to Michael's jaw, and he tipped his face up. "If I was an angel, I'd be more than happy to kiss your nose. I'd be happy to kiss you lots of places."

Michael swallowed, his throat suddenly dry. The months of teasing and wanting and fighting crumbled around him and only the wanting was left. "Lucky for me you aren't an angel, then, isn't it?"

"Hmm." Gil bent his head, his eyes dropping to Michael's mouth. "Sure about that?"

A dozen smartass answers competed in Michael's head, but he surprised himself by being honest instead. "I'm not sure of much of anything right now."

Gil nuzzled the side of his face with a stubble-covered jaw, and Michael caught his breath. "Be sure of this; when I say I want you, I'm not messing with you. And I won't hurt you. I promise."

"You can't promise that."

"Watch me."

They'd shared a couple of casual kisses, usually when Michael had been drinking and his resistance was low, and once or twice as hello or good-bye when the cocktails made him feel loose and flirty. This was different. There was nothing casual about the hand that slipped around Michael's waist, pulling him in. And once Gil's mouth settled onto his, there was nothing casual about the kiss either.

Michael's heart took up a rapid drumming against his sternum. He had plenty of opportunity to pull away, but he didn't. Instead he gripped the soft cotton covering Gil's wide shoulders, his fingers curling in the fabric, and when Gil slid his tongue along the seam of Michael's lips, he opened to him with a soft, welcoming sound.

Michael loved being surrounded by Gil's size, and the feel of the hard body under the cotton shirt was going to prove addictive. He ran his hands over the mounds of muscle on Gil's chest and made a soft sound, curling his tongue around Gil's. When Gil had held him in his arms the night before, it felt like coming home to a place he'd never been but had always craved. Tonight, he knew going in this was a dangerous, dangerous thing to do. Dangerous to his peace of mind, to his resolve. In fact, he felt his usually steadfast willpower taking a hit with every swipe of Gil's tongue over his.

When Gil pulled back, Michael made a sound of protest he'd have found embarrassing if he hadn't been so far gone. He was so hard he ached, pressing against the inside of his snug jeans. Gil leaned his forehead down against Michael's, his eyes closed and his full lips slightly parted as he took several deep breaths.

"Michael," he said finally. "I have to stop now."

"Why?" Michael asked, stretching up to nuzzle the flesh under Gil's chin. Gil grunted softly.

"Don't."

"Why?" Michael rubbed his hands over Gil's chest, marveling again at the size of him, the shape of him. He was like a giant, muscled playground.

His nipples were hard and pressed against the fabric, and Michael fingered them softly. When Gil grunted, Michael did it again.

Gil caught his hands and held them in front of his chest. "I'm already at the point where I don't want to stop, okay?"

"So am I," Michael murmured.

"You've been pushing me away for months. I don't—"

Michael pressed his lips over Gil's, stopping the words. He lingered, sliding his tongue along Gil's lower teeth before pulling back.

"Isn't it enough that I'm not pushing you away now?" He grabbed Gil's T-shirt, rucking it up, leaning forward to place his lips over one small, copper-toned nipple. He flicked the center with his tongue, then nipped it with his teeth, and Gil arched his back with a soft hiss. "Like that, do you?" Michael moved to the other side and suckled hard on the erect nub. Gil's hand lifted, fingers spearing through Michael's dark hair. One of Michael's roaming hands slid down, and he found the thick ridge of Gil's cock caught between the worn denim and his sturdy thigh. He felt the girth and weight, and he squeezed.

"Goddammit, Michael." Gil's hands lifted to grip Michael's head between his palms. He forced his face up until their eyes met. "What are you doing?"

Michael slid his palms over the smooth skin on Gil's sides and back. "Wanting you, Gilbert." He nuzzled his face into Gil's palm. "Isn't that enough?"

Gil sucked in a deep breath. "Yeah." He sighed. "If it's what you're willing to give, it's enough."

Then they were kissing again, Michael with an intensity that battled with the tenderness Gil was trying to show. Finally Michael grabbed his shoulders and simply jumped up, wrapping his long legs around Gil's hips and his arms around his thick neck. Gil grunted, curling his fingers into the back of Michael's thighs. "The things I want to do to you, little man."

Michael shuddered, his lips on the lobe of Gil's right ear. "I'm not that little," he hissed as Gil carried him through the dining room and down the hall to the bedroom.

He dropped Michael onto the high bed, pulled him to the edge, and whipped Michael's shirt off over his head.

"No." Gil studied him with admiration, "you're not that little. You're perfect."

Feeling scorched everywhere Gil's gaze touched, Michael knelt, precariously balanced on the soft bed as he pulled Gil's shirt up and off. Michael knew his lean body was nothing compared to Gil's. The man had caps of muscle on his shoulders, wide, full pecs, and a striated stomach with more than six "packs." Michael didn't look like that; he was pale and slender. He had pecs he'd worked on, but no matter how many sit-ups he did, his stomach was flat, with no bulging muscles, and his legs were long and whipcord lean. Michael thought his body looked better in clothes than out of them, but none of his insecurities seemed to bother Gil. He reached for the fly on Michael's jeans, popped them open, and pushed them over his hips. Michael lay back and shimmied to help the snug fabric along, then kicked them off over his feet. Gil paused when Michael straightened, his gaze avid as he ran his palms over the soft hair covering Michael's thighs. Michael shuddered, painfully aware of the erection pressing insistently against the front of his gray briefs.

Gil made a pleased sound in his throat, running the back of his fingers up Michael's length. When he turned his big hand and gripped him, Michael pressed forward into the engulfing heat. Gil moved his fingers up and down experimentally, and Michael grabbed on to his shoulders to steady himself. The sensation of Gil stroking his dick made his knees weak. After several minutes of the almost tortuous sensation, Michael pulled away to lie down on the bed, and pushed off his briefs. His cock curved up toward his belly, and he grabbed it hard around the base, holding back what was rapidly becoming an embarrassingly quick orgasm. The look on Gil's face as he stared down at him wasn't helping matters any.

"God, you're beautiful," he said almost reverently as he stared at Michael.

"Do you plan to join me?" Michael held out his hand. "Come on, Gilbert."

Gil grinned, shoving down his pants and briefs, his long cock flopping out, full and thick between large, strong thighs.

Michael whistled softly. "Wow. That's… proportional."

Gil climbed onto the bed, lifting one thick leg to straddle Michael's hips, bracing himself on his hands and knees over his body. His cock brushed Michael's thigh, a warm weight. "Thanks." Gil gave him a wry grin. "I think."

"Oh, it's a compliment. No one ever told you that before?"

"Not that I can recall." Gil leaned down, still holding his weight on his hands and knees, and kissed Michael gently.

Michael looped his arms around Gil's neck. "Come here," he whispered. "Lie on me."

"I'm too big."

"Gilbert, shut up and lie on me."

Michael lifted his head and caught Gil's lower lip between his teeth, biting gently. Gil grunted, following him when Michael pulled, gingerly lowering his body.

He was big, there was no mistaking that. Big and heavy. But all the strength and size, covering him, was also warm, pressing him into the softness of the duvet. And safe. Michael sighed, feeling safer than he'd been in his life.

"Too much?" Gil asked, muscles stiffening as he prepared to lift away.

"No." Michael tightened his arms around Gil's neck and he gingerly relaxed. "I like it."

"You can breathe okay?"

"For fuck's sakes, Gilbert. What kind of whiny bitches have you dated?"

Gil looked startled, then laughed, and Michael felt Gil's stomach muscles flex against him with each chuckle. "Very whiny ones, apparently." He slid his arms between Michael and the bedding and rolled, and Michael found himself sprawled over the big body. Gil ran his hands down the curve of Michael's spine, and he stretched like a cat, rubbing his hard cock into the warm space between Gil's groin and thigh. Gil moaned softly, filling his hands with Michael's ass. Gil rolled his hips up, massaging the round globes he held, and the heavy heat and pull of skin on skin against Michael's cock made him shudder. He opened his mouth on Gil's throat, teeth scoring the bronzed skin.

"Ah, he bites." Gil laughed breathlessly, and Michael nipped a little harder. In retaliation, Gil's hands moved to Michael's sides, and he tickled him. Michael scrambled up, batting at his hands, until he was sitting astride Gil's hips. He spread his hand between Gil's pecs, noticing how small it looked against all Gil's bulk. He grabbed a couple of chest hairs and yanked.

"Ouch!"

"Tickling will not get you laid."

Gil rubbed the spot. "Pulling out chest hair won't help you get laid either."

Michael smiled down at him, slowly leaning forward to press a kiss to Gil's chest. "Oh, I'm not worried about getting you—interested again."

"Is that right?"

"Uh-huh." Michael shifted back, pausing at Gil's knees, then curled his long fingers around Gil's heavy cock. He lifted it, moving his fingers over the velvety skin and the patchwork of swollen veins. "This is pretty amazing, Gilbert." He slid his hand up toward the tip, moving the skin over the hardened core. As he slid his hand back to the base, it grew firmer in his grip. He leaned forward, giving Gil a teasing smile as he patted his cheek with the swollen tip.

"You planning to play around down there all night?"

Michael's smile widened; then he stuck out his tongue, licking the fat head. "You think I'm teasing?"

Gil reached down, running his fingers through Michael's thick hair. "God, I hope not." He closed his fist around dark strands, trying to ease Michael's head lower.

"Ah ah ah." Michael grabbed several tufts of wiry, curly pubic hair, pulling them taut but not hard enough to hurt. "I do this at my speed, Gilbert."

Gil quickly released Michael's hair, spreading his hands. "Whatever you say."

Michael released the pubes, patting Gil's thigh. "He can be taught. Now...." He turned his head one way and then the other, studying the cock in his hand. He held it gently, licked from base to tip, then curled his lips around the head and hummed. He smiled around his mouthful when he felt the muscles in Gil's thighs tighten. He swirled the tip of his tongue over the slit and tasted a burst of salty bitterness. Michael pulled back, licking his lips. "Yum."

Michael saw Gil's hands curl in the bedding instead of reaching for his hair, and he smiled, deciding he'd teased him enough. It wasn't false modesty to say he gave a killer blow job, but he wasn't sure even he could get all that cock past his gag reflex. Curling his fingers around the thick base, he lowered his head and opened his mouth to begin taking him slowly in.

"Oh God yeah," Gil groaned. Michael pulled off just as slowly, tongue pressing along the underside, swirling around the glans until he popped off.

"If you promise not to pull my hair, I'll see how deep I can take this."

Gil lifted his hands, then stacked them behind his head with a grin. "I'll be good."

"Then so will I."

"Oh, isn't he cute?"

Michael met his eyes as he curled his palm around the base, noticing his fingers were nowhere near touching. He'd had lots of dicks in his mouth, but he didn't think there had ever been one this size. It was a challenge he welcomed. Making sure to cover his teeth with his lips, he lowered his mouth onto Gil, keeping the ring of his mouth taut, savoring the salty, musky taste of his skin with his tongue. His lips felt the rush into the veins that filled the thick cock, the blood that made it thicker, harder. Michael loosened his jaw and relaxed his throat, swirling his tongue as long as he could until his mouth was just too full. He breathed carefully through his nose until his lips connected with his hand and the tip of Gil's cock brushed the back of his throat. Once there he pulled back, using his mouth and his lips and tongue to slowly drive Gil insane.

Gil's stomach muscles were shuddering within minutes, and his legs were tense. Michael pushed them apart, reaching past the base to grip the large, heavy sac of testicles in his hand. He fondled them gently, tugging slightly as he lowered his mouth down Gil's length again. He was able to go farther this time without gagging, to get more of the amazing prick down his throat, so much so he could swallow, moving the walls of his throat to caress the sensitive head. Gil gasped and a hand landed on the back of Michael's head, but he didn't grab hair or try to force his head down farther. He just touched Michael's hair, running his fingers through it while his back arched, his hips moving restlessly. Michael pulled off.

"There's lube in the nightstand, if you'll get it for me."

Gil groaned. Michael continued to move his hand as Gil rolled to his side and yanked open the drawer, rummaging without being able to see what he was searching for. He grunted in satisfaction as his hand closed around the tube.

"Damn." He studied the bottle in his hand for a moment. "Jackson pops for the expensive stuff."

"Pretty sure David insists on it." Michael held out his hand.

"Did he plan to get laid this weekend? I'd have thought he'd take it with him."

"And I'm pretty sure he buys it by the case." Michael made a *gimme* motion with his hand and Gil handed it to him. Michael flicked the top open with his thumb and sat astride Gil's thighs, squirting some lube onto his fingers and palm. He closed the bottle and dropped it on the bed, then leaned down and took Gil's thick cock into his mouth again. When he reached behind himself, Michael watched Gil's avid expression as he slid two fingers into his own ass, working to stretch the tight ring of muscle.

"Want me to turn around so you can watch?" Michael asked with a teasing smile. Gil nodded. Michael turned around, dipping his head over Gil's groin, then eased long fingers into himself. He heard Gil's breath shorten, felt his cock thicken in his mouth as he pulled out the two fingers and worked three slowly inside.

It was dirty and perhaps one of the sluttiest things he'd ever done. It was also liberating and thrilling when Gil rubbed up the back of his thigh, then caressed one asscheek almost reverently.

"You're so beautiful, Michael," he murmured. "So fucking beautiful."

In response to the praise, Michael pushed his fingers in to the base, lowering his mouth to Gil, making a temporary detour to pull one of the hefty balls into his mouth. He rolled it around, sucking on it for a few minutes. By the time Michael went back to his cock, Gil's legs were moving restlessly on the soft duvet and Michael had swallowed a healthy dose of precome.

"You're driving me crazy," Gil gasped. "You know that, right?"

"I'm hoping." Michael grinned at him over his shoulder before taking his cock back in. This time Michael made it until his nose touched the tip of curly pubes, and he breathed in slowly through his nose, allowing his mouth to go sloppy about the big dick. He tightened his lips again as he pulled up, nearly letting the thick meat fall from his mouth, then going down again. Up and down, slowly at first, then faster. Saliva dripped down Gil's cock and Michael used his hand in conjunction with his mouth, sliding up and down the hardened flesh. Gil pulled Michael's hand from his ass and slid in one of his thick fingers, then a second as he curled them and pressed against Michael's gland. Michael came off Gil's dick, gasping.

"Like that, do you?" Gil teased. He sounded as breathless as Michael felt. Michael went back down on him, sucking hard and swirling his tongue around Gil's tip. Another rush of precome filled his mouth.

"Michael," Gil warned, sounding breathless.

"Hmm?" Michael didn't even slow down, moaning when Gil moved his fingers inside him.

"Michael," Gil repeated, sounding more intent. "I'm close, baby," he said. "Real close. You'd better…."

Michael pulled off and eased around to face Gil.

"Condom, Gilbert." Even Michael could acknowledge that he sounded breathless. He felt breathless. Gil had never closed the drawer, and his hand went back in. He came up with a condom faster than he had the lube. He handed it to Michael.

"Extra-large," Michael mused with a saucy grin, tearing open the foil wrapper with his teeth. "I don't know if it's wishful thinking for Jackson, but for you, it's dead-on." He scooted back on Gil's thighs, slipped the rolled latex over the tip of Gil's cock, then lowered his head to roll it down his length with his lips.

"Oh Jesus," Gil moaned. "He's multitalented."

Michael came back up with a smile. "Oh, baby. We're just getting started."

He rose up onto his knees, scooting forward, and reached behind himself to grab Gil's dick. He held it upright, slid the tip behind his balls to his hole, then slowly breached himself as he lowered a fraction of an inch at a time.

It wasn't easy. By the time he was halfway he was panting, sweat standing out on his forehead and slipping beneath his glasses.

"You're so fucking gorgeous," Gil murmured, his hands sliding up Michael's thighs, finding the caps of muscle above his hip bones with his thumbs. "So fucking gorgeous, Michael. You feel so good, baby. So tight, so hot."

It might have been hokey, or so Michael thought, but the words whispered with such obvious adoration made all the difference. Michael's muscles relaxed and he slid down, his ass coming to rest on Gil's groin.

"God, Michael," Gil groaned, his hips lifting slightly. Michael thought if he moved much more, he'd be able to feel him in the back of his throat.

"My pace, Gilbert," he warned. "This isn't a Vienna sausage you've got here. Go too fast, and I won't be able to walk tomorrow."

Gil made an obvious effort to lie still, his hands curling in the duvet. "You take it, babe. I'll just lie here."

"That's my big, strong housepainter," Michael teased. He moved gingerly up, then down, angling his hips and hissing when each movement dragged the thick prick inside him over his prostate. He began to move faster, pushing up, letting gravity bring him back down. Gil filled a trembling hand with lube, then curled his hand around Michael's cock. His erection had flagged; taking a prick the size of Gil's wasn't easy, and the concentration necessary to relax key muscles, to find the right angle, took its toll. But Gil brought him back to life with the slick, firm grip of his hand, and within minutes Michael was pushing down onto Gil's cock, then thrusting forward into the tight hold.

"That's it, baby." Gil's other hand moved up to touch Michael's torso, hands sliding from Michael's pubic bone to his pecs. Gil gripped a hard nipple, and Michael gasped when a jolt of pleasure shot from his chest to his ass.

"That." Michael threw his head back. "That."

"This?" Gil gripped the firm nub and twisted, and the resulting rush of sensation was almost too much. Michael cried out, pulsing into Gil's hand and onto his chest, his sphincter clamping down so tight he could scarcely move.

"Oh Christ." Michael hovered on the most exquisite edge of pleasure and pain, and he shuddered. His body convulsed before everything tight within him let go and he collapsed onto Gil's chest.

Gil wrapped his arms around him. "Are you okay?" he whispered against Michael's ear.

Michael couldn't muster the muscles required to nod. "Yeah, I'm—no, I'm dead."

Gil laughed, and Michael realized he was still hard inside of him.

"You didn't come," he moaned, finally able to command his hand to move. He ran it over Gil's shoulder, then down to his forearm. "I'll…."

"I'll get there. Just tell me when you're okay."

"Mind… blown," Michael muttered. Gil's hands moved over his back, his shoulders, over his hair.

"You're so amazing," Gil whispered. "So fucking amazing, sweetheart."

"Amazing fucking, anyway." Michael forced himself to swallow. "I think my brain is back."

"Are you loose enough?"

"I'm not sure there's any such thing as loose enough with you, Gilbert, but I'm not as tight as I was."

Gil angled his hips up, lifting Michael, pressing his dick farther inside of him. Michael whimpered when Gil's cock moved against his prostate. "Jesus God."

"Jesus God *good*? Or Jesus God *bad*?"

"Jesus God, was your dad an elephant?"

Gil let loose some startled laughter, then grabbed Michael around his waist and rolled them over. Michael made a shocked gurgling noise when Gil grabbed his legs and pushed them up to his chest. Gil went still.

"Does it hurt?"

"No, it doesn't hurt," Michael answered. "It's just—intense."

"Intense isn't bad." Gil gave a shallow thrust and Michael caught his breath, his eyes rolling back in his head. "Too much?"

"Just—stop talking, Gilbert," Michael managed, his hands digging into Gil's biceps.

"I can do that."

Gil began to move again, his thrusts shallow, and Michael whimpered. His body was so hypersensitized, his ass so stretched, his prostate vibrating almost constantly. He'd have thought it impossible, but he was hard again, and each of Gil's thrusts sent a jolt up his spine. Shocking him, because it had never happened to him before, a slow-rolling second orgasm rocked him. He didn't come much, but he came hard, his head back and his mouth falling open on a silent cry. Moments later Gil stiffened, his muscles going rigid. When Gil slowly collapsed on top of Michael, he encircled the big body with his arms and held him, so swamped with tenderness that for a moment he thought he might weep from pure joy.

Gil turned his head, his stubble-covered jaw coming to rest against Michael's cheek. "You're incredible."

Michael snorted, pushing the softer feelings down. "You just came, so everything seems dandy to you."

"Oh, shut up and take a compliment, you brat."

Startled by the description, Michael laughed.

Gil kissed his cheek. "You have the best laugh, Michael. I just wish I heard it more."

"Keep calling me creative names, then. I haven't been a 'brat' since I was thirteen."

"Oh, I beg to differ." Gil pushed up onto his hands. "I'm going to pull out, okay?"

Michael tried to stay relaxed. It wasn't easy, but it didn't hurt as much as he'd thought it might. He lay limp-muscled on the bed, unwilling to move. He heard Gil get up and pad barefooted down the hall; then the light went on in the bathroom. Water ran, and he heard Gil talking to Scooter.

"Hey, princess. You want a treat, huh?"

Gil went to the kitchen and Michael was dozing by the time he returned. Gil washed off his belly with a warm, damp cloth and Michael made a sound of contentment deep in his throat. A few moments later Gil climbed onto the bed with him, pulling a blanket up over Michael's shoulder.

Michael instinctively cuddled into the broad, warm chest, tucking his head under Gil's chin, nearly whimpering again in pure delight at the feeling of his big, hard body. Gil tenderly cradled the back of Michael's head in his palm.

"It's okay, baby," he said against Michael's ear. "I'll keep you safe."

Michael hummed and fell asleep, knowing he could.

CHAPTER SEVEN

SAFETY AND sweet heat surrounded him, and Michael pressed deeper into the sensation, fighting the distant knowledge he had to wake up at some point. It wasn't until the third time he floated to the surface that he thought to question the big arms around him, or more urgently, the large, semierect cock pressed into the crease of his ass. Michael remembered who it was attached to, and he was abruptly wide-awake. He stiffened.

"Oh, don't do that."

Michael turned his head slowly, looking over his shoulder. Gil's face was right there, so close he could kiss him if he wanted. And he wanted to, for just a second. It took every bit of self-control he had not to.

"What time is it?" Michael noticed the room had started to lighten, a soft morning glow coming in around the blinds.

"Just after six. The guys will be here in about forty-five minutes."

"I need to get up." Michael tried to pull away again, but Gil didn't release him. "Gilbert, let me go."

"Not yet." Gil nuzzled the back of his neck. Every muscle in Michael's body was tight, fighting against the desire to melt back into Gil's wide body and his soft, warm mouth. "Ah, Michael. You're not going to turn all weird on me now, are you?"

"What do you mean, weird?" His lips felt stiff and his voice sounded tight.

"Weird, like, I've held a lovely, warm snuggle bunny all night—"

Michael made an affronted sound. "'Snuggle bunny'? What the fuck—"

"—and now you're stiff as a board and I can feel the heat leaching out of you. So, talk to me, Michael."

Michael rolled to his side, palms flat against Gil's chest and more than ready to push away. This time, reluctantly, Gil let him go. He gave Gil an exasperated look.

"Snuggle bunny?" His voice dripped disdain, and Gil smiled.

"Hey, if the bunny slippers fit, baby." He spread his palms.

Michael growled and sat up, pushing at his hair, swinging his legs over the side of the bed. Gil reached out again and grabbed one of his arms.

"Michael." Gil pulled on his wrist. "Look at me. Please." Michael sighed but turned to look at him. "What's going on?"

He studied the wide hazel eyes, the broad, handsome face, and some of Michael's stiffness softened. "I don't want you to think this was more than it was."

"Meaning?"

"Meaning... I know you've been making noise about finding someone and settling down permanently, but that isn't me, Gilbert. I'm not capable of that kind of commitment. Last night was fun—"

One of Gil's brows arched. "Fun? Just fun?"

Michael rolled his eyes. "Fine. Really fun."

Gil grinned. "Thank you."

"But it doesn't mean anything more than that. I'm not a 'settling down permanently' kind of guy. I don't want you to expect more than I'm capable of giving."

Gil's smile faded slightly. "How can you be sure you aren't a 'settling down permanently' kind of guy?"

Michael sighed. "Trust me, I know." He scooted away and stood up. "I like you, Gil. But you can't expect anything more than that. I told you last night...."

"I know," Gil said behind him, deep voice soft. "You were clear. I shouldn't expect more than you were willing to give."

Michael nodded, not sure he could trust his voice any longer. Gil sounded so sad, and Michael hated that he was hurting him. But he'd told Gil....

He turned away, pausing long enough to separate his clothes from Gil's, then scooped them up off the floor. He felt Gil's gaze on him until he was out of the bedroom door. It was hard to be dignified while completely naked, but he thought he managed.

He didn't let the façade drop until he was behind the closed bathroom door. Then he leaned against it, his head back against the wood and his eyes closed. He'd thought scratching the itch might make it finally go away, but now he knew he'd made a huge mistake. This was only going to make it worse.

What the fuck had he done?

VERNON AND Manny were right on time, and by then Michael had showered and started the coffee, fed Scooter, straightened up the living room, and stripped and remade the bed while Gil was in the shower. He even started a load of laundry before joining the others in the kitchen.

"Well, look who's just a little energizer bunny this morning," Vern teased when Michael finally entered the kitchen.

"Oh, fuck you, Vernon," he snapped, pouring himself a cup of coffee.

"A cranky bunny."

Michael shot him a venomous look.

"Maybe drop the bunny jokes, okay, old man?" Gil muttered. He shot Michael an apologetic look, which he chose to ignore.

"I'm going to McDonald's for an Egg McMuffin." Michael put his mug down on the counter hard enough that some of the steaming coffee sloshed out on the counter. He grabbed a paper towel with a jerky motion and wiped it up. "You have exactly two minutes to place an order. Then I'm leaving without it."

"I'd like the burrito breakfast." Manny offered Michael a tentative smile. "No hot sauce."

"A Mexican who doesn't like hot sauce." Vern shook his head. "That's just unnatural, man."

"I'm Puerto Rican, you Neanderthal," Manny shot back. "And not all of us like hot food, okay?" He looked at Michael and shrugged. "It gives me heartburn."

"Me too." Michael turned to the others. "Anyone else?"

"Two sausage biscuits," Vern said. "With hash browns."

"Fine." Michael looked at Gil, managing not to meet his eyes. "Gilbert?"

"Two Egg McMuffins." Gil dug in the pocket of his jeans and held out his keys. "Take the truck."

"Why?"

"Your windshield is broken, remember?"

"Oh." Michael sighed. "Right. Okay." He took the keys, then turned and left the room.

"Jesus, who shit in his Wheaties?" he heard Vern say behind him.

"Shut up, Vern," Gil grumbled. "Drink your damned coffee."

THE MEN had eaten and prepped the trim by the time the neighbors began to arrive, and Michael was pleased to see that most of them seemed more than qualified with a paintbrush. As the bright cranberry color cut into the beige and the mossy green, the house came alive. He walked out to the curb several times, huddled in his bulky coat because it truly was cold as hell. He remembered hearing David's dad call it "brass monkey weather" once, and smiled faintly as he recalled the explanation.

"It means it's cold enough to freeze the balls off a brass monkey, Michael. Pile on the layers!"

He'd envied David the relationship he had with his father, right up until he'd shared his grief when the man died. Maybe his decision to keep his distance from people was the only way to function.

He kept his distance from Gil all day, and was grateful when Gil didn't press it. He painted trim on the other side of the house from where Gil directed the neighborhood troops, and he chatted with Beverley and Jordyn when they brought trays of sandwiches around noon. He handed out cans of soda pop and small bags of chips, and he tried to be as friendly as possible to their volunteers as the work seemed to get done almost by magic. At three o'clock the house was painted, and the equipment was cleaned and loaded into the back of Gil's truck. A guy from a windshield replacement company was using a small hydraulic lift and handheld suction cups to take out Michael's shattered windshield and drop in a new one. It was costing him more than a hundred bucks, but it was worth it not to see the horror on David's face when he saw the shattered windshield. Jackson called at four, and Michael was relieved to be able to tell him that everything was done.

"It really looks great. He's going to love it."

"That's good." There was a pause on the other end of the line, and it was like Michael could hear Jackson thinking. "Michael, are you okay?"

"Yeah, I'm fine," he answered blithely.

There was another pause. "You sure?"

"Yes, Jackson. I'm sure." He knew he sounded more irritated than the simple questions warranted, but he couldn't seem to help it. "Just—bring him home before dark so he can see how great it looks, okay?"

Jackson hummed, and Michael hated that even Jackson's murmurs were too knowing.

The neighbors left when the work was complete, but Manny, Vern, and Gil remained, waiting for David and Jackson to arrive. Anxious not to be trapped in the house with just the four of them, Michael offered to make a run to the store for beer and snacks while the guys turned on a football game. Gil gave him a level look that told him he knew exactly what Michael was doing, but Michael ignored him, running out the front door with his car keys in his hand.

He stalled at the grocery store, but there was only so much time one could spend in an Albertsons. He bought Fat Tire, now a convert to the beer, and added chips and pretzels. He even bought a bouquet of flowers to put in a vase on David's dining room table. But eventually he had to return to the house. He was standing in the kitchen, arranging the bright spring flowers in a vase, when heavy hands fell onto his shoulders. He jumped.

"Jesus Christ," he fumed when he turned and found Gil standing behind him. "I've got a knife in my hand."

"Sorry," Gil said, but he didn't look particularly regretful. He removed the knife from Michael's hand and set it next to the crystal vase on the counter.

"I need to finish that." Michael crossed his arms over his chest defensively.

"You can spare two minutes to talk to me. You've been running from me all day."

"No, I haven't," Michael countered, but he had been, and Gil had him.

Gil gave him a wry look, not even bothering to argue the point. "I just wanted to tell you that I get it, okay? You never pretended you were interested in forever. It was fun, but it's cool, all right?" He caught Michael's upper arms in his hands and squeezed. "Just… don't turn weird on me, okay? We have to be able to work together."

Michael studied Gil's earnest face, the muscles that had been rigid since he woke that morning slowly softening. "Yeah, okay."

Gil smiled. "There, that wasn't so hard, was it? We can be grown-ups."

He winked and walked away, just as easily as that. Something contrary inside of Michael was mildly insulted that it seemed so easy for him. Recognizing that it made no sense, Michael jammed small red lilies in the vase and carried it to the dining room table. He was setting it down when Manny spoke from near the front window.

"They're here."

They all exchanged a look, then opened the door and piled out onto the porch, Scooter in the lead, yipping happily.

David was already out of the truck, standing on the front walkway, his hands stacked over his mouth. When Scooter came to dance around his knees, he bent long enough to greet her, his blond hair soft and blowing in the breeze and his eyes wide behind the lenses of his glasses.

"Oh my God." David straightened, staring at the house. Jackson got out of the truck and scratched Scooter behind her ears when she ran to him, smiling as he joined his fiancé on the sidewalk.

"You like it?" he asked. David turned to him, hands going to his hips. "You did this?"

"The hell." Vernon scowled. "He was too busy doing you. We did this."

David looked between Jackson and the men on the porch, then did a little dance, jumping in place and doing everything short of squealing, making them all laugh. He ran to the front porch, hugging each of them in turn.

"It's so beautiful!" he cried, throwing his arms around Michael. "Did you pick the colors?"

"No, actually, Gil did that."

"They're perfect," he gushed, moving on to Gil, who hugged him with a laugh. Vernon allowed himself to be hugged with an indulgent eye roll. Even Manny accepted a hug with good grace. Then David had to walk around the entire outside of the house. It was overcast and near dusk, but there was enough light for him to see everything, and he was so excited that it almost made up for the reasons his house had to be painted to begin with. Almost.

Eventually they were all inside, sitting around the fireplace with the football game muted on the large TV. Michael got David a glass of wine and Jackson a beer, they asked about their weekend and their cabin and the lake, but he knew they were all just stalling. Finally, he gave Gil a look he hoped said *Can we just do this?* Gil nodded once, and Michael could only assume he read his intent. Then David gave him the perfect opening cue.

"Did you always plan to paint the house this weekend?"

Jackson took David's hand. "Not exactly. I'll let Michael explain."

David turned to him, and Michael had a sudden urge to tell Jackson *Gee, thanks, pal.* Instead he leaned forward in his corner of the couch.

Unnoticed by any of the others, Gil, seated next to him, touched his back fleetingly. It helped.

"About four hours after you guys left Friday night, I heard a noise out in the driveway. I remembered what you'd said about raccoons getting into your trash, so I put Scooter on her leash and went out to chase them away." He paused, hating that he was going to have to wipe the happiness off David's face. "It wasn't raccoons."

As he'd feared, the further into the explanation he got, the paler David became. When he talked about the man who chased him into the house, David covered his mouth with his hand, and Jackson encircled his shoulders with a steadying arm.

"Michael." David reached out and curled his hand around Michael's forearm. "Oh my God, Michael. You're okay?"

"Yeah, I'm all right."

"He didn't hurt you?"

"No, I managed to get back in the house and the door closed and locked." David looked down at his little dog, who was all but sitting on his feet. "She's okay too."

David's trembling hand went to her head. "But how terrifying. My God."

The worst part was when they told him about the graffiti. He wanted to see it, of course. Gil had taken photos with his phone and he handed it over, cued up to the images. Michael's heart ached as David's eyes filled with tears.

"I don't understand," David murmured. "What have we ever done to anyone that they'd want to do this?"

"Nothing, sweetheart, and that's the hell of it." Vern's deep voice was ragged. "You didn't do a damned thing. You're alive, and you're young, and you're in love. And for some people, us being any of those things is enough."

"They called the police, and Mitchell is already on it," Jackson said.

David turned to his fiancé. "You knew about this?"

"We weren't going to paint your house without getting someone's permission," Gil teased. "You should also know you have some amazing neighbors."

David wiped his fingers under his lower eyelids. "We do?"

Gil told him the story of how the neighbors had gathered, offered to help, and basically created a neighborhood watch group to help keep an eye out.

"That is nice." Michael could see David trying to pull himself back together.

"Oh, and David—" He leaned toward his best friend. "—it wasn't Trevor."

David inhaled, then let it out slowly. "You're sure?"

"Oh yeah." Michael would never forget the black eyes so close to his. It would be so much easier if they had belonged to Trevor Blankenship. "I'm sure."

"I don't know if that makes it better or worse," David said, mirroring Michael's thought. "It's better that it isn't someone I know. But it's worse because that means… we have no idea where it's coming from. Do you suppose they thought no one was here?"

"I've been thinking about that," Gil answered. "Jackson usually parks his truck in the driveway, and it wasn't there. Maybe he did think the house was empty."

"But my car was in the driveway," Michael countered. "And David and Jackson had only been gone a couple of hours when I heard the noises."

"What're you saying, Michael?" Manny asked.

Michael looked at the faces gathered around him, their expressions solemn. "I think," he said carefully, "that whoever it is had been watching the house, and he figured doing this when I was here alone was simpler than possibly coming up against Jackson."

David sagged against Jackson's side. "But… why do it at all?"

No one seemed to have an answer for that.

"The police will figure it out." Michael wished he felt as sure of that as he sounded.

CHAPTER EIGHT

AFTER A nearly sleepless night, muscles so tight they ached from jerking awake at every sound outside the window and out in the hall of his building, Michael left his downtown studio apartment at eight fifteen for his usual six-block walk to A.F.I., leaving time for a side trip to Starbucks for the largest coffee he could get. That morning he wondered if half a gallon would be enough. He let himself out through the main lobby door and drew up short when he saw the large man in a knit Seattle Seahawks hat and black jacket leaning against the shiny blue pickup parked at the curb.

"You're running late." Gil studied him in amusement.

"What are you doing here?"

The big man gave him a lopsided smile. "Holding the parking place. What do you think I'm doing here?"

"I have no idea."

"I'm going to give you a ride to work, Michael."

Michael stared at him, aghast. "What? Don't you need to be at work? I thought you were starting up at the O'Banyon house this morning."

"I've been there since six, but I'm on a break." His grin grew cagey. "I have an in with the boss."

"Gilbert, what the hell? I can walk to work by myself. I'm a big boy."

Gil waggled his eyebrows. "I seem to recall."

Michael huffed in exasperation, but he was very much afraid he was blushing. "I can walk the six blocks to work without an escort."

Gil shrugged. "That's up to you. I'll just follow you."

Michael glared at him. "Go. Away."

Gil shook his head slowly. "Not on your life."

"Why are you doing this?"

Gil straightened away from the truck and sauntered toward Michael, his hands going into his deep pockets. When he spoke, his voice was quiet but emphatic. "Michael, whoever hit David and Jackson's house Friday night saw you. Up close and personal. Until the cops have a lead on him, I'm going to be your new very best friend."

Michael sighed loudly. "And what if they never get a lead on him?"

Gil gave one shoulder a lazy shrug. "Then we might as well get married, babe, because I'm always going to be here."

Michael gave him a sardonic look. "You're an idiot."

"And you're wasting my break. So, are you going with me, or am I following you, cuz daylight's burning."

"Fine." Michael stalked to the passenger side door, waiting for Gil to unlock it. Instead, Gil reached around him and opened the door, holding it wide. He gave an expansive gesture with his arm, and a bow, then winked when Michael sent him a baleful look. "My mom always told me to be polite. How am I doing?"

"You're an asshole." Michael stepped up into the cab.

"Okay, so needs work, then." He shut the door, and Michael pulled on his seat belt as Gil jogged around the front of the truck. He opened the door and got in, pulling on his seat belt before starting the engine.

"I stop at Starbucks," Michael informed him archly as Gil pulled away from the curb. "Are you going to let me get out and walk in?"

"See, I'm betting since you always walk, you've never noticed"—he turned and looked at Michael—"it has a drive-thru window."

Michael huffed. "You're obnoxious."

Gil's grin widened. "So I've been told."

The Starbucks drive-thru was around the back of the building, and in truth Michael never had noticed it before. He gave Gil a startled look when he ordered his flat white.

"How do you know what kind of coffee I like?"

"I've made the coffee run before."

Michael frowned, trying to remember. Then it came to him. It had been the first time they'd had an actual meeting concerning how to go forward with Delta Restoration, Renovation, and Design. Michael stared at Gil's strong profile. "That was December."

"Yeah, so?" Gil shot him a quick look as he lifted his hip to pull his wallet from his back pocket. "Has your preference changed since then?"

"No, I—" Michael blinked, then turned away quickly, staring unseeing out the window. He couldn't have said why he was moved by Gil remembering his coffee order months later, but he was.

"Here ya go."

Michael turned back to find Gil holding out the large coffee. He took it from him, grateful for the warmth of the cup in his hand. "Oh, you can't pay…." Michael reached for his wallet in his jacket pocket, but Gil waved him away.

"Get the next one."

Michael still felt off-center when he got out of the truck at A.F.I. and pulled open the front door.

"Hey, Michael!"

He turned back, standing in the open vee of the doors. "What?"

"See you at four thirty, baby."

Candy from reception and Debra from textile acquisitions walked up together at that moment, heads swiveling as they looked between Gil in the big truck and Michael in the doorway. He stepped aside for them to enter while giving Gil a withering look. By the time he got upstairs, the information that a man in a big truck was calling Michael *baby* would be all over the floor, and he felt the beginning of a headache behind his eyes.

"You're determined to drive me insane," he told Gil.

"No. Just determined to make sure you're safe."

When Gil said stuff like that, Michael thought, what was he supposed to do? He shook his head as he entered the bustling lobby.

THE NEXT few days were a weird combination of Gil's reassuring presence and Michael's remaining fear from his encounter with the vandal. Work began on the O'Banyon mansion, mostly prep stuff for the crew and web searches for the different artisan and antique reproduction materials needed on the design side. Michael and David were still discussing the best time to leave A.F.I. and hadn't come to a consensus. They were going to make enough money that they didn't need the day jobs anymore, but there were several contracts outstanding, and David wasn't comfortable just leaving the company in the lurch. Michael couldn't have cared less, but he took his cue from David in that regard. He certainly wasn't going to quit and leave David alone there.

Michael spent hours each night huddled in his studio apartment, leaning over his laptop, searching for the perfect fabrics and wallpaper. He'd turn on the TV, eat something fast and easy, then dive into the Internet. He was making good headway on procurement, even if he wasn't sleeping much. Staying busy was intentional; after waking the one morning held in Gil's arms, his narrow bed was cold and lonely, and he hated it. When he did sleep, invariably he dreamed he was being chased by a masked man with a shovel, and he'd wake shaking, his head pounding, with a blinding headache. He started driving his car to work, and even though he wasn't walking anymore, Gil was still there each morning and afternoon, following him in the pickup, lingering until Michael was inside A.F.I.'s doors or in his apartment building. Michael wondered how Gil was managing to be there twice a day; he and Vernon and a hired crew were working at the mansion, supposedly prepping the walls and ceiling in the entrance hall. Michael felt almost guilty that Gil spent so much time as his private security detail. Almost.

Gil texted him each evening, just to be sure he was okay once he was home. The texts were reassuring, but the element of flirtation was gone. Michael couldn't really complain; he'd made himself clear. He hadn't wanted anything other than a hookup, and they'd had that. He still checked his phone several times a day, disappointed when the only texts he received were from David.

Then Detective Mitchell called, wanting to see all of them at the house the next afternoon. He had interviewed David and Jackson, but he hadn't spoken to Michael and Gil since the night of the incident. Now he wanted to see them all, and Michael resigned himself to another sleepless night.

He wasn't the only one who wasn't sleeping. David looked exhausted when he arrived at work the morning of the meeting. So much so Michael told him to go home and take a nap, and he took the two meetings on David's book that day. After the meetings, where pointless information was discussed and nothing was decided, Michael was twenty minutes late arriving to meet with Mitchell. When he pulled up, Gil's truck was already parked out front. The snow was gone and the lawn was beginning to green up. It was the first time Michael had seen the new colors with sunlight on them, and he smiled in spite of his exhaustion; the house looked darling. It also had a neighborhood watch sign in the front window and the small logo of a security company in the flower bed. Jackson had installed security cameras on the porch and above the garage, and Michael wished all the steps had done anything to make David feel safer. They hadn't.

He rang the bell and was slightly surprised when Gil opened the door. "Oh, hello."

"You're late." Gil gave him a mildly reproving look as he held the door open wide. "You said you'd be here by three."

"I got held up in a meeting." Scooter gave a happy bark and met him at the threshold, tailless butt wagging. He bent and stroked his hand down her back. "Hey, pretty girl." He straightened. "And don't nag," he muttered at Gil. "Hey, Jackson."

David's fiancé was sitting in the rocking chair, and he gave Michael a nod. "Where's David?" Michael took off his jacket and hung it on the coatrack.

"He's still asleep. Mitchell got held up and won't be here for a few more minutes, so I didn't wake him. I'd love to think this meeting will help him feel better, but somehow I doubt it."

Michael couldn't help but agree. He sat in the corner of the sofa, aware of Gil's attention trained on him.

"David isn't the only one not sleeping," Gil muttered.

Michael thought the large frames of his glasses and the judicious use of concealer had hidden the dark circles under his eyes, but it had been eight hours since he'd applied it. Apparently it had worn off.

"Bad dreams last night?"

Michael could feel them watching, seeing more than he wanted them to see. "I'm fine," he said brusquely.

"Michael," Gil persisted.

"Gilbert, leave me alone."

Gil huffed. They were saved from further discussion when the doorbell rang.

When Gil opened the door, Detective Mitchell greeted him with a wan smile. "Mr. Chandler."

"Gil, please." He shook the detective's hand. "Come on in."

The detective crossed into the room, offering his hand to Michael as Jackson stood up.

"I'll go wake David. He hasn't been sleeping worth a damn, and I wanted him to rest as long as he could. Be right back."

The silence that remained in his wake was anything but comfortable. Mitchell slipped his hands into his slacks pockets and rocked back on his heels. Gil turned and looked out the window, but Michael doubted he was enjoying the view. Murmured voices came from the bedroom, and then Jackson returned.

"Can I get anyone a cup of coffee?"

"Yes." They all spoke in unison, then exchanged amused looks.

"Cream? Sugar?"

"All of the above," Gil answered.

"I'll help." Michael stood, wiping his damp palms on his jeans. He didn't know why he was so nervous. "So how pissed off is David that you let him sleep?" he asked when he arrived in the kitchen, opened the fridge, and took out a bottle of creamer.

"Pretty pissed off." Jackson got a tray out of an upper cupboard, his tone mild. He set five mugs on it, then added a sugar bowl filled with packets of sweetener and poured the flavored creamer into a small pitcher. "He'll get over it. He needs the rest."

"He needs to be treated like a grown-up." David bustled into the kitchen on a wave of hair-gel-scented air. He'd clearly just redone his hair, and his eyes were bright and clear even if there were bags under them. Michael suspected Visine drops. "We need sugar too. Some people don't use sweetener."

"Okay." Jackson found another sugar bowl in a cupboard, and David went to the walk-in pantry to get sugar. When he came back out holding a small box of sugar cubes, Jackson took it out of his hands, then slipped an arm around his waist. "And I always treat you like a grown-up." He pressed a lingering kiss to David's lips, and Michael saw the stress begin to bleed from his friend's shoulders. He turned away with a slight smile.

"You don't, but I know you're just thinking of me."

"I am," Jackson agreed. There was the sound of another kiss, and this time Michael grimaced.

"Can you two put a cork in it? At least until after I get coffee?"

He took the pot out of the coffeemaker and poured the liquid into mugs. He'd teased David about his old-school coffee machine, but secretly he loved the smell of the coffee brewing. He inhaled with pleasure.

"How did the meeting with Snyderman's go?" David leaned around Jackson's arm and put both the sugar bowls on the tray.

"Fine." It had been annoying from beginning to end, but David didn't need to know that.

David gave him a sardonic look. "Liar."

"Then why did you ask?" Michael took the tray from Jackson, added the creamer, and carried it into the living room. He set it on the table and began to doctor his coffee.

Once everyone was settled, Mitchell on a dining room chair Jackson carried in and placed near the door, the detective cleared his throat. He leaned forward, linking his hands between his knees.

"I wish I could tell you we have a suspect," he began without preamble, shaking his head. Michael was struck by how much he resembled a hound dog. "We don't. We are seeing a recent uptick in hate crimes, however. And we think where your group of friends is concerned, it might all be the same perpetrator."

"So what does that mean?" Gil had never settled, and he stood near the door, a scowl on his face.

Mitchell turned to look at him. "We think this was the same guy, all the way back to the damage on Jackson's truck."

David and Jackson exchanged another of their looks, the one that said they didn't need to speak to know what the other was thinking. Michael looked away.

"There are earmarks," Mitchell went on. "Similarities in style that lead us to believe it's being done by the same person. Symbols almost like a signature on the graffiti. We've got a receipt from a store downtown, so we know the point of purchase. Unfortunately it's a busy store, and the cashier who rang up the sale doesn't remember who purchased it. It's also a very common brand of paint."

"Don't they have video surveillance?" Michael frowned. "I mean, don't all stores have that now?"

Mitchell grimaced. "The camera pointing at that register wasn't operating. And it's an old part of town; the business owners have been slow installing video cameras."

"Well, crap."

David looked at him with a small smirk. "The king of understatement, that's our Michael."

"It's a somewhat milder sentiment than the one I expressed to the store owner." Mitchell grimaced.

"So, basically you've got nothing?" Gil asked. He sounded angry, and Michael looked up to see that his skin was flushed. Michael stared until Gil glanced at him, and then turned to look away toward the windows.

"I didn't say we had nothing," Mitchell countered calmly. "The paint didn't match your car, David. I still haven't come across anything like that paint. The paint samples do match your truck, however." He turned to look at Jackson.

Jackson's dark brows rose. "But it's a common brand, right?"

Mitchell nodded. "It is, but in my experience vandals and taggers use the same brand of paint over and over. They also tend to sign their work. The tag signature was the same on Jackson's truck and David's car. We think the only reason he didn't sign what he'd done here was that Michael interrupted him."

"So, it's one guy who took a bat to Jackson's truck, then David's car, and now did the damage here?" Gil glared at Mitchell. "How fucking hard can one guy be to find?"

"One guy is actually harder to find than an organized hate group." Mitchell shook his head. "The difference this time is that… we have an eyewitness." He gestured to Michael.

Michael felt cold slip down his spine, like someone had taken an ice cube to his bare skin, the memory of those black eyes chilling him. He straightened, forcing himself to lift his chin. "I didn't see anything but his eyes through the mask."

"You also know how tall he is, what his build is like, and that he has a mark above his right eye. Which is a lot more than we had before."

"So your theory is that this is some… rogue homophobe?" Gil's voice had gone from irritated to confrontational.

"Gilbert, for God's sakes." Jackson turned to look up at him. "Cut the man a break. This isn't his fault."

"I know it's not his fault," Gil shot back. "But what he isn't saying is that whoever this is, he's escalating."

David put out his hand, and Michael hated that it was trembling. He settled a comforting touch on his friend's thigh, squeezing gently.

"Is that true?" David looked from face to face, finally settling on Mitchell's. "That he's escalating?"

Mitchell pursed his lips. "Yes, I'm afraid so. In the beginning he seemed satisfied with malicious mischief and property damage, and that may just be a function of the fact he wasn't caught. But when he picked up a shovel and physically threatened someone, he upped his game. I think it's safe to say if he'd caught Mr. Crane the other night, at the very least, he'd have hurt him badly."

A wave of fear curdled Michael's stomach. He'd seen it in those vicious eyes; if the man had caught him, he'd have been lucky to get out alive.

"The main reason I wanted to see you all this afternoon is to advise you to be very careful for the foreseeable future. Be aware of your surroundings. Don't take unnecessary risks. I saw that you've started a neighborhood watch; who is your police contact?"

"Officer Dwyer," Jackson replied. "He met with us last night. David's and my mom are designated window watchers, and trust me, after last weekend no one is going to get past them."

Mitchell gave them a slight smile. "That's good. You'd be amazed how many suspects have been apprehended by neighborhood watch groups. As for the rest of you"—he looked from Michael to Gil—"I can only advise you to be vigilant. It might be wise to consider getting a roommate if you live alone."

Michael glanced at Gil, then quickly away. It was tempting, but that was a very bad idea.

"You're moving in here." David grabbed Michael's hand, and Michael flinched. David's hands were freezing, and Michael covered them with both of his, squeezing. "Just for a while. If anything happened to you…."

Michael wasn't going to quibble. Frankly, he was scared. Even with Gil as escort to and from his building, he'd been looking over his shoulder almost constantly. "Thank you," he murmured.

"Gil, see if Vern can't move in with you temporarily," Jackson said. "That trailer he lives in is as secure as a tuna can."

Gil's jaw was hard. "I'll convince him."

"Also, you have a doggy door, right?" Mitchell looked at Scooter, who was happily gnawing on a cowhide chewy in her bed.

"Yeah, we do." Jackson glanced at Scooter. "Why?"

"Consider locking it and only taking her out on a lead. Try to prevent her from eating anything she finds in the yard or on the street. Keep any new toys or balls that might just show up and turn them over to your police liaison. Animals have been targets in situations like this before."

David's grip on Michael's fingers became almost punishing.

"The main thing is to be vigilant. We did get a few clues here. Because he was interrupted, he wasn't as careful as before. He paid cash for the paint, and the area he purchased it in could be significant. There is a possible suspect on a CCTV feed, but he knew where the cameras were and managed to completely cover his identity with gloves and a hooded sweatshirt." Mitchell looked from face to face. "I just want to reiterate; you need to be careful for the foreseeable future. We'll get this guy, but we don't want any collateral damage in the process."

Mitchell left not long after, and the silence that remained felt heavy.

Jackson pulled David against his side, rubbing his hand up and down his fiancé's arm. David still held Michael's hand in a hard grip, but Michael was looking to Gil. The big man was leaning against the door, the expression on his face resolved.

"I've got you." Gil's deep voice moved over Michael's raw nerves, a settling presence, larger than life. Michael felt his gaze like a fierce hug.

Gil dipped his chin in acknowledgment, and Michael tried for a small smile.

He failed.

GIL HAD apparently been in earnest when he told Michael he "had him." He went with Michael to his studio apartment within minutes of Mitchell's departure and helped him load most of his wardrobe into the back of his car. He teased Michael over the amount of grooming products he owned, but he carried everything to the car without complaint. When they got to David and Jackson's, he unloaded it all with the same good spirit and installed everything in the closet of the spare bedroom.

While they'd been gone, Jackson had put a piece of wood across the doggy door, something Scooter didn't approve of at all. David was terrified now that someone would try to poison her. In fact, David seemed more frightened and frail than before, and Michael was concerned about him. He promised to never let Scooter out of his sight, and that seemed to mollify David somewhat, but there was no mistaking he was shaken.

Frankly, so was Michael. His little apartment wasn't much, but it was close to A.F.I. and it was home. He loved David and Jackson, and he loved the house, but he certainly hadn't planned on moving in with them. Three men, two of whom were very fussy about their appearance, living in a house with one and a half baths wasn't a recipe for happy cohabitation.

Michael had his laptop and his phone, but it wasn't the same as being in his own private space, doing what he wanted, eating when he wanted. It was a bit like moving home to his parents' house, although there he'd have had an entire floor and no one would have given a damn if he was there or not. Having to adjust to the idea that there were people who cared enough about him to be smothering was new.

When Gil was ready to leave, Michael walked him out to his truck.

"Thank you," he said as Gil unlocked his blue Ford pickup. It was even bigger than Jackson's truck, which he thought was frankly ridiculous. He'd heard, even made, jokes about men compensating for other possible shortcomings by buying a huge truck. Michael could attest Gil certainly didn't have that problem.

"For what?" Gil tossed his jacket into the back seat of the cab. It was slowly beginning to warm up, although it could turn viciously cold overnight again. March coming in like a lion and all that.

"For helping me get my stuff." Michael glanced back at the house. "I feel like I moved in with Mom and Dad."

Gil smiled slightly. "Well, I feel like I'm moving my cranky Aunt Nancy into my spare bedroom, so I hear ya."

A breeze picked up the front of his hair, and Michael shoved his hands into his pockets. "I really hate this," he admitted finally. Gil closed the truck door and walked around the hood, coming to stand close.

"Which part?"

"All of it. Giving up my privacy. Seeing David so scared." He hunched his shoulders. He felt short of breath, and his heart lurched inside his rib cage. "Being so fucking scared myself."

Gil reached out, slipped a big hand around Michael's nape, and pulled him in. Once he was in contact with Gil's bulk and heat, he felt himself melt into his chest. Gil tucked Michael's head under his chin and held on to him, simply held him, until Michael's breathing evened out and his heart rate settled into a slow, steady beat.

"Okay now?"

His deep voice rumbled under Michael's ear, and he nodded. Gil pressed a kiss to the top of his head, then took a step back.

"I'll stay here until you're in the house, okay?"

Michael nodded, reluctantly turning to go.

"Michael." He paused and turned back. "God help anyone who would be foolish enough to hurt you." Gil's voice was low, rough with emotion.

Michael felt a surge of gratitude. "Right back atcha, big guy."

Gil grinned, and Michael could feel his gaze all the way back to the porch. The truck's engine didn't start until he was in the house, the door closed and locked behind him.

LIVING WITH Jackson and David was… weird.

It wasn't that they were bad roommates or interfered in his life. If anything, they bent over backward to be the exact opposite. David took him grocery shopping the first night to make sure there was food he liked in the house. He already had a key and the codes to the alarm system, so that was seamless. It was living with other people for the first time since college; it reinforced Michael's belief that he was better off living alone.

It was little things. He was a night owl, and Jackson, because of the early hours he worked, was in bed by ten. Usually Michael retired to his room, when at his apartment, he more often than not fell asleep in front of the TV. He usually showered at night before he fell asleep, but the bathroom shared a wall with the master bedroom, and his noise disturbed Jackson's sleep. David was very apologetic when he asked him not to shower at night, but to do so in the morning meant he was jockeying with Jackson and David for time in front of the mirror. He got to the point where he showered in the afternoon when he got home from work, but then by the next morning, his hair was impossible to get right. He knew it was a little thing, and that they were just worried about his safety. He was also a bit of a whiny prima donna; he could admit that about himself. After the first week, what he wanted more than anything was to just go home.

Living with people he worked with was also problematic. There was no "away from each other" time. He and David loved each other, but it was like they were siblings; nobody else better say something critical, but they were jabbing at each other more than normal. At one point Jackson said he was going to send them both to time out until they figured out how to get along. They'd laughed and that had cleared the air, but Michael knew it was only a matter of time before they were at each other again.

They'd been in a frustrating Skype meeting with a client who owned a midlevel hotel chain. They had lots of money and zero vision, and by the time the call ended, Michael was ready to tear his hair out. To get him out of the office so his head didn't explode, David sent him to the O'Banyon mansion with the color chips for the exterior, so Richard could approve the final selection and Gil could order the paint. Richard had seen the colors online, but David wanted him to see the actual chips before they invested in five hundred gallons of paint.

The weather had warmed up, mid-March now more lamb than lion, and the team had decided the best way to advertise the work going on at the high-profile site, aside from the four-by-eight Delta sign in the front yard, was to renovate and upgrade the exterior. Michael thought the new color scheme—pearl gray, charcoal gray, and black—would be dramatic and make the old home look larger, grander. It also went with the river rock foundation and wouldn't take away from any bride's color scheme. It was something they could use as a sales point until the old mansion became the wedding destination of choice for the Inland Northwest. Michael had no doubt, once the work was done, it would be only a matter of time before every wedding from Seattle to Butte would be held in the grand old house.

When he arrived at the mansion, he parked on the street, glad the icy season was behind them. He passed Gil's blue truck as he walked up the long drive, but he didn't see the big man or Vernon anywhere. Knowing they had to be on-site somewhere, he climbed the long staircase that led to the porch and rang the front doorbell.

It took a couple of minutes, but Richard finally answered the door. He wore slim-fit jeans, a hoodie, and running shoes, and he made the casual wear look expensive.

"Michael!" He smiled, teeth very white against his salt-and-pepper beard and tan skin. "David rang up to tell me you were on your way over." He stood back and invited Michael into the entryway. The scent of wallpaper paste and wet paint instantly hit him, and he could see that the walls had been finished. He admired the pale celadon paint with the dark wood. "It looks great, doesn't it?"

"It really does." Michael smiled in delight. There were some pieces of woodwork missing, but the floor looked as it must have when it was brand-new, and when he gazed up, he could see the peacock had been repainted. Now, instead of a childish-looking mural with a smirking bird, it was an elegant depiction of a proud animal with a tail that almost seemed to glow. "Oh," he breathed. "Wow."

"It's beautiful, isn't it?" Richard said with a smile.

"Yes, it is."

The ceiling background was soft blue fading to white, the colors of the sunrise reflected in pink- and lavender-tinted clouds. The peacock, who had seemed so ridiculous before, was now the epitome of elegance, body angled so that it was looking over its shoulder, comb picking up the glow from the rising sun. The bright blue body led down to the sweeping tail, long feathers with the distinctive iridescent eyes following the line of the wall, spreading along the curve. It was spectacular, and Michael recognized the same fine hand that had done the murals at the children's hospital. It was whimsical without being childish, and Michael sighed.

"He did that in two weeks," he mused aloud, shaking his head and walking a few steps to look at the mural from a different angle.

"Actually, he did it in about a week." Richard studied it as well, arms folded over his chest. "He said he wanted to get it done so that Lyle and I didn't have to live with scaffolding blocking the front door. We mostly come in through the back anyway, but he wouldn't hear of it. He worked very long hours, but I couldn't be more pleased with the outcome."

Michael moved again, standing so that he could see the ceiling and brilliantly colored Tiffany windows. "When you have a photographer in to do new photos, you'll want to make sure they get the ceiling and the stained glass windows from this angle, in one shot."

"Oh, I agree. The way Gilbert lined it up, the bird on the ceiling looks like it was part of the window and just flew to a new perch, doesn't it?"

He was right, and it was brilliant.

"So, David said he wanted me to check the color chips for the exterior?"

"Oh yes." Michael dug them out of his breast pocket. Richard took them and walked into the ballroom where the light was better, and Michael followed. Through the floor-to-ceiling windows he saw scaffolding stretching across the back of the house.

"Oh yes, these are very fine. Don't you think?"

Michael turned to find Richard studying him, dark brows raised. "I do."

"I especially like the slight luminescence in the pearl gray. It will look like this on the house, yes?"

"Yes. We've used it before on corporate jobs, and it makes all the difference between the pearlescent and flat gray. The color changes with the light applied. It's very modern-looking, particularly when banded with the black."

"Lovely." Richard handed the chips back. "Let's get it ordered."

Michael smiled. "Excellent. I'll just take these out to Gil."

Richard directed him to go through the kitchen, and Michael left him with a slight smile.

When Michael walked out through the back door, he could hear men talking and the sounds of laughter. Vernon was on a ladder, busily sanding the woodwork around the ballroom windows, and up one floor on scaffolding, two men were patching cracks in the stucco between the main Tudor-style beams. He searched, and farther along the back of the huge house, he saw Gil. He was up high, level with the third-floor windows, standing on a wide piece of steel-enforced wood, big legs braced. He was sanding in an area that had been patched on one of the dark beams. He'd stripped off his jacket as the day had warmed, and his broad shoulders stretched the white T-shirt he wore, his bald head gleaming in the sunlight.

"Hey, Hostess," Vern called. He grinned at Michael, waving the sander in his hand. "How you doin', cutie pie?"

"Hey, old fart. I'm just dandy." Michael gave him a big fake grin. "I see they let you out of the home today."

The two new guys hooted, laughing as Vernon flipped Michael off with a saucy grin of his own.

"Now, what kind of an example are you two setting for our client, acting like that?" Gil looked down on them, his hands on his hips, but there was a grin on his handsome face. Michael walked down to the section of scaffolding holding him, his head back as he looked up.

"Doesn't it bother you to be up that high?" Michael called.

"Nah. I've been higher."

"There's the God's honest truth," Vern shouted, and the new men laughed again.

"Watch yourself, you old coot." He gave Vern a scolding look, then turned his attention back to Michael. "What brings you out here?"

Michael held up the paint chips. "Final decisions for the exterior. David told me to get Richard's final okay and then give them to you."

"Excellent. I'll be right down."

Gil gripped the support bars of the scaffolding, and Michael couldn't help but admire the way he moved. For someone his size, Gil was surprisingly graceful and very agile. He swung his leg over, angling his big body easily up and over the side bar so he could climb down. He'd gone down one rung when there was an ominous creaking sound, and he froze.

The three-story tower of metal and wood groaned and shuddered. Instinctively, Michael took a step forward, hands outstretched as if to hold it in place.

"Michael, get back," Gil shouted.

Michael jerked away, tripping over his feet in his haste to follow Gil's instructions. He almost fell, but as he steadied, the tower gave another groan and an ominous pop.

Michael turned back as the entire structure collapsed in a pile of twisted metal and wood.

CHAPTER NINE

THE GROUND beneath Michael's feet shuddered with the force of the collapse. A cloud of dust blew up, obscuring his vision. Michael inhaled the fine particles of dirt and began to cough even as Vernon bolted off his ladder and shoved him out of the way.

"Gilbert?" Vern shouted, plowing into the cloud. "Goddammit, Gil, answer me!"

The other two men flew down their tower of scaffolding, but after that they didn't seem to know what to do. The dust took several seconds to settle, and by then Vern was picking up the long planks and throwing them aside.

"Get your asses in here and help me," Vern screamed, and that spurred them into motion. The tower had collapsed in on itself, and now the heavy planks were stacked like matchsticks atop the metal framework. For a moment it was almost as if Gil had simply disappeared, but then Michael saw the sole of one of his heavy work boots sticking out from beneath the rubble.

"There, Vern," he shouted, wading in between the men and pointing. "He's there."

Richard came out through the back door, a cell phone to his ear, watching as between the four of them, they managed to move enough of the planks and metal rubble to reveal Gil's upper body. His arm was up over his face, and he was covered in the fine dust. The two men Michael had yet to meet grabbed a plank and threw it aside, and Vern cursed.

"Fuck. Stop. Stop!" he yelled. "Michael, call 911."

"I've got them on the line." Richard stepped in between them, looking at Gil's prone form. "Is he conscious?"

"No, he hasn't moved," Vern answered. "And we just uncovered—that."

Michael couldn't really see anything but the ripped leg of Gil's khakis and blood. "Oh God." His voice was unsteady.

Richard was talking but his voice sounded far away, and Michael just kept looking from the arm covering Gil's face to the torn pants and the blood spreading beneath his awkwardly bent leg.

"Michael!"

Michael jerked when Richard shook his arm hard. "What?"

"Can you get to his head without jostling him at all?"

Michael blinked, then looked at the twisted metal frame and the planks around Gil's head. "Yeah, I think so."

"Do it, and see if he's conscious. Don't touch him, just talk to him."

"Okay, yeah."

Michael studied the twisted rubble, then began to pick his way toward Gil's head. Vern and the other guys tossed aside anything that wasn't directly on his still form, and that helped. When he was finally by his head, Michael knelt in the dust.

"Gil." He leaned in close, his hands aching to touch him. "Gil, baby, can you hear me?"

Gil didn't move, didn't respond. And from this angle, Michael could see an ugly spreading bruise above his right eye. "He hit his head," he told Richard. "It's already bruising."

Richard relayed that information into the phone, but Michael had turned back to Gil.

"Come on, Gilbert," he said, his voice louder. "No one is impressed with this dying-swan routine. Come on, you big asshole. Wake up!"

But he didn't, and Michael's breath grew short, his eyes stinging with dust and threatening tears.

"Call Jackson, Michael." Vern's stern voice cut through his growing panic. Michael looked up at him. "Call Jackson. He has his medical power of attorney."

Hands shaking, Michael dug his phone out of his back pocket. He stared at the screen in incomprehension, then managed to pull up his contacts. He had to press the button twice, but he was finally able to get a ring on the other end.

"Hey, Michael," Jackson answered, voice clipped. "What's up?" A siren wailed in the distance.

"Jackson," Michael gasped. "Jackson, it's Gil…."

That was as far as he got before his voice failed him.

"Michael? What about Gil? Michael? Michael, answer me."

The phone was plucked from his trembling hand.

"Jackson, this is Richard Lawrence. There's been an accident."

Michael listened to Richard, but he couldn't make sense of what was being said. The siren got louder, then cut off abruptly, and moments later two men in blue uniforms appeared around the corner of the house, one carrying a large red bag, followed by three more men in bulky fireman's jackets with reflective tape around the arms, chest, and hips. Richard went to meet them, and Vern and the two guys who'd been sanding the stucco stood off to one side, looking pale and shell-shocked.

The two paramedics arrived by Gil's side. One of them knelt instantly by his feet and ripped the leg of the torn khakis away. Gil's phone fell out of his pocket, and Michael bent and scooped it up, shoving it into his jacket pocket. He looked away from the wound in Gil's leg; he didn't consider himself squeamish, but there was so much blood.

"Sir?"

Michael looked up into the face of the other paramedic. He looked very kind, and very young.

"I need to get in there. I'm sorry."

"No, no, it's okay." Michael stood up, staggering a few steps. The paramedic caught his arm.

"Are you all right?"

"I'm fine. Take care of him."

Michael backed away, watching the paramedic near Gil's feet open the red bag and remove nitrile gloves, pulling them on while the other cautiously moved the arm Gil had over his face to study the knot forming above his right eyebrow. Michael didn't want to see the damage to his leg, but it was impossible not to look. The paramedic near his feet straightened the misshapen leg cautiously, and Michael cringed, but Gil didn't respond at all. The young man pulled something else from the kit, removing a thick square bandage. His hands flew efficiently as he tore the plastic wrap from the bandage, then placed it over the open wound and pressed. Blood welled around the edges as he used a roll of tape to secure it in place, then added another bandage on top of it. Michael closed his eyes against the vision now seared behind his eyelids—torn flesh and so much blood.

The three firemen carefully moved the rest of the long planks and twisted metal out of the way while the paramedics worked feverishly over Gil. The one at his feet wrapped more bandages tightly around his leg, then fastened two long, rigid plastic strips, one on the outside and one between, tied at his knee and ankle. The other grabbed equipment Michael didn't recognize from the kit and returned to Gil's head.

"McCrory," he said briskly, and the paramedic by Gil's feet moved to join his coworker, his body blocking Michael's view. He shifted in time to see them angle Gil's head, one holding it in place while the first inserted something into his mouth. Michael crossed his arms, his nails digging into his upper arms. He'd seen enough TV medical shows to understand Gil was being intubated.

"I'm in." The first man pulled something from the tube, and the second connected a breathing bag. They attached a cervical collar around Gil's neck and fastened it in place. The bruise on his forehead was spreading, and there was a knot the size of a golf ball under his usually smooth skin.

The paramedic who had wrapped his wound was speaking into a radio attached to the shoulder of his uniform, and Michael heard him say "… compound fracture of the right tibia and fibula" and "…contusion above right eye, with loss of consciousness." He turned and looked up at Michael. "How far did he fall?"

The image of the scaffolding collapsing passed through Michael's mind. "Three stories."

The paramedic went back to his radio. "Victim fell three stories with impact to front of his head above his right eye. He's been intubated. Request transport to Sacred Heart trauma unit." The radio popped and a voice responded, but Michael didn't understand what was being said.

A large arm came around Michael's chest, and Vernon pulled Michael back into his hard body, holding him tight. "He'll be okay." He pressed his lips against the side of Michael's head. "He's the toughest son of a bitch I know. He'll be okay."

Michael couldn't take his eyes off the bruise on Gil's head, the way the big body lay limp while the five men worked together to roll him slightly to the side and slip a long plastic board beneath him.

Dimly Michael was aware of another siren stopping on the other side of the house, and moments later two more paramedics appeared, pulling a rolling gurney between them. One medic pulled his pack together and gestured the others into place around Gil.

"On three," he said, then counted softly. On *three* the seven men picked Gil up and transferred him to the gurney. The medics quickly strapped him into place.

"Where we taking him?" one of them asked.

"Sacred Heart Trauma. They're expecting him."

They pulled the gurney back up and began to walk away, and Michael broke free from Vern's embrace, going after them. "I'm coming with you."

One paramedic opened the doors on the back of an ambulance, and the two men loaded the gurney into the back. All Michael could see was the bottom of Gil's big boots.

"I'm coming with you," he repeated, attempting to climb in through the doors. The medic caught his shoulder, stopping him, and Michael turned on him. He must've looked fierce, because the man held up his hands.

"You can't ride in the back, sir. It's the rules."

"I don't give a shit about your rules," Michael retorted, his voice trembling. "I'm going with him."

"You can ride up front with me," the other medic offered. "But we need to move."

"Michael?"

He turned back to Vern. "I'm going with them to the hospital."

"We'll meet you there," Vern called after him.

Michael climbed into the passenger seat, slamming the door.

"I'm Michael." He offered his hand to the driver.

"I'm Blaine." He squeezed Michael's hand. "Let's move."

Blaine started the engine, turned on the siren, and pulled forward to the end of the drive.

"Seat belt, Michael."

He hastily strapped in. There was a small window between the cab and the rear, and Michael turned, staring through it. Gil was still unmoving, even as the paramedic started an IV in his arm.

"His name is Gil?"

"Yeah. Gilbert Chandler."

"You're good friends?"

Michael had to swallow the sudden lump in his throat. "Yes. Very."

Blaine didn't say anything else, didn't offer any platitudes about how Gil would be just fine. Part of Michael wanted him to, even if the words were meaningless. The haste with which they'd gotten Gil ready to transport and into the back of the ambulance had been both reassuring and terrifying. Reassuring because of their obvious expertise, terrifying because of what they weren't saying but what Michael could see on their faces. "He's critical, isn't he?"

Blaine glanced at him, then turned a stoic face forward. "I'm not a doctor, Michael. There's no way for me to know that."

Michael inhaled and forced himself to hold the steadying breath for a moment. "Yeah, okay." He licked his dry lips, but it didn't help much. "Is the trauma unit different from the regular ER?"

Blaine took a moment before answering. "Yes, it's specifically for more serious injuries."

Michael wasn't stupid; he knew that. He guessed he'd just needed to hear someone say it, so he could wrap his head around it. Big, powerful, happy, teasing Gil was seriously injured. This was serious. The man who just that morning had followed him to work, then given him a smartass smile and salute before he drove away, was lying in the back of an ambulance, and he wasn't moving. Inside his core, Michael began to tremble.

Blaine pulled the ambulance into a short bay behind the hospital.

"Please keep off to the side." Blaine put the ambulance in park. "If you can remain out of the way, they'll let you stay longer."

Michael got out of the ambulance when Blaine did, hurrying to the back, but followed his instructions and stayed out of the way. Gil was removed from the back by the paramedics and wheeled through the doors, and the medical staff started talking back and forth. Michael didn't understand most of what they were saying. He heard "CT" and something about a pupil being fixed and dilated, but he wasn't sure what it meant. They rushed Gil inside and into a large, brilliantly lit, curtained area. The staff, with the help of the paramedics, transferred him from the gurney to a larger bed. A nurse immediately began to cut away his filthy clothes, and Michael acknowledged the slight nod Blaine sent his way as he and his partner left. Michael stood off in one corner as the rags were removed from Gil's body, as the big legs and hips came into view. The splint and bandage were left in place on his leg, and Michael tried to ignore the blood seeping through the bandages.

"Okay, what have we got?"

A slender woman wearing gold wire-framed glasses, with brown hair cut in a soft, modified shag, entered the area. She had on a white lab coat over pale blue scrubs, and her ID tag read Dr. Gail Shumway.

"Compound fracture of the right tibia and fibula and a contusion with swelling above the right eye, with possible TBI," a male attendant responded. "He's been unconscious since the fall, which was at least thirty minutes ago, and his right pupil is fixed and dilated. BP is 156 over 95. Pulse sixty-five."

Another nurse was standing near Gil's head. "We also have a small amount of blood in his right ear."

"We'll need to get a CT first. Call Angelo in ortho for a consult on the leg. We'll talk to neurology once we know what we're dealing with." She sounded so calm and competent that some of the knots in Michael's stomach began to unravel.

They cut Gil's T-shirt off, and Michael noticed for the first time that he was wearing plain white Jockeys. His cock and balls made a soft bulge between his thighs, and Michael wanted them to cover him, to do something to preserve his modesty. This was so unfair, to leave him exposed like that when he was helpless.

"Can't you cover him, please?"

Everyone in the room turned to him.

A male nurse in dark blue scrubs approached him. His dark skin gleamed in the lights and his chocolate-brown eyes were kind. "Sir, you don't belong back here. Let me take you to the waiting room—"

Michael held his ground, seeking out the doctor's face. "Cover him, please. He'll be cold. And he wouldn't be comfortable with all of these people... seeing him like this—"

To his horror, Michael's voice broke and tears blurred his vision.

Dr. Shumway crossed around the table and came to him, holding out her hand. "I'm Gail Shumway."

Michael had to swallow several times before he was able to speak. He shook her hand. "Michael Crane."

"And he's your friend?"

He nodded. "Yes. His name is Gil Chandler."

"I promise that we'll cover Gil with a warm blanket as soon as we can, but this is the easiest way for us to assess his injuries. Are you by any chance his medical representative?"

"No. That would be another friend of ours, Jackson Henry. I'm sure he's on his way."

"Good. And now you really are going to have to go out to the waiting room. Gil is headed for a CT scan, and I'll come out and speak to Mr. Henry just as soon as we know anything conclusive about his head injury, all right?"

"Aren't you going to fix his leg?"

She slipped her arm behind him, gently guiding Michael toward the doors. "Just as soon as we can. Right now, his head injury takes precedence." Michael paused in the doorway, looking back at the big man who lay so uncharacteristically still under the bright lights.

"Please cover him so he doesn't get cold. Please."

She turned to one of the staff. "Sandy, please get a warm blanket to cover Mr. Chandler. And now Lee will see you to the waiting room, all right, Michael?"

The male nurse grinned at him, his teeth very white against his dark skin.

Michael looked back one last time, willing Gil to lift his head, to open his eyes. At that point he'd have been happy if he moved his fingers, but there was nothing.

"This way." Lee caught Michael's elbow and pulled him gently from the room, taking him down a short hallway. Michael allowed himself to be led to another set of doors, and Lee pressed a large silver button on the wall. The doors swung silently open, and Michael found himself standing in a small waiting room done all in shades of green. "Here you go. There's a small coffee bar just around the corner and a café in the basement."

"No bar?" Michael was only half joking.

Lee chuckled. "Don't I wish, but no, unfortunately." He turned to go back through the doors.

"Lee?"

He stopped, an expectant look on his attractive face.

"Please—" Michael's throat thickened again, and he fought to get the words out. "—he's important to a lot of people."

Lee's smile gentled. "We'll take good care of him. And you're lucky; Dr. Shumway is the best. She's completely thorough."

"Okay. Thank you."

"Sure."

With one last smile, he disappeared back through the double doors, and Michael found himself standing in the waiting room, alone. After stumbling to a line of chairs upholstered in spruce-green fabric, he sat heavily, rubbing his temples. He closed his eyes but didn't leave them closed long, however; when he did, he kept seeing the scaffolding collapsing on a loop, over and over again. He whimpered softly, his heart aching.

"Please, God," he whispered. He wasn't much for praying, and the words felt awkward in his mouth. "Please. Please."

He wasn't even sure exactly what he was praying for. He just knew Gil needed help, and if there was a God and he was just, then he'd listen.

TIME SEEMED to have lost all meaning to Michael. He wasn't sure how long he sat there alone, repeating "please" over and over again in his mind. Footsteps finally filtered through, and he looked up as David and Jackson came down the hall. He must've looked really bad, because David rushed forward and knelt in front of him, pulling him into his arms.

"Oh, sweetheart," David sighed, squeezing him tight. "I'm so sorry this happened."

Michael's eyes began to sting again, but he refused to cry. If he let go, he was afraid he'd never stop. He pressed his forehead into David's shoulder, squeezing his upper arms. One of David's hands lifted to his hair; his other arm squeezed his shoulders.

Finally Michael sat back, rubbing his hands over his face.

"Are you all right?" David asked him, his voice soft. He sat in the chair beside him.

"Yes. No. I don't know." Michael ran his fingers up through his hair, not even caring how it looked when he was done.

"Michael, I don't want to push." Jackson looked like he regretted speaking, but needed to. "But I have to know...."

"Jackson." David shook his head. "Not yet."

"Babe, I have to figure out what was wrong with the equipment. Then I have to call Gil's family. I need to know what to tell them."

"It's okay." Michael stretched his neck to one side, trying to get the ache out of it. It didn't help. "What do you need to know, Jackson?"

Jackson pulled a chair over and sat in front of him, his extraordinary blue eyes red-rimmed and solemn. "Just tell me what happened."

Michael inhaled and blew out a noisy breath. "I went to the house so that Richard could okay the paint colors. Then I went out through the kitchen because the scaffolding covered the back of the house. Vern was sanding around the windows on the first level, and the two new guys were on scaffolding up on the second floor, patching the plaster between the beams. Gil was on a three-story unit on the main patio area, sanding the beams at the very top of the house. I told him Richard had okayed the colors, and he said he'd be right down. He swung over the top of the scaffolding tower, and...." He stopped, seeing it again in his head. David grabbed his hand, holding on. Michael closed his eyes. "There was this weird noise, like the scaffolding was groaning. Then it shook and I reached out, and Gil...." He had to stop for a minute, take several breaths. "Gil yelled at me to get back, and there was a snapping sound...."

"A snapping sound?"

"Yeah, like something broke."

"Metal or wood?"

Michael frowned. He hadn't thought of it that way, but now that he did, there was no mistake. "Metal."

"You're sure?"

"Yeah, I'm no expert but I'm pretty sure."

"Okay, then what happened?"

"Then the whole thing just... collapsed straight down."

"It went straight down?" Jackson pressed, as if to clarify. "It didn't lean?"

"No, it collapsed down right on top of itself. This big cloud of dust shot up, and when it cleared, Gil was under part of it—" He stopped, unable to continue. He held his hand up, shook his head.

"That's okay." David squeezed his hand. He looked at Jackson. "That can be enough for now, can't it? Maybe Gil will have more to add—later."

Jackson nodded. They heard voices in the hall, and moments later Vern and Manny came into view. They hurried their pace when Jackson stood up.

"How is he?" Vern asked. He looked like he'd aged a decade in the last hour.

"We don't know anything yet." Jackson reached out and caught Vern's big bicep, squeezing. "But he's strong as an ox, man. You know that better than anyone."

"Yeah." He rubbed one of his gnarled, bent hands over his jaw. He looked at Michael. "How you holding up, baby boy?"

Michael shrugged. Why the question made his throat tight, he couldn't say.

"I need to make a couple of calls," Jackson said. "I'll be right back."

The others looked at each other, then settled in to wait.

THEY SAT in a group, pulling the chairs close to one another as if making them into a huddle could protect them from anything worse happening. David went to get everyone coffee, but after a single sip, Michael didn't touch his again; every time he looked at the cup, he could see Gil's big hand curled around it, holding it out to him with a wide, teasing grin. His right leg kept shaking, but he couldn't seem to stop it, short of holding it down. The afternoon grew longer and the sky outside the windows darkened, and the only person who'd come through the double doors that led to the trauma unit was a woman with forms for Jackson to fill out, authorizing treatment. Every minute that passed felt like an hour, and finally Michael couldn't sit still any longer. He shot up out of the chair, feeling the eyes of his friends as he crossed to the windows. He wrapped his arms tightly, protectively over his chest as he stared out into the darkened parking lot. Moments later hands landed gently on his shoulders.

"He's going to be okay."

Michael looked back, surprised to find Manny behind him. "How do you know?"

Manny's hands lingered for a minute; then he squeezed before letting them fall away. It was the first time Manny had ever touched him.

"When I was in the hospital—this one, actually—" Manny gave a self-conscious shrug. "Vern just kept saying 'You're going to be okay.' Over and over. One day, when I was feeling particularly sorry for myself, I asked him how he could know that. I didn't fucking feel okay. And then he said— 'I know you feel like shit, and I know this is hard, but you're never going to be okay if you keep dwelling on the fact that you aren't.' It took a long time. But one day, I realized I was okay. And Vern said, 'See, I told ya.' He's such an asshole."

"I heard that," Vern announced. He was still sitting next to Jackson, his fingers linked at his waist and his eyes closed.

"Fucker has ears like a bat," Manny murmured.

Michael allowed himself a small smile.

"You just have to hang on to the thought, Michael," Manny went on. "Gil is tough. And he's going to be okay. Just keep thinking it. He's going to be okay. And when you can't think it anymore, we'll think it for you. We've handled worse than this."

Michael took a deep breath. "Thank you."

Manny's small smile was beautiful. "We've got you."

Michael looked at the men still sitting together. They were watching him, but for Vernon, who was still pretending to be resting his eyes. Jackson's face was solemn and David's eyes suspiciously bright, but the support in them was undeniable. Michael realized he'd never had friends like this before in his life.

The swish of the electric doors sounded and Michael whirled, his heart in his throat. Dr. Shumway walked through. She looked so calm; Michael took his first deep breath in what felt like hours. If she had terrible news for them, she wouldn't look so calm, would she? He hurried over when Jackson stood.

"Mr. Henry?" she asked, looking from face to face.

"I'm Jackson Henry."

She studied the anxious faces, then settled on Jackson's. "You're Mr. Chandler's medical representative?"

"Yes."

She looked apologetic. "I'm actually only supposed to speak to you."

"Anything you say to me, I'm only going to repeat to them anyway. And Gil wouldn't want them kept in the dark. You can trust me on that."

"All right, I will, then." She slipped her hands into her deep coat pockets. "As I'm sure you know, Mr. Chandler sustained a badly broken right leg in the fall. Anytime there is an open fracture, particularly in an environment like a construction area, there's always the concern of infection. We've started him on a series of strong IV antibiotics in hopes of heading off anything like that. He also struck his head when he fell, and that is actually of more concern than the broken leg."

"Okay." Jackson swallowed nervously. "Height and impact… it did a lot of damage?"

"Significant, yes. When he hit his head, he sustained an injury to the tissue surrounding the brain," she explained patiently. "There are layers

135

between the brain and the skull. When blood collects in these areas, it's called a subdural hematoma. Sometimes this kind of injury can be relatively minor and resolve on its own. Unfortunately, we don't believe Mr. Chandler's will. I've consulted with a neurosurgeon, Dr. Aadi Pillai, and he feels the accumulation of blood pressing on Mr. Chandler's brain is reaching dangerous levels. I agree with him."

"So, what happens next?" David asked.

"The doctor will go in and drill two holes in his skull to clear the hematoma and relieve the pressure," she answered. Michael groaned before he realized he'd made any sound. David slipped an arm around his waist, holding him tight. The doctor spoke directly to Michael. "We have to relieve the pressure, and this is the least invasive way. We'll suction out the accumulated blood and insert a tube, which will allow for continued drainage until the injury stops bleeding, hopefully without compromising brain function. We'll start with this approach in hopes we won't need to do anything more invasive."

"Could there be a compromise of brain function?" Michael asked, terrified by the thought.

She gave him a steady look. "There's always the risk of permanent damage with a head injury, but we won't know that until he regains consciousness. And even then, there could be lingering effects. For now, this is what needs to happen to reduce that possibility."

Michael felt a sick swooping sensation in his stomach. Could brain surgery ever be considered anything but life-threatening? And what if there were permanent effects? The idea made him feel sick.

"What about his leg?" Vern asked, looking as pale as Michael felt.

"That requires surgery as well. We feel like putting him under anesthesia once is preferable to waiting and doing a second surgery, so they'll be doing the surgeries concurrently. Dr. Scott Angelo and his team are going to do his leg, and there's no finer orthopedic surgeon on our staff. They're prepping him now and will be taking him up shortly." She looked from face to face, her eyes kind. "He's young and physically in excellent condition. Both of those things weigh heavily in his favor."

"Thank you. Should we stay here?" Jackson asked. "Or is there someplace closer?"

"I'll send a nurse to take you upstairs." She patted Michael's shoulder before she turned away. "Hang in there. These surgeons are the best we've got."

He inhaled deeply, forcing himself to nod. *Hang in there* and *He's going to be okay*. It was all just words.

How was he supposed to cling to platitudes when he was scared to death?

CHAPTER TEN

AS DR. Shumway promised, a perky young nurse named Hayley with a blonde ponytail came out and took them upstairs to the surgical waiting room. She provided a bit of levity by trying to flirt with Manny, turning him bright red. Vernon took advantage of the opportunity to tease him after she sent him a winsome smile as the elevator doors closed behind her.

"She was sure cute, Emanuel." Vern took a seat, arching a brow at Manny. "Think of the backflips your mama would do if you brought her home for dinner."

"Fuck off, Vernon." Manny sat next to him, hitting him in the shoulder.

"Careful, Manny. He's old." Jackson gave Michael a slight wink as he and David took seats across from them. Vernon flipped him off, which pulled a reluctant smile from Michael. It felt completely wrong on his face and faded almost instantly.

"You should call his brother," David murmured to Jackson. "You told him you would when you had news."

"Oh yeah." Jackson made a face, reaching into the pocket of his denim jacket for his phone.

"He's better than the sister." David reminded him with a sour expression, as if discussing her was distasteful.

"Which isn't saying shit," Vern muttered. Manny kicked the bottom of Vern's shoe. "What? It's the truth."

"Are they that bad?" Michael glanced between Vern and Jackson as they exchanged a long look.

"He really isn't," Jackson finally replied. "He just isn't gay-friendly, which makes him the same as half the country. His sister, on the other hand, wants her hands on their parents' money and doesn't much care how she gets it." He pressed a kiss to the back of David's hand, then stood and walked a short distance to the bank of windows. His voice drifted to them. "Yeah, Don. It's Jackson…."

"Sometimes I think I'm the only one of us who has a decent sibling," David said, pulling Michael's attention.

"My brother is all right," Vern growled. "As long as I don't have to see him."

"I love my sister," Manny said. "She's pretty cool. She just lives in Oregon."

"And she makes the best *pasteles* I've eaten in my life," Vern agreed. "I'd marry Anitza to get her to cook for me."

Manny smirked. "She has a straight husband and four children who might protest."

"I'm an only child." Michael sat in the chair beside David. "And my parents were so bad at it, it's probably a good thing they only had one."

David gave him a sad smile and took Michael's hand. "They really are pretty hopeless."

"That's being very kind."

David ran his thumb over Michael's knuckles. "Are you okay?"

"I'll live. I just hate the waiting. You know how bad I am at this."

"Sweetheart"—Vern's voice was rough—"I don't think any of us are great at it."

Jackson finished his conversation and came back to his seat.

"Well?" David searched his face.

"He said to call him when there's news."

"God forbid he get his sorry ass over here himself." Vern made a face, sinking lower in his chair.

"They live in Moses Lake, Vern, and they've got little kids. I imagine he'll get here when he can."

Vern didn't respond, but his sour expression spoke volumes.

After that they settled into a restless pattern. They bought horrible coffee from a vending machine around the corner, then didn't drink it. Beverley and Shirley arrived with a picnic basket full of sandwiches, apples, and cookies, and two thermoses of fortunately truly excellent coffee. Michael couldn't force himself to eat anything, but Bev's coffee was always welcome. The moms didn't stay long, departing with hugs after their sons promised to call when there was news.

At the two-hour mark, a short man with cinnamon-toned skin, wearing dark red scrubs, came through the doors to the waiting room. The gathered men went still, watching him. He approached and studied them, looking from face to face. "Mr. Henry?"

Jackson stood and offered his hand. "I'm Jackson Henry."

"I'm Dr. Pillai. I just operated on your friend, Mr. Chandler?" His English was impeccable, even with his noticeable Indian accent.

"How is he?"

"He's stable. I was able to evacuate the subdural hematoma, and the pressure in his brain has returned to near normal levels. There is a drainage tube in place that should prevent the hematoma from reforming. If the bleeding tapers off or stops, he should improve dramatically."

"And if it doesn't?" Jackson rubbed his hands on the side seams of his Levi's, the only indication of his nerves. "If it doesn't stop the bleeding?"

"Then we'd probably need to consider a craniotomy, where we remove a section of the skull to get to the bleeder. For now, I don't think that's necessary. The next twenty-four hours should tell us."

"But he came through all right?" Michael's voice trembled, and his diaphragm was shaking.

"Considering what he's been through today, he's actually doing quite well. Blood pressure and pulse are near normal, and his right pupil is now reacting to light, which is a good sign. I'll be able to tell you more once he regains consciousness. Dr. Angelo is still setting the broken leg, but he should be in to see you all before long."

He gave them a slight smile before he went back out through the double doors.

"That's good." Vern studied them in turn. "Isn't it?"

"It is." Jackson sat down, stretching his long legs out in front of him. "One surgery down, one to go."

It was after six and they were getting anxious again by the time Dr. Angelo came through the doors. He apologized for the delay. "He's a big man, and his bones are heavy. Fortunately the breaks were clean, and the paramedics did a terrific job cleaning the wound." He pulled his surgical cap from his head, and his dark hair spilled over his forehead. "He'll set off the metal detectors at airports from here on out, but as long as we can avoid infection setting in, I'm optimistic about his prognosis. He's in recovery now, then they'll be taking him to the ICU."

Michael's mouth was dry. "The ICU... isn't that bad?"

The surgeon shook his head. "The fact he didn't regain consciousness before surgery makes us want to keep a close eye on him, that's all. Don't worry. He's in great physical shape, which helps."

After he left, Vernon stood up. "I know where the ICU is, at least."

Manny bumped Vern's arm with his elbow. The fond, unguarded look the older man gave him in return showed precisely how much he cared about Manny.

They trooped into the elevator again, then into the waiting room connected to the fifth-floor ICU. When Michael sat in his third hard, crappy waiting room chair of the day, he grimaced.

He wasn't made for this; this hour upon hour of sitting vigil. He wanted to see Gil, to see for himself that he was going to be okay. He needed to touch him, to have those hazel eyes open and look at him. His unconsciousness had been the scariest part of all this. Gil was so very alive, so much larger than life. What if he wasn't okay? What if something still went wrong? He had to battle the thoughts back before they overwhelmed him.

He looked down, noticing for the first time that the knees of his gray skinny jeans were dusty. He batted at them, which was almost no help at all.

"I think they're going to have to be washed." David ran his fingers over Michael's right knee. "That seems to be ground in pretty good."

"Lovely." Michael glanced across the room to his reflection in a window. His hair was a disaster, hanging in a wonky hook over his right eye. He tried to push it back, but there wasn't much he could do about it. "Well, I look like crap."

David gave him a wan smile. "Do you honestly think if he's awake, he's going to care how you look when he finally sees you?" He shook his head. "You don't get it, do you?"

Michael shifted, feeling awkward. "I don't get what?"

"Gil really cares about you, Michael. He has for a while. I think he'd take you any way he could get you."

What Gil wanted… that had been clear all along. The problem lay with Michael, with wanting to keep his fucking distance, and he knew that. But he'd never imagined losing Gil completely, how death might come to such a vital man and take him forever. It left him sick and shaking.

"Are you gentlemen here for Mr. Chandler?"

An unfamiliar nurse wearing Mickey-and-Minnie-Mouse scrubs had come to the door.

Jackson shot to his feet. "We are, yeah."

"I'm his nurse, Pam. If you can all keep the noise to a minimum, I'll take you back to see him. It's almost eight, so I'm afraid you won't be able to stay very long."

"We can all go at once?" Vern popped to his feet too.

"Not theoretically, but I don't think you're going to turn me in, are you?" Her smile was mischievous.

Michael couldn't imagine why he was nervous, but as they walked silently down the long hall of the ICU, his palms began to sweat. They passed several rooms with glass walls and privacy curtains, some closed but most open at least a few feet. In many of the rooms there were visitors around the patients. The large cubicles looked like regular hospital rooms but for the sheer volume of equipment. There was more noise from all of the machinery too, pops and whirs and the sound of ventilators. When they were across from the nurses' station, Pam directed them to an open door. It was dim inside the room, and there was so much equipment surrounding the bed, it was hard to see who was in it. The bed was slightly elevated, and Vern made a pained sound. When Michael got closer, he saw why.

A narrow bandage wrapped from front to back on Gil's bald head, a tube coming from behind his ear attached to a machine. The bruise that had looked huge earlier now encompassed most of his face on the right side, and his eye was so swollen, Michael couldn't imagine how he could open it. He was dressed in one of those hospital gowns that ended at the knee, and his cast was visible from just below his knee to his ankle. He had IVs in each arm and a tube in his mouth attached to a ventilator. Bruises blotched his other leg and arms, reminding them how far he'd fallen. All in all, he looked awful.

"Try to remember that just because the bruises and swelling look worse, it doesn't mean that he is worse." Pam had come to stand beside him, and she spoke softly. "The bruising on his face and arms will probably be at its worst in a day or two. But it will get better."

People kept saying that, or a version of that, and he wanted to believe it, he really did. But he was so afraid. Afraid now that someone had gotten past his thorny defenses, now that he cared, he'd lose him.

Each of them walked to the side of the bed, got as close as they could, and bent to murmur something to their friend. Vern spoke softly, then pressed a kiss to the small stretch of forehead above his left eye that wasn't bruised. Manny bent near his ear, holding his hand. David hung back and let Jackson walk forward, and Michael nearly lost it when he heard Jackson's voice break and saw him wipe away tears.

When it was finally his turn, Michael stumbled closer, stopping beside the bed. He curled his fingers around one of Gil's big hands and stared down into his battered face. His broad shoulders stretched the fabric of the gown tight across his chest. Michael looked over his shoulder at Pam, who still stood near the door. "You don't have a gown that will fit him?"

"That's the biggest they had in the ER. I'll see if I can't find one for him in the morning."

"Thank you." Michael turned back to Gil, stroking his hand over the bruises on his arm. "You're a mess," he whispered. "You're bruised all over, but I guess that makes sense when you fall three floors." He leaned forward until his lips were next to Gil's ear. "You scared the shit out of me, you asshole. Have you any idea what that was like, watching you fall…?" Michael bit his lip, refusing to cry. "You have to wake up so I can yell at you, Gilbert. I've earned the right."

He closed his eyes and pressed his forehead against the tight fabric covering Gil's shoulder. "Wake up, Gil. I need you—" His voice broke, and he paused before trying again. "I need you to come back."

"I'm afraid I'm going to have to ask you to leave." Pam sounded truly regretful. "But you can come back at eleven in the morning."

"You have my number," Jackson said. "I'm his medical contact."

"I promise, if there's any change, I'll call you."

The men left the room, Michael pausing at the door, watching the bellows in the ventilator moving up and down, up and down.

"Is it breathing for him?" he asked impulsively, hoping he didn't sound as frightened as he was.

Pam shook her head, a soft smile touching her lips. "Not completely. It's assisting."

"Okay."

She pressed her hand briefly to his. "Try not to worry."

Michael gave him one last, lingering look, and left the room.

The five men walked to the elevator in silence, and Michael wondered if they were all feeling at the same loose ends he was. An unfamiliar cell phone tone sounded along with buzzing in his pocket, and Michael looked down in bewilderment.

"That's Gilbert's phone," Vern said.

Remembering he'd stuffed it into his pocket, Michael took it out and looked at the screen. "What's Brookline?" he asked.

"Oh shit." Vern held out his hand. "I'd better take that one."

Michael handed the phone over, his eyes going to Manny. "What's Brookline?"

"That's the assisted-living place where his dad is."

"Oh." Michael watched Vern as he took the call. He could hear him telling someone Gil had been in an accident, then listening to their response. It wasn't a long call.

"I guess I'm going to have to make a run up there." Vern came back to them. "Gil Senior is out of soap and popsicles."

"Seriously?" Jackson asked. The elevator doors opened and they stepped on. "They call Gil for popsicles?"

"And soap. Listen, the old guy has Alzheimer's. Whatever makes him happy at this point is worth a stop by the grocery store." Vern looked at his watch when they arrived in the lobby. "I'm going to need to go feed Pixie too."

"What's Pixie?" Michael frowned.

"Pixie is a pain in my ass." Vern scowled. "He was Gil's mother's cat, and he inherited him."

"She named a boy cat 'Pixie'?" Michael grimaced. "That's just wrong."

"Well, right or wrong, the damn thing has to be fed, and Gil Senior needs his popsicles. I'll take you back to your car and then head up, Manny."

Impulsively, Michael stopped in front of Vernon. "Let me help."

Vern looked at him in surprise. "What?"

"Let me help you. I can buy popsicles or feed a cat. I'd rather do any of it than sit around waiting for visiting hours to start again."

Vern pursed his lips, studying him. "Okay. How about tonight you take Pixie, and I'll do the popsicles."

"Okay." Michael patted down his pockets, searching for his keys, grateful to have something to do. He found his key ring in his coat. "I need to go get my car. It's still at the mansion. You'll have to tell me where the food is and stuff…." He looked up to catch Jackson giving Vernon an irritated look. "What?"

"Nothing. And we'll take you to get your car. I can fill you in on the cat." Jackson stopped by the doors to the parking lot. "Vern, do you want me to get ahold of the guys? I'm sure Richard and Lyle will understand if we need to delay the paint for a few days."

Vern shook his head. "No. Gil will have my head if we get behind just because he's down."

Jackson dropped his hands into his back pockets. "You know it's going to be a long time before he's back up, right?"

"Yeah, I know. We'll manage."

"I can help out," Manny offered. "My load is light right now."

"We can also hire more guys." David gave Jackson a quick look, and he nodded in agreement.

"Let's just—take it a day at a time, okay?" Vern looked away, his eyes somber. "As soon as Gilbert is up to barking orders again, we'll do it how he wants us to."

"Whatever you say, man." Jackson patted him on the shoulder. "We can be here in shifts."

"I'll come by and see him in the morning." Vern dug his keys out of his jacket pocket. "Besides, you're the guy they'll want if he—needs anything."

"You have that meeting in the morning." David gave Jackson a pointed look.

"Oh, that's right. Leave the scaffolding that fell where it is, okay, Vern? Insurance guy needs to see it."

"The Fire Department moved most of it, but we'll leave it where it is now."

They walked into the parking lot and paused at the back of Vern's pristine '66 Mustang.

"If they call you—" Vern paused, his eyes searching Jackson's.

"I'll call you. Try not to worry. He's in good hands."

Vern didn't look convinced.

Manny threw his arm over Vern's broad shoulders. "It's okay, old man. Let's go so we can get popsicles."

"We?" Vern arched a brow.

"Yep, we're going to take care of Gil Senior, then you're getting clothes so you can come stay with me."

"You think I'm going to sleep over your uncle's garage?" Vern shook his head. "I don't think so, Emanuel."

"I think that's a great idea," David piped up. "And Manny's loft is very nice."

"Loft." Vern rolled his eyes. "Dandy." He glared at Manny. "Get in the damned car."

CHAPTER ELEVEN

MICHAEL PEERED at the note Jackson had written giving him Gil's address and directions. He slowed as he turned the corner. Gil's house wasn't far from David's, but the neighborhood was very different. Where David's neighborhood was filled with turn-of-the-century homes, a few post-World-War-II-era places thrown in, Gil's looked like the construction had taken place mostly in the fifties and sixties. There were lots of ranch-style and split-level homes, and he passed an elementary school that looked as if it had been built in the seventies. He checked the address again, then tried to see the numbers on the curb. He was in the 1200 block, and Gil's address was 1720, so he picked up speed slightly, pausing briefly at the corner. The streetlights overhead shone through the canopy of branches that met over the street, new, bright spring leaves shifting in the breeze and throwing weird shadows over worn, painted house numbers. He slowed, car rolling to a stop when he finally spotted the address at the curb.

He stared, startled. The house he was looking at was totally different than the other houses in the neighborhood. A long and low A-line made up the roof, meeting at an off-center peak, and a light from inside showed through the large floor-to-ceiling paneled windows on either side of the front door. Michael got out of his car, locking it as he stared at the house. The front door, shown clearly in the bright porch light, was turquoise. Skillful landscaping, almost like a Zen garden, created a winding rock stream beneath a wooden bridge constructed of slender pieces of hardwood that had been laminated together. It spanned the gap between the sidewalk and the long, narrow front porch. Two large blue ceramic urns sat on either side of the door, ferns that were just beginning to add new growth falling gracefully toward the tile porch. The exterior was about as quintessential a midcentury modern design as he'd seen in town, and a bubble of excitement floated in his stomach.

He used the key to unlock the door, then sighed in quiet pleasure as he stepped through. He was in a large square patio, enclosed from the street but open to the sky. There were wooden benches built into the walls on two sides, and at the center was a wood-burning, freestanding fireplace. He imagined there would be furniture in the space when the weather turned warmer, and plants in more of the ceramic urns. He could almost see it.

To his left was the sliding glass door entrance to the living room, and he went up the three steps, then slid the door open. The living room had hardwood floors, a geometric-patterned area rug under a long, low sofa upholstered in oatmeal-toned fabric. Michael recognized the designer and ran his hand over the back of the couch in pleasure. There were two armchairs with wooden arms and legs, and a wooden sideboard against the far wall with a huge flat-screen television sitting on it. Everything was simple and masculine and impeccably clean. It was also Michael's dream house, right down to the glass-topped coffee table and the vase-bottomed lamps in three different jewel tones, all sporting the same squatty beige shades. On the wall was a metal starburst wall clock, and Michael stared at it for several seconds. He had a starburst clock of his own, but his wasn't nearly as fine.

Walking up another three steps, he moved through a shadowy dining room featuring a long blond wooden table and eight chairs. Five hanging medallion lamps with beige shades in different geometric shapes hung above. A counter separated the kitchen and dining room, three simple stools at the poured concrete surface, more pale wooden cabinets along the wall above a very modern range and beside a stainless-steel fridge. The combination of eras was seamless and perfect, and Michael ran his hand over the smooth, polished concrete, making a soft sound of pleasure.

He'd had no idea Gil loved midcentury modern as much as he did. But then, he didn't know very much about Gil, full stop. He knew he was handsome and a teasing smartass and an amazing lay, but he'd held him at a distance, hadn't let him close enough to find out anything about him. Basically, he'd refused to discuss him with David; he hadn't wanted to know anything about him. Michael looked around the impeccably decorated space, clearly revealed in the light shining from under the fan hood above the stove, and shook his head. He'd been so stupid.

There was a garden window across the room with several framed photos sitting among containers holding herbs, and he crossed to look at them.

There was a picture of Gil, Vernon, Manny, and Jackson, all wearing snow gear and holding snowboards. This must have been pre-David, or Michael's best friend had been doing his version of "skiing"—sitting in the lodge with a hot toddy. There was another photo of a young Gil with a full head of medium brown hair, posing with another boy who looked a lot like him and a very pretty girl with waist-length blonde hair. Michael wondered if they were his siblings. There were also portraits of a beautiful woman with bobbed hair and jewelry à la Doris Day in the fifties, and a handsome man with a smile like Gil's in a World War II Army uniform. Gil looked like his parents, Michael thought. He had his father's bone structure but his mother's soft mouth. Michael sighed and put the pictures back in the window, turning to look for the cabinet Jackson had told him held the cat food. And froze, his breath catching in his throat.

"Jesus God," he muttered.

Across from him on the concrete counter sat the biggest cat he'd ever seen. It was white and orange, with a white breast, muzzle, and front paws, butterscotch-orange face, and full, bushy tail. Dark orange markings curled around its back, and it had a huge pink nose. Large, vivid green eyes studied Michael, and the tufts of orange fur sticking up on the tips of its pointed ears twitched. The beast sat at least three feet tall; Michael could tell just by looking it had to outweigh Scooter.

"They named you 'Pixie'?" The cat's ears shifted at the sound of its name. "Someone had a very twisted sense of humor." The cat stood and stretched, then jumped down from the counter almost silently on its enormous feet before he approached Michael.

He stiffened. "If you eat me, I can't feed you."

The cat sniffed at his legs, and if it wanted to stretch a bit, Michael's crotch wasn't out of reach. Instead it wound around his legs, making an odd chirping sound.

Michael's brows shot up. "Dude, really? That's the best you've got?" The cat's noises grew louder, and Michael was torn between surprise and the urge to laugh.

He found the cupboard with the cat food and looked down at Jackson's note. "Okay, so you get a full can and a full bowl of the dry stuff. Huh, I wonder why Jackson would know that." He took out a can, and the cat's noises rose in volume.

"Yeah, yeah, I get it." He found the bowls in a far corner, sitting on a place mat with the face of Garfield on it, the words FEED ME in capital letters. He chuckled, picking up the two large earthenware bowls. Once they were filled, he put them back down, and the cat attacked the food like he hadn't eaten in weeks. Michael watched him for a moment, then decided to take a tour of the rest of the house.

A long hallway led to a bathroom, an office, and a guest bedroom. Around a bend was the master suite, with a king-size bed. A white tufted-leather headboard took up most of one wall, and lamps sat on small tables on either side. Linens in a white-and-turquoise repeating circle pattern covered the bed. The attached bathroom was beautiful, with a backsplash of clear and green glass tiles, trough sinks, and a huge glass walk-in shower. It smelled like Gil, and Michael noticed a towel hung neatly over the shower door. He went to it and touched it, feeling the slight whisper of dampness in the folds. He closed his eyes and pressed his face into it, inhaling the scent of Gil's morning shower.

When he came out and studied the master bedroom, he saw the bed was neatly made and there weren't any clothes tossed carelessly around. He was persnickety about his surroundings, but Gil apparently was too. Michael didn't leave a mess when he left his apartment in the morning because he hated coming home to it. There wasn't a thing out of place in the large bedroom, leading him to believe Gil was the same.

Michael paused near a portrait hanging on the wall. It was the same woman he'd seen in the kitchen, only older, a soft smile on her face. Her image had been lovingly rendered, her blouse and the background done in soft greens and blues. Even before he looked at the signature, he recognized the technique. He wasn't surprised to see *g.chandler* scrawled in the corner.

When he walked back through the house, no longer as awed by the décor and design, he paid closer attention to the art on the walls. Some of it was by other artists. When he bought other people's art, Gil tended toward modern works or black-and-white photography. A series of stunning male nudes hung on the wall of the office, and a pastel depiction of stylized flowers was on the wall of one of the spare bedrooms. In the dining room was another of Gil's pieces, a beautiful image of an old man sitting in a battered Chevy pickup truck, leathered arm propped on the open window, a cigarette hanging from his mouth. Michael stared at it for several minutes.

Whoever the man was, Gil clearly loved him. He'd rendered every line on the old face, every seam in the battered Seattle Mariners hat pulled low on his brow, the scratches and dents in the faded paint of the truck's door. It was a stunning painting, and Michael wondered why Gil didn't use his talent doing portrait art instead of painting houses.

He was still staring at the painting when Pixie came into the dining room and began rubbing against Michael's legs. His purr sounded like the motor of a small car.

"So, I'm your friend, huh?" He bent and gingerly ran his hand over the huge, leonine head. "You are enormous. Beautiful, but like a Lab in a cat body."

Pixie butted his head against Michael's knee, then turned and jumped effortlessly onto the dining room table, stretching out across the surface. Michael gave him a narrow-eyed look. "Why do I get the feeling you're not usually supposed to do that?"

The cat merely returned his look with a slow wink and then a steady gaze.

"Fine. Since you're big enough to eat my arm, you can stay right where you are." He paused long enough to run his fingers through the luxurious, orangesicle-colored fur. "I'll bet you're every bit as high maintenance as I am. And clearly your boy is out of his damned mind, wanting both of us." He hesitated. "At least I hope he still does. Wouldn't that be the ultimate irony? I decide I want him, and he's gotten bored waiting on me?" He sighed softly and left the house after locking up carefully.

He drove to David and Jackson's through the residential streets, his mind full of Gil's house, Gil's paintings, Gil's cat. By the time he pulled up in front, he had dozens of questions, none of which could be answered before Gil regained consciousness. He jogged up onto the porch, and when he unlocked the front door and walked in, he found David and Jackson lying spooning on the couch, Jackson in back with his arm around David's waist. They were watching a basketball game on television. Michael knew it must be love; it was eleven o'clock at night and his completely sports-ignorant best friend was watching basketball.

He closed the door and glared at Jackson. Scooter ran to him and danced around his knees as he bent to pet her, then stopped to sniff his pant legs. Her batlike ears flattened. "I know, you think I've cheated on you. Well, that's because your daddy is an ass."

"What did I do?" David asked.

"Not you." Michael pointed at Jackson. "Him."

"What?" Jackson asked, going up onto his elbow, his brow furrowed. "Pixie? Really?"

Jackson fought it, but finally laughter won out and he dropped back down, burying his face in the back of David's neck.

"Did you know about this?" Michael asked David.

"What? He's a cat."

"A really fucking big cat! For God's sakes, that animal could've eaten me if he'd been hungry enough. He's the size of a mountain lion."

"Aw, come on, Michael," Jackson finally managed. "Don't exaggerate. He's a nice cat. Besides, if you want to blame anyone, you're going to have to go to Vernon. He's the one who set you up."

"Oh, believe me," Michael promised. "The old man and I are having a chat next time I see him." He looked at David. "And I'm not going into work tomorrow. In fact, depending on how Gil does, I may just be done at A.F.I."

David didn't look surprised. "Why does it depend on how Gil does?"

Michael looked away, his face heating. "Because depending on how soon he can come home, he isn't going to be able to be alone, and I'm the most expendable."

"How do you figure that?" David sat up, a frown furrowing his brow.

"I'm your assistant, which you wouldn't want to live without, but you could. And everyone else is scheduled to work on the mansion."

"Well, you're a bit more indispensable to me than you seem to think." David ran his fingers through his hair. "And actually, I've been thinking we should both be done."

Michael smirked. "What about letting down the poor owners?"

"Shut up," David grumbled. "Things are different."

Michael's amusement faded. "Yeah. They are." He pushed away from the door. "I'm going to make a sandwich, then I'm going to bed."

David stood and went with him. "We haven't eaten yet either. I can warm up some spaghetti, or we can order pizza."

Michael gave him an irritated look. "You didn't have to wait on me."

David looped his arm around his shoulders. "Yeah, we did. Come on. You can make the salad."

"Oh, sure." Michael nudged David with his elbow. "I can tear open a bag with the best of them."

David gave him a small smile. It was a weak attempt at humor, but it was the best Michael had.

MICHAEL DIDN'T sleep well. Every time he dozed off, the vision of Gil falling replayed in his mind, over and over. He finally dozed off about dawn, then jerked awake an hour later when Jackson's truck started up in the driveway outside his window. He sat up groggily, pushing at the hair twisted over his face. After slipping on a thick pair of socks, he opened the bedroom door and, lured by the scent of coffee, padded into the kitchen. David was standing at the counter, dressed in nice slacks and a neatly pressed dress shirt. He'd clearly already showered and shaved, and even so, he looked tired.

"Good morning," he murmured around the cup he held near his lips.

"Hey." Michael went to the cupboard and got himself a mug, taking it to the coffeepot. "You look nice." Scooter came to lean against his leg, and Michael bent to pat her on the head.

"I'm going to go in to A.F.I. and tell them we're leaving." David straightened and reached for a Pop-Tart when it sprang up in the toaster. "I figure it's the least I can do."

"You aren't going to give them two weeks' notice?" Michael grabbed the other Pop-Tart. "The art department is going to shit."

"They'll get over it."

Michael arched a brow as he leaned against the counter. "You better hope Delta takes off, big boy. If it doesn't, you'll never get a reference out of the brass at A.F.I."

"It will take off." David spoke decisively, as if he was trying to convince himself. "And you better be nice, or I won't let them know you aren't coming back either."

Michael gave him an exasperated look. "I can do that."

"Why? I'm your boss and I can handle it. Besides, don't you want to get back to the hospital?"

"Well, yeah." Michael frowned at the skinny pastry in his hand.

"Then get a shower and get dressed and go to the hospital. I can handle the rest of this."

"That doesn't seem exactly fair, somehow."

David shrugged one shoulder, taking a nibble of his Pop-Tart that indicated he wasn't much interested in it.

"How was Jackson this morning?" Michael asked, taking a healthier bite of his own.

"Exhausted. He was up calling the hospital every hour all night."

"Is everything…. Did he find out anything?" Michael's pulse kicked up as nerves skittered under his skin.

"Gil's holding his own, which is about as good as we're going to get right now, I'm afraid."

"So he's still unconscious." Michael tried to ignore the sinking disappointment.

"The nurse, Pam, told Jackson it might take a couple of days for the swelling in his brain to go down."

Michael stared into his cup. "Do they think he'll have permanent brain damage?"

"They haven't ruled it out." David's hand curled around his forearm. "But they haven't said it's indicated either. Let's take it one day at a time and not jump to scary conclusions, okay?"

"Yeah, okay." Michael wanted to believe it but doubted he could.

"Okay, I'm going to go." David walked into the dining room, taking a jacket off the back of one of the chairs. He made a noise of irritation and picked up a soft-sided red lunch bag from the table. "Jackson forgot his lunch. Again."

"He's got a lot on his mind today."

David's frown immediately changed from irritated to melancholy. "True. I'll run it by the mansion on my way downtown."

"Why don't you let me take it?" Michael offered. "I can't get back into the ICU until eleven anyway."

David turned to him. "You don't mind? They won't have moved the scaffolding yet."

It was a slight shock to his system to understand what David wasn't saying. They hadn't moved the scaffolding yet. Which meant there was probably still a big red stain from Gil's compound fracture on the cement. He forced himself not to react, with his expression at least. "It's okay. I don't mind dropping off Jackson's lunch."

"You're sure?" David looked anything but convinced.

"Don't fuss, David." Michael grabbed the lunch bag and started back to the kitchen. David caught his hand, stopping him. He felt like a jerk when he saw the genuine concern in his friend's eyes. "It's fine," Michael reiterated. "Now, unless you plan to call to tell them you're going to be late on your way to quit, you'd better go."

David slipped into his coat, then kissed Michael on the cheek. "I'll see you at the hospital later."

"Yeah."

Michael watched him until he left the house, then returned to the kitchen to throw away the dried-out Pop-Tart. He'd completely lost his appetite too. Scooter eyed it, though, and Michael broke off a tiny corner with no frosting or filling. "You can have this." He handed it to her and tossed the rest into the can, then went to shower.

MICHAEL PARKED in front of the massive house and walked up the driveway with Jackson's lunch bag in his hand. The weather had turned mild, with temperatures in the low sixties and blue sky above dotted with white clouds. There seemed to be a lot of cars in the long driveway. He recognized Jackson's truck and Vern's Mustang, but the cute little red BMW and a large dark sedan didn't belong to any of the guys he knew.

He saw scaffolding being set up on the driveway side of the house, Manny and the new guys stacking the tower, Vern on the ground directing them. Michael walked up to him and watched for several minutes before he spoke. "Aren't you concerned about someone messing with it if it's sitting out here in the open like that?"

Vern turned to him, brows lowered over his eyes.

"We aren't going to be leaving it up." Vern's voice was gruff. "We'll be taking it down each night and storing it in the carriage house." He gestured toward a garage off the back of the drive, its doors standing open. "Richard said we could lock it up in there."

Michael turned and looked at it. "Isn't that a huge inconvenience?"

Vern's mouth twisted. "You could say that. But I won't take any more chances with these guys."

Michael studied him, frowning. "Vern, Gil's falling wasn't your fault. It wasn't anyone's fault."

"Yeah, well, we'll wait to see what the cops have to say about that."

Surprise widened Michael's eyes. "The cops? Who called the cops?"

"Jackson did. Something about the whole thing got his back up. He's got Mitchell out there now with a couple of other guys, poking around. Like I don't have anything to do without the fucking cops hanging around. No!" he shouted and Michael jumped, then realized he was yelling at the guys setting the towers. "The pins go on the inside. How many times do I gotta tell you that?" A cell phone rang, and Michael recognized Gil's ringtone. Vern pulled the phone out of his pocket, looked at the screen, and cursed. "Son of a bitch." He sighed, then answered. "Gil Chandler's phone—" He stopped to listen, and Michael saw his face darken and his nostrils flare. "She doesn't have authorization to do that. Goddammit, I'm telling you. Check his file. The only person who can do that is Gilbert. Okay, okay. I'll get there as soon as I can." Vern punched the button to disconnect the call.

"What was that?"

Vern turned to Michael after shoving the phone back in his pocket. "Gilbert's sister is up at the home, trying to get old Gil to sign some papers."

Michael remembered the conversation about Gil's sister, and anger spiked in his chest. "Let me go."

Vern made a face and shook his head. "I'll take care of it, Michael."

"Vernon, you can't do everything. It's two hours before I can get into the ICU. Let me do this."

Vern stared at him for several seconds, his eyes narrowed. "Do you even know where it is?"

"No, but you can give me directions, you old fart."

Vernon put his hands on his hips, but Manny climbed down, smiling. "Brookline is up on Sixty-Sixth behind the grocery store. Just drive past it and make a left at the gates, then follow the road through the entire complex. The memory care units are in the very back. You go into a small lobby and ring the doorbell. They'll let you in. Just tell them you're there to see old Gil."

Vern glared at him. "Thank you so much, Emanuel."

"Anytime, Vernon." Manny smacked the old man on the butt.

"Boy, you're turning into one big pain in my ass," Vern grouched at him.

"You love me." Manny turned to Michael. "Take orange-and-vanilla popsicles. The old man will love you, and everything else will sort itself out."

Michael held the lunch pail out to Vern. "Give this to Jackson, will you?" Vern sneered at him. "I'm not your servant boy."

"Oh, for God's sakes, you obnoxious old shit." Manny rounded on him, his own brow furrowed. It was as angry as Michael had ever seen Manny. "We're all worried about him and we all feel bad. You don't have the market cornered on feeling guilty. Stop taking it out on Michael." Manny held out his hand, taking the lunch pail. "I'll give it to him."

"Thanks." Impulsively, Michael threw his arms around Vern's neck, hugging him tight. "You didn't do anything wrong, Vern," he whispered near his ear. "It's not on you, okay?"

Vern hugged him fiercely for a moment, then pushed him away, sniffing, looking more irritated than anything. But Michael knew what a big heart beat in the old chest, and he gave Vern a small smile before he turned away.

"Orange-and-vanilla," Vern shouted after him as he walked to his car.

"Got it." Michael waved without looking back.

HE STOPPED by the grocery store, less than a block from the assisted-living place, and bought a box with twelve orangesicles inside; he even bought one of those foil-lined bags so the ice cream treats wouldn't melt. When he left the store parking lot, he followed Manny's instructions, found the open gates, and pulled through. Trees lined each side of the road, and lawns that were greening up nicely surrounded the buildings. The whole place looked like an upscale apartment complex with two-story buildings on one side and duplexes on the other. He drove through the buildings that looked like a vague blend between Victorian and Craftsman, all painted butter yellow with a darker yellow trim. There was another set of gates, and just like Manny had said, there were two buildings at the end of the cul-de-sac. They looked like one-story residences, homey with flower beds and lots of large windows. Michael didn't know what he'd expected a memory care place to look like, but this wasn't it.

He parked and got out of his car, nervous for the first time. The old guy had never seen him before, and the staff had no reason to listen to him; he could only hope they didn't throw him out.

He opened the door into the enclosed entry and signed the book next to the locked interior entrance before ringing the bell. It made him feel sad, that Gil's dad had to be in a locked unit. Voices approached from the other side of the door; then it popped open. A very pretty Asian girl wearing a burgundy smock with a name tag that said Chow answered, giving him a friendly smile.

"I'm here to see Gilbert Chandler?"

"Are you family?"

"No, I'm actually a good friend of Gil Junior."

She gave him a compassionate look. "We heard about his accident. Is there any word?"

"He's holding his own."

Her smile was bright. "Oh, good. I like Gil. He's a good son." She stood aside. "Come on in."

Michael entered a room that looked like the living room in a comfortable home. Two long couches hugged the walls and four cushy chairs sat across from them. Several older residents were dozing or watching what looked like an episode of *Gunsmoke* on television.

"I brought popsicles." Michael held out the insulated bag.

She laughed. "He's going to have enough of these for a month. Vernon brought some last night. Mr. Chandler is in the dining room." She started to lead Michael through the room, then paused, her smile fading. "His daughter is here."

"So I understand."

She nodded. "Vernon told you we called?"

"He did." They exchanged a knowing look.

"Let's go see if we can interest him in a popsicle."

She walked ahead of him into a large dining room with several cloth-covered square tables, small vases with a few spring flowers in the center of each. At one sat an older gentleman, his white hair combed back and his mouth set in an obstinate line. A woman stood next to him, hovering near his shoulder.

"Malarkey!" Mr. Chandler said, shaking his head.

"Dad, just your name. Right there." She pointed, then tried to hand him a pen. "Someone needs to be able to look after you, and right now Gil can't."

"Malarkey!" he announced again. "Malarkey, malarkey, malarkey!"

Chow smiled. "He saw Vice President Biden on the TV use that word, and ever since it's been a favorite."

"And appropriate," Michael muttered under his breath, and the aide smiled.

"Mr. Chandler," Chow announced, "aren't you popular today. You have another visitor."

The old man didn't turn, but the woman did, and she frowned as she eyed him. "Who are you?"

"My name is Michael Crane. I'm a friend of your brother's."

Her cool gaze moved over him from his head to his toes and back again. She sniffed. "I'm sure you are."

Michael gave her a level look. "Charming." He walked around her and smiled at Gil senior. "Hi, Mr. Chandler. I'm Michael."

His hazel eyes, so much like Gil's it was startling, moved over him. "Malarkey." He crossed his thin arms over his chest. At one time he must've been Gil's size; Michael could tell he was tall, but now his rangy frame was very thin. He searched for something to say, unaccustomed to talking to someone Mr. Chandler's age, let alone one with his issues. Finally, inspiration struck.

"Balderdash," he announced clearly. "Now, would you like a popsicle? I brought some, and I understand they're your favorite. Orange-and-vanilla."

Gil senior's face brightened. "Popsicle."

Michael took the box from Chow and took out an ice cream bar. He pulled off the wrapping and handed it to the old gentleman.

"I'm trying to speak with my father," Gil's sister—he thought her name was Heidi—said, clearly annoyed.

"I noticed." Michael thanked Chow when she handed the older man a paper napkin. "But your dad seems to want a popsicle."

Gil senior took a bite of the popsicle, then looked up at Michael. He swallowed the ice cream.

"Balderdash."

Michael grinned. "Poppycock."

Chow laughed, the old gentleman smiled, and Michael decided he wanted a popsicle too.

CHAPTER TWELVE

MICHAEL SPENT about ninety minutes with Gil's dad. Heidi finally got really irritated and stormed out after about twenty minutes, but Michael found, to his total surprise, that he was enjoying sitting with the older man. They each ate two of the orange-and-vanilla popsicles and came up with increasingly outrageous words for silliness. Michael pulled up an online thesaurus on his cell phone. His personal favorite was *flummery*. Old Gil had a few moments of consideration for *twaddle* and *tomfoolery*, but ultimately he returned to *malarkey*. God love Joe Biden.

He left Brookline at ten thirty and drove straight to the hospital, parked in the lot, and carried in his messenger bag. He rode the elevator to the fifth floor, then entered the ICU quietly. New nurses were on duty, and Michael noticed someone had finally found Gil a gown that fit, but he was just as still as he'd been the night before, and that concerned him. The neurologist, Dr. Pillai, came in and checked Gil's pupils, reporting that the pressure in his head was within normal ranges and his blood pressure and pulse were still good.

"When will he wake up?" Michael asked, looking back at Gil's face. The bruises now were truly spectacular, green and purple among the black and blue. There didn't seem to be a spot on his body that wasn't discolored or swollen, so Michael confined himself to touching the back of his hand.

"It shouldn't be too much longer," the doctor answered kindly. "The CT this morning looked promising, and there's little drainage. All head injuries are unique, and each patient responds differently." He patted Michael on the shoulder. "All indications are positive at this point. Try not to worry."

He left the room, and Michael exhaled in irritation. "Try not to worry." He studied the swollen half of Gil's face and the bandage on his head, the tube coming from behind his ear that attached to a machine. They'd pulled the breathing tube that morning and told Michael he was breathing well on his own, but he remained unconscious. Looking at the big man lying so deathly still made Michael's chest hurt. How in the world could he do anything but worry?

Vernon and Manny arrived at six, entering the room on quiet feet.

"Hey, baby boy." Vernon spoke quietly, then walked to the edge of the bed and looked down at Gil. "Damn, I hoped he'd be awake by now."

"Me too." Michael closed his laptop and slipped it into his bag. He'd spent the afternoon working on procurement samples for the mansion and texting with David. The fact they were both quitting had been received at A.F.I. about how they expected—not well at all. David put in his two weeks' notice and told management Michael would not be returning at all. Fortunately the O'Banyon job ensured they could put Michael on salary, so he could at least afford to pay his bills.

"Has the doctor been in?" Manny asked, standing near the door with his hands shoved in his front pockets. He looked miserable as he studied Gil's battered face.

"The neurologist said his tests look good. The orthopedist said there's no indication of infection. Everything seems to be real positive. He just hasn't woken up."

Vern straightened. "Well, he always has been a contrary son of a bitch, so I imagine he will when he's good and ready. As for you, Hostess, you need to go eat a decent meal and get a good night's sleep. Emanuel and I will stay until they throw us out at eight. You've done enough time in that chair today."

Michael's gaze went back to Gil's face. "You'll call me if he wakes up?"

"First thing, sweetheart. Now get out of here."

It was dark when Michael walked out to his car. The days would start getting longer soon, but for now as he walked across the lot, it felt like midnight, and he was tired. Traffic was awful, crawling up the hill. David sent him a text and asked if he could pick up coffee, which he was more than happy to do, but that made him even later. By the time he walked into the house, carrying a bag with coffee, bananas, and a frozen pizza, he was ready for some shitty food and a bed.

David and Jackson were sitting on the couch, facing one another. Michael paused with the door open, studying their faces. They looked so somber, particularly when they turned to him.

"What's wrong?" Fear shot the length of Michael's spine and his breath grew short. "What happened? Is it Gil? Did Vern call?"

David stood and quickly came to him, his hands raised. "Relax. We haven't heard anything. As far as we know, Gil's the same."

"Then"—he looked between them—"what's wrong, because something is."

David looked at Jackson, who sat back, his expression pensive. "Up to you, babe," he told David.

David grabbed Michael's hand and pulled him into the room. "Come here." He urged him to sit in the rocking chair. "If we discuss this with you, you have to promise to listen and not overreact."

Michael looked between the two of them. "Overreact to what?"

David sat next to Jackson, turning to him. "You spoke with Detective Mitchell. You tell him. I'll just get the details wrong."

Jackson studied his fiancé for a long moment. "Okay." He turned to Michael, who was watching him, heart thumping uncomfortably hard. "I just got off the phone with Mitchell. You know I met with the police this morning at the site."

"Yeah."

"I've worked with Gil and Vern a lot. I've even helped them put up scaffolding more than once. There is no one more careful about how the towers are assembled than Gil. He tests all of it himself, goes over every single plank to make sure there aren't any weak spots. And if he finds one, he fixes it."

"Okay." Michael frowned. "So?"

"It seems unlikely," Jackson went on, "that Gil would miss something that brought down an entire tower."

"But the tower fell. I mean, I watched it. It went straight—" Michael stopped, suddenly feeling like someone had punched him in the solar plexus.

"It did," Jackson agreed. "It went straight down. If it was a structural defect, that isn't how it should have fallen. One break wouldn't have brought the whole thing down. Even if more than one was faulty, it should have leaned, then toppled."

Michael felt sick to his stomach. "You think someone tampered with it."

Jackson hesitated, then nodded, his expression solemn. "We know someone did."

Michael blinked, registering Jackson's emphasis.

"I told Mitchell about your description of how the tower went down. It sounded wrong to me. I trust your powers of observation, and I'm sure it happened just the way you said. They're still looking at it, but it appears the scaffolding was intentionally damaged."

"Intentionally damaged... how?"

Jackson leaned forward, his hands linked between his knees. "It's hard to explain if you haven't built scaffolding, but the towers have two areas where they connect. One tower slides into the top of another, creating a seal, and then there are crossarms that connect to pins on the inside of the side poles."

"I watched Vern supervising the other guys for a few minutes this morning. I know what you're talking about."

"Okay, good. Once the towers are stable, then the planks can be set in place. I know for a fact that Vern and Gil built the towers first thing yesterday morning. When you told me there was a snapping noise, it sounded like one of the pins broke. But one broken pin wouldn't have brought an entire tower straight down."

"Just tell me." Michael stuffed his hands, which were suddenly freezing, under his arms. "I know you're building up to something."

Jackson sighed, and David ran his hand down Jackson's arm.

"It's okay," David murmured.

Jackson turned to Michael, the corners of his mouth tight. "The crime lab found the tower supports were cut part of the way through in several places, all on the side where Gil tried to climb down. No one would have noticed the damage unless they were specifically looking for it. You haven't worked on scaffolding before; there's enough overlap in the bars that unless you knew where to look for the cuts, you wouldn't see them. The whole thing was set up the day before. None of the guys would assume it was tampered with overnight. There was no one on-site after dark, and the traffic sounds would cover the sound of a saw. According to Vern, Gil had only been up for a few minutes and he'd climbed up on the side that hadn't been tampered with. When he swung over on the side that had been cut, his weight pulled it off-center, and one of the weakened places failed. It put stress on the others. As he fell, he took the rest of them out."

"They're sure?" Michael asked, his voice sounding hollow to his own ears. "That someone did this... on purpose?"

"Yeah. There were hacksaw cuts in the steel. Richard and Lyle aren't living in the house yet, but they wouldn't have heard it anyway. Whoever it was used a handsaw. With the traffic noise in the area, and the back of the house not visible from the street—" He shook his head.

"They don't have cameras?" Michael looked between Jackson and David.

"They don't. They plan to install some, but the work hasn't been done yet." Jackson's lips tightened into a hard line. "Whoever it is doing this shit isn't stupid. Mitchell said they had to have staked out the mansion before that night, and knew there were no cameras. It was also a full moon with no cloud cover. They'd have been able to see without even needing a flashlight."

The level of sophistication involved was intimidating. This was no petty vandal.

"Do they think it was the same guy who vandalized this house?" Michael's heart was racing, fear and adrenaline making his chest tight.

Jackson gave him a level look. "Mitchell thinks it seems likely, yes."

Michael shot to his feet, patting down his pockets, finding his keys and pulling them out.

"Where are you going?" David asked, frowning as he stood as well.

"Back to the hospital." Michael headed for the door.

"Michael, stop. What good is that going to do?"

He turned on David. "I'll be able to keep an eye out. You just told me someone tried to kill him yesterday, didn't you? The same guy who came after me with a shovel?"

"They tried to hurt someone from our crew. We don't know they were targeting Gil."

"Even if they weren't targeting Gil, they were trying to hurt one of us, and they succeeded. Which is why I'm going back." Michael opened the front door.

"Michael, they aren't going to let someone just waltz into the ICU. Besides, they won't let you on the floor," David protested. "Visiting hours are over at eight, and it's quarter to now."

"Then I'll sit in the waiting room watching the fucking door. But I'm going. I'm not leaving him alone down there and defenseless."

"Goddammit, Michael." David was so upset he actually stamped his foot. "None of us slept last night, and I know you're exhausted. You have to sleep."

"I don't." He knew he sounded unreasonable, and he didn't care. He felt a little wild and his body trembled. "I need to make sure no one gets to him."

"They have security at the hospital. We can call."

"Just stop." Michael glared at him. "I'm going back, so stop arguing with me." He rushed out through the front door, slamming it behind him, so angry he didn't even notice no one had followed him until he was in his car and on his way back.

IT WAS eight twenty when Michael walked back into the hospital. Most of the foot traffic was exiting the lobby, not going in, which was a relief, but he was so determined to get to the fifth floor they'd have had to tackle him to stop him. When he got as far as the ICU waiting room, he began to recognize the flaw in his plan.

First of all, there was no way for him to get into a room directly across from the nurses' station without someone noticing him. He glanced down the hallway; the lights were dimmed and the floor was quiet but for the noises of the machines. That hadn't lessened a bit. A woman with dark hair stood behind the desk at the nurses' station, and he couldn't see a way to sneak past her. He turned and went back into the waiting room, flopping into one of the uncomfortable chairs. He'd told David he would watch the door if that was all he could do. Well, apparently, it *was* all he could do.

He was soon sorry that in his haste to get there, he hadn't at least pulled into a drive-thru to get a hamburger on the way downtown. He hadn't eaten since the popsicles that morning, so busy on his laptop at lunch he hadn't even noticed his hunger. He yanked another chair over and lifted his feet onto it. He'd text David to bring him drive-thru in the morning. If David was still talking to him, after his flounce from the house. He leaned his elbow on the arm of the chair and rubbed his forehead, trying to think what he could text that might help make David forgive him.

"Hello."

Michael looked up, startled to see the blonde nurse, Pam, from the day before standing in the doorway.

"Oh, hi." Michael dropped his feet self-consciously to the floor. "Sorry."

She grinned. "You honestly think your feet can hurt one of those chairs?"

"I doubt World War III could hurt that chair."

"So, after the apocalypse, there will be cockroaches and these chairs?"

"And Cher."

She laughed. "Okay, so who is David?"

Michael blinked in surprise. "David—Snyder?" She nodded, brown eyes sparkling. "My best friend."

"I sort of figured that, actually. You see, I just got off the phone with him. He told me you were headed down here and determined to spend the night sitting out here watching the door to the hallway. So, you plan to stay until tomorrow morning, huh?"

Michael felt his face heat. "Someone hurt him," he said softly.

"Gilbert?"

"Yes. On purpose. They sabotaged some of his equipment, and that's why he fell. And I can't just stay at home… not and leave him here alone." He had to stop talking. His voice had thickened, and he was afraid if he kept going he was going to end up breaking down.

"Do you really think you could stop them if someone came here and decided to go after him?" Her voice was gentle. That was almost worse than if she'd laughed at him.

"I have no idea." He straightened his shoulders. "But I'd damn sure try."

She studied him for a long moment. "I like you, Michael. It is Michael, right?"

He nodded.

"I thought that was what David said, but I like to be sure. Anyway, because I liked you when you were here earlier, I went to my supervisor and got permission for you to stay in Gil's room."

Michael stared, able to feel how wide his eyes were. "You liked me? Why?"

She grinned. "You remind me of my brother. Anyway, she said it's okay for you to stay."

"She can do that?"

Pam shrugged. "Management wouldn't love it, but what they don't know won't hurt them. And it is discretionary. We're pretty quiet right now. If we get a new case sent up, you'll have to come back out. Or if for some reason Gil's condition were to worsen, but that isn't likely to happen."

"You sound so sure." He knew he sounded needy, but he couldn't seem to help it.

"Pretty sure. I've been doing this a long time, and Gil's having no problem holding his own."

"But he's not awake yet."

"He will be. Cut the guy a break, Michael. He fell three stories. Takes the brain some time to come back from something like that, but it will."

Michael took what felt like the first deep breath he'd managed in hours. "Thank you."

"You're welcome. Now come on, before my boss changes her mind."

Michael stood and followed her. They moved quietly by the open doors to the other rooms. There had been at least six patients that afternoon, but only three of them were occupied now, and it was a lot quieter than it had been. When they arrived at the nurses' station, the dark-haired woman on the phone looked up, giving him a slight nod.

"Thank you," he whispered, hoping she could see his appreciation on his face. She waved him away into Gil's room with a small smile.

He walked in, studying all of the equipment. The bellows in the ventilator moved up then down with a rhythmic hiss, and he watched the numbers on the screen across from the bed. Everything looked exactly the same as it had when he left, and he exhaled slowly.

Pam came around behind him, pushing the recliner from the corner until it was right beside the bed.

"Here you go. And I'll get you a blanket and a pillow."

"Thank you," he said, meaning it. His stomach rumbled, and he covered it with a sheepish look.

"And maybe a turkey sandwich?"

"That would be amazing."

She gave him a wink and headed toward the doors, pausing before she walked out. "I don't know if anyone mentioned it to you earlier, but talk to him. I can't tell you the number of people who tell doctors they could hear their loved ones while they were comatose. It will make him feel better to know you're here."

Michael carefully curled his hand around Gil's, and perched on the edge of the chair. "I'm here," he murmured, squeezing Gil's hand. "Right here. And it's time for you to wake the fuck up."

Pam returned with the promised blanket and pillow and a turkey sandwich on wheat with a bag of chips. By the time he dug in, his stomach had begun to feel hollow; the food helped a lot. He adjusted the chair until it was closer to the bed, took off his jacket and shoes, then covered his legs with the blanket. He still found it impossible to relax.

When he'd been there about an hour, and he knew he was overtired and jittery at the thought someone out there had hurt Gil intentionally, he scooted to the edge of the chair, one hand curled around Gil's fingers. The other moved up and down the bruised skin of Gil's thick forearm, and he leaned forward, suddenly exhausted, gingerly pressing his forehead against the solid wall of Gil's shoulder.

"Pam said to talk," he began, feeling awkward. "I think she probably meant more than me just telling you I'm here, over and over again." He lifted his head and studied Gil's black-and-blue forehead, the bandage that now had some pinkish discharge coming through the gauze. They'd drilled two holes in his head; the thought made Michael shudder. He wanted to fix it, to somehow make it better with the brush of his fingers. It was stupid, but it was how he felt.

He concentrated on Gil's long dark brown eyelashes. "It's been a damned long day and a half, Gilbert," he started, trying to talk to him as if he were awake. "And by the way, I have a bone to pick with you. Who in their right mind named that saber-toothed tiger you live with 'Pixie'? It's like that neighbor of David's naming their poor corgi Bootsy. There should be a law that you're not allowed to humiliate your animals with stupid names. That cat could eat you in your sleep, Gil. You should have been nice and named it something butch, like Clint Eastwood or Bruce Willis." He smirked. "Although Pixie could be a good drag queen name. With that bushy tail of his, it's like he carries his own boa. So maybe the name isn't so bad after all."

He shifted his gaze to the hand under his, studying Gil's nails. There was a spot of gray paint on his thumbnail. "So what else shall we talk about?" He picked at the small gray spot. "This is easier when you're being a snarky smartass, you know; I'm not much for monologues." He snorted softly. "I can just imagine what you'd say to that. 'You're full of shit, Michael.'" He slipped his fingers between Gil's thicker, beefier ones. "Sometimes I am full of shit. And so dumb. You must be unconscious if I'm admitting that." He rested his other elbow on the edge of the bed and leaned his forehead on his hand. "I'm going to tell you something you aren't allowed to hold over my head later, okay? I'm sorry I kept pushing you away. I didn't want to. But you scare me, Gil. You really, really scare me." He clenched his hands around one another. "I guess I have to explain that, don't I?"

He thought of the morning he'd wakened safe and secure in Gil's arms, how right it had felt. How terrified he'd been. How terrified he'd been for five years.

"I went to the University of Washington. I don't think I've ever told you that, have I? I'm one of those snotty, rich frat brats. And I'm actually the worst of the worst; I'm a legacy brat. Both of my parents went to Washington. My mother was even the president of her sorority. And if you met her, you'd be able to see it all over her, right down to the four-carat rock on her hand and her cultured pearls." He chuckled, but there wasn't any humor in it. "I think it was the only thing my parents actually expected of me in my life—that I'd go to the U, pledge a fraternity, graduate with honors. Two out of three isn't bad, right?" His smile faded and he stared at the pattern on Gil's gown, let his eyes go unfocused. "Or so you'd think."

His mind slipped back to a too-bright fall day and the pair of blue eyes that stole his breath. "I pledged a fraternity. I even pledged the old man's fraternity, though I had no fucking intention of being a lawyer. Then I met a guy." He huffed out a ragged breath. "How cliché is that, honestly? You change your major, change your life, because of 'some guy.'" His voice softened. "His name was Evan Coldwell, and I met him at a party during freshman rush. I was the freshman, he was a junior, and I fell for him before he'd ever opened his mouth."

Evan told him he hadn't wanted to attend the stupid party, and he'd been putting away Solo cup after Solo cup of microbrew without ever getting sloppy drunk. Michael had been so impressed by his self-possession. He'd been pretty well toasted himself, and he let Evan pick him up. That night had been a turning point in a lot of ways; at eighteen Evan was the first guy Michael actually had sex with. He'd done a lot of making out and fooling around. But this was fucking, and some pretty spectacular fucking at that. It had changed his life. Or so he'd thought.

"Evan was living in an apartment off campus, and I ended up never moving into the frat house. Fortunately for me, the frat got itself put on probation the first weekend and wasn't allowed to rush a freshman class. It was like a gift. It was move in with Evan or the dorms, and my parents were a whole lot more willing to pay rent than for some crappy dorm room. God forbid the son they spent eighteen years ignoring should sully the family name by living in a dorm." He exhaled, and it was shaky. "Wow,

Michael. Bitter much? I guess that's the other thing you should know about me; my relationship with my parents sucks, and I'm a whiny bitch. Anyway, Evan." He ran his fingers delicately over Gil's arm, wincing anew at the bruises.

"I was young and supremely stupid, and I gave him… well, whatever he wanted. He'd found himself a meal ticket with a trust fund, and I thought he was as in love with me as I was with him. I never questioned it when he didn't want to discuss his family; after all, I had issues with my parents. I had no trouble believing he had issues with his. We lived together for two years, made all of these plans for how our lives would be when I finally got out of school. He was going on to law school when he graduated, and I found it hilarious that my father would be getting a lawyer in the family, even if it wasn't me. Anyway, the weekend he graduated, I'd planned a party for him. He'd mentioned in passing his family wasn't coming, and I felt sorry for him." He shook his head. "Stupid, so stupid.

"I went to commencement, so proud when he walked across the stage. He looked so handsome in his cap and gown. He told me we'd meet up at home, that he didn't want to fight the rush to try to get to me in the crowd once the ceremony was over. I planned to pick up his graduation present and some stuff for the party, and then we'd catch up at the apartment. I thought we could maybe have a little private party before our friends got there." He let his forehead come to rest gently on the back of Gil's wrist, taking a shaky breath. "Have I reiterated enough that I was stupid?

"I got home carrying bags full of pretzels and chips and a small velvet gift box containing a truly awful University of Washington class ring inset with amethysts and a single diamond. Looking back, it was gaudy and so not Evan's style, but then, I guess I really wasn't either. When I unlocked the door to our place"—he remembered the shock, the disbelief, the cold that had spread from his face down—"everything was gone. I mean, all of it. Evan's clothes, his pictures, his desk, everything. There were dents in the carpet where the furniture had been, but it was gone, like it vanished into thin air. Even the plates, the silverware, and the towels in the bathroom. Four hours before it had all been there, and now it was gone. It was mostly all his to begin with, but… I wasn't thinking clearly, and I thought we'd been robbed. I went to the on-site property manager, hysterical, and he told me Evan had arranged for him to let the crew in, and he just assumed we were moving."

Michael lifted his head, sniffing. He hadn't noticed the tears until they were slipping down his cheeks and off his chin. He rubbed them away in irritation.

"I even thought maybe it was some sort of surprise. Maybe he'd moved us to a nicer apartment without telling me. But then I found my stuff in the closet and tossed in a corner of our bedroom. I tried calling him but got a recording, saying his phone was disconnected. I was frantic; I had no idea where he was or what happened. I mean, we'd made love that morning and he was fine, although in retrospect it seemed he was uncharacteristically gentle." He cleared his throat roughly.

"I found out later that he hadn't cut off his relationship with his family at all. I just wasn't part of it. I stayed with friends that night, still trying to make excuses, to come up with rational reasons for why he'd just abandon me like that. I was so distraught that my best friend, Hayley, went online and did a search of Evan's name, something I never thought to do. He'd told me he was from Champaign, Illinois, but there was no record of the family name there. Hayley is nothing if not thorough. She finally found him in Oklahoma City."

He was so weary, his body felt like his bones were dissolving. The only other person he'd ever told this story to was David, and remembering the details of the day his life fell apart always exhausted him.

"The more Hayley found out, the more things began to make a horrible sort of sense. His family was prominent in Oklahoma politics. His dad was a city councilman and his mother, like mine, headed up a dozen charitable organizations. Evan apparently never came out to his family. As far as they knew, their big old straight son went to the University of Washington for four years of freedom before returning to the family fold and doing what all good sons do—finish grad school, pass the bar so he could enter the family firm, get married, and start working on those two point five grandchildren. He married his high school sweetheart within weeks of getting home. The Evan I knew was as big a lie as everything else about his life." Michael was suddenly cold and wrapped his hands in the blanket.

"I made a decision after that. I decided if I could live with a man for two years and never know I was his dirty little secret, I couldn't trust my judgment. I'd never let anyone close enough to make a fool of me again. And I haven't. Except for David, but there was never anything romantic there, not from the beginning. We looked at each other and were just – best friends. Anyway, I graduated from the U with my degree in fine art and saw an ad on an industry Web page for the job where I met David. It did two things I needed for it to do—it gave me an income, and it got me out of Seattle and away from my parents. And that, as they say, is that."

Michael took a deep breath, held it for a moment, then slowly released it. "So now you know why I wouldn't let you close. You scare the living shit out of me, Gilbert. I've been fighting my feelings almost since the day we moved the stuff out of your dad's house. But…." He rubbed the back of his arm across his eyes. "I don't think I can do it anymore. Seeing you fall like that, seeing how badly hurt you were—are, I just…." His emotions were slipping out of control as his eyes filled again, and the tears he couldn't stop streaked his face. "I love you, Gil." He touched the battered face with gentle fingers. "You have to open your eyes. You have to wake up so I can give you grief for scaring the shit out of me like that. Because listen to me, you asshole. I need you. I need you to—"

He cut off his sentence when he saw movement behind Gil's left eyelid. The right was still too swollen, but his left lid was definitely twitching, and his lashes were trembling. Michael's heart rocked in his chest, abruptly hammering at the base of his throat. "Gil? Baby, can you hear me?"

Gil's arms moved, and he made an odd noise, like the cross between a gasp and a groan. Then he coughed, and his left leg shifted under the blankets.

"Gil? Oh my God, Gil." Tears streaked down Michael's cheeks. His gaze was glued to Gil's face, and slowly, his left eye opened. It rolled, as if he were searching the room, then stopped when he spotted Michael.

Michael smiled. "Hey," he whispered, his voice breaking.

"Hey." Gil's voice sounded raw, like someone had abraded the inside of his throat with sandpaper. He closed his good eye, and Michael felt a moment's panic. That couldn't be it; Gil couldn't pass out again, not when he'd just come back to him.

"Gil!" Gil's eye immediately opened again, and his poor, swollen lips pulled up at the corners.

"You can't take it back," he rasped.

"Take what back?" Michael held Gil's hand between both of his.

"I heard you, Michael. You said you love me, and you can't take it back."

Michael's smile trembled and he pressed his lips to Gil's knuckles, his tears wetting the bruised skin. "I won't take it back, baby. I'll take out an ad in the fucking paper if you want me to."

Gil's grip was weak when he turned his hand and caught Michael's fingers between his, but it was there. "On Sunday, widest circulation day."

Michael's laugh was ragged. "You're on."

The corner of Gil's lips curled up in a slight smile. "And I love you too."

Michael kissed his poor bruised knuckles again, then dropped his forehead to Gil's hand.

CHAPTER THIRTEEN

EVENTUALLY MICHAEL got up from his chair to alert Pam, and then there was a rush of activity and he had to leave the room. Different doctors than the ones Michael had seen before moved in and out of the room, and he stood watching from the doors to the waiting room as he called David and ended up speaking to Jackson.

"He's awake?" Jackson sounded as anxious as Michael had felt.

"Yeah, he is."

"Is he okay?"

Michael knew what he was asking. They'd talked all around it, but from the moment Dr. Shumway had told them there could be repercussions from the injury to his head, they'd been afraid of what that could mean. Michael knew they weren't out of the woods by any stretch. "He seems to be okay. He knew who I was, and he talked to me."

"Thank Christ." Michael heard the stark relief in his voice.

"Yeah. I'm not much for praying, but I've been doing a lot of it. In fact, I may owe God my firstborn."

Jackson gave a ragged laugh. "Well, good luck with that."

They moved Gil out of the ICU that night, and by morning he was in a room on a lower floor that at least had a view of downtown. Michael walked with them as he was moved and met the nurses who would be taking care of him on the orthopedic floor. The visiting hours were much looser outside of the ICU, and they didn't seem to have any problem with Michael spending the night in yet another recliner.

Once he was moved, Gil was exhausted, and more asleep than he was awake, but when he did open his eyes he searched for Michael. He dozed, holding Gil's hand, waking every time the nurses came in to check his vitals or bring him medicine. They assured Michael Gil's exhaustion was absolutely normal, and the relief he felt every time Gil wakened was so complete he was almost light-headed with it.

Vern and Manny were there by six thirty, and their relief was reflected on their faces when Gil clearly knew who they both were.

"What the fuck were you thinking, Gilbert?" Vern demanded. He sounded stern, but Michael knew it was just Vern being Vern.

"Thought I could fly," Gil answered.

"Well, I hope this disabused you of that notion. Because I can guarantee, your big old ass didn't do anything but fall. And another thing, you jackass—you gonna scare ten years off my life, you need to start paying me better."

"Don't listen to him." Manny smiled as he held Gil's hand. "He's just pissed off cuz you're getting a vacation, and his tired old butt has to do all the patching and repair on the exterior of the O'Banyon place."

"Damn straight," Vern grumbled. "That fucking place is huge."

"I'll be back before you know it." Gil's eye drifted closed. "After a nap."

Manny and Vern left not long after, and within an hour Jackson and David came through the door. While Jackson sat beside Gil, talking to him softly, David pulled Michael into the hall.

"How is he?" David caught Michael's hand, squeezing it.

"Sleepy. I'm just so fucking relieved he's awake at all…."

"I know. Listen, we need to talk about how much time you're going to be spending here."

Michael stiffened, withdrawing his hand. "Have the police found the guy who did this yet?"

David sighed. "No, not that we've heard."

"Then I'm here."

"Michael…."

"David. As long as someone is out there willing to sabotage his equipment"—Michael spoke through stiff lips, winding up—"and he's as helpless as he is right now, I'm not going anywhere. I can keep working on procurement on my laptop—"

David reached out and grabbed Michael's shoulder. "Stop. Will you let me talk?"

Michael pursed his lips, but subsided. "So? Talk."

"Jackson and I have been talking about it, and you can't be here all day, every day."

"Watch me."

"Oh God, you're infuriating. Shut up."

Michael arched one brow, waiting.

"All I mean is that there are enough of us that we can… do it in shifts, or something."

"David, the other guys are working on the mansion. We can't put Richard and Lyle off."

"We won't," David assured him. "But you can't exhaust yourself by being here, never getting a decent night's sleep. And you might as well resign yourself to the other guys periodically coming in and throwing you out. Jackson is insisting on it."

Michael studied David's resolute face. "Gil told me he loves me." Michael wasn't sure where that came from, wasn't even sure he'd meant to say it, but there it was.

David's frown faded, and his eyes softened. "Did he? And what did you say?"

Michael felt a tiny flare of giddiness in his stomach. "Actually, I told him first. I just didn't know he was awake to hear me."

David's smile grew. "Is that right?"

"Pam, the nurse, said I should talk to him, that people who woke from comas told doctors they could hear. It was weird at first, you know? Just… talking? But—" He took a deep breath. "—I told him about Evan."

David squeezed his arm.

"I don't know if he heard that part, but I told him. And I guess I realized something."

"What?"

"That in order to love someone, you have to let them in. I've been pushing him away since… probably that day at his dad's house, because he scared me. Evan hurt me so much, I figured not allowing myself to care was the only protection I had. Then he fell."

Michael shuddered, his throat growing tight, and David stroked a hand down his arm. "That had to be so scary."

"It was. But you know what scared me more than watching him fall? The idea that I've spent months pushing him away, and I might never have a chance to tell him that I do love him. But he heard me. He told me I'm not allowed to take it back." He laughed, feeling it wobble. "He wants me to put an ad in the paper, on Sunday, because more people read that day."

David made a soft sound, then wrapped his arms around Michael, hugging him hard. "I'm so glad," he said against Michael's ear.

175

He squeezed David back. "I love him so much. So, when you fell in love with Jackson, and you told me it scared you? God, do I get it now."

David leaned back, smiling. "Do you also remember me telling you that it would happen to you someday too?"

Michael groaned softly. "I knew that would come up."

"Oh hell yes, it would. Have you any idea how nice it is for me to be able to say 'I told you so'?" He laughed softly. "More than anything, I'm just so fucking glad."

"Me too." Michael smiled weakly. "Pissing myself, but glad."

David laughed and hugged him again.

AS THE days went by, Gil was more and more lucid. The physical therapy people had him sitting up in bed the second day, then moving cautiously to the recliner the next. The orthopedist was satisfied that his blood counts indicated he'd managed to dodge infection, and the neurosurgeon came in and pulled the tube from his head on the third day, pleased with his improvement. He also changed the dressing, and Michael cringed inwardly when he saw the two short incisions closed with staples. This man had drilled holes into Gil's skull. Michael was so damned glad the doctor knew what he was doing, he didn't think he could ever express it.

Dr. Pillai was pleased with the way the incisions were healing and that the swelling had gone down. He taped on a clean bandage, telling Gil he'd have to come into his office to have the staples removed. He also said there could be some side effects, but their severity remained to be seen.

"What sort of side effects?" Michael's hands curled around the railing on Gil's bed until his knuckles were white.

Dr. Pillai sat on a stool near the foot of the bed, setting Gil's chart aside. "Well, first of all, allow me to reiterate how unbelievably fortunate Gil's been throughout all of this. Falling three floors onto concrete, by rights, could kill you. So far I see remarkably few indications of long-term problems. But you need to understand; his brain got bounced around in his skull, and to think there would be no bruising is naïve." He studied Gil's face. "I expect there to be continuing headaches. If they increase in severity, you're to come right back here. There could also be a general…

malaise. The tiredness will probably continue. You may notice your balance is off, which is worrisome with your leg compromised. But since you aren't exhibiting any other indications of more extensive injury to the part of the brain where the hematoma was, I have to say—" He shook his head. "You're a very lucky man."

Gil looked at Michael and gave him a soft smile. "Yeah. I really am."

FIVE DAYS after Gil fell, Michael's phone rang, displaying a local number he didn't recognize. Gil was napping, so he stepped into the hall.

"Hello?"

"Michael Crane?"

"Yes?"

"Michael, this is Detective Mitchell. We met at David Snyder's home?"

"Oh yes. Hello, Detective."

"How is Mr. Chandler?"

Michael leaned against the wall. "He's doing well. They're discussing releasing him tomorrow."

"That is good news." Mitchell paused for a moment, and Michael could hear papers rustling. "Michael, we'd like for you to come in for a few minutes at four this afternoon."

Michael frowned. "Why?"

"We've arrested a suspect in the vandalism of Mr. Snyder's home."

He stiffened. "You have?"

"Yes. A patrol officer actually picked him up tagging a bridge downtown last night. We recovered some other evidence from a backpack that was in his possession that leads us to believe he might have been involved in your attack. We'd like to put him in a lineup and see if you can pick him out."

"He was wearing a ski mask, Detective. How would I be able to identify him?"

"You said you thought his eyes were distinctive."

The angry black eyes flashed through his mind, the red discoloration on his right eyelid. Could he identify the man from just that? He thought perhaps he could.

"What about the vandalism on the scaffolding?"

There was a pause. "We haven't been able to tie him to that yet, but believe me, we're working on it."

When Michael walked back into Gil's room, he was awake and looked up at him with a soft smile. His face was still black-and-blue, more green and yellow slipping into the vivid bruising, but the swelling had gone down enough that he looked more like the man Michael fell in love with.

"Hey."

"Hey, yourself." Michael sat down beside him, and Gil reached for his hand.

"I'm getting used to this." He squeezed Michael's fingers. "When I wake up now, and your hand isn't within reach, it feels weird."

Michael lifted the big hand. "I just got an interesting phone call."

"Oh yeah? Who from?"

"Detective Mitchell." He watched Gil's gaze sharpen. "They've arrested someone in connection with the vandalism at David's."

Gil's hand twitched in Michael's grip. "Do they think he might have tampered with the scaffolding?"

Michael ran his thumb over the scraped knuckles. "They aren't sure, but he said they're working on it." He looked away from Gil's close scrutiny. "They want me to come down and see if I can identify him in a lineup."

A weighted silence settled between them.

"Are you okay with that?"

"Honestly?" Michael squeezed Gil's hand. "It kind of scares me. But do I want them to be able to hold him? Yeah, I do."

Gil sighed. "I wish I could go with you."

"I wish you could too. I need to call David. I might be willing to do their lineup, but I'm not leaving you alone."

Gil linked their fingers. "Babe, I'm fine. What are you afraid is going to happen if I just lie here and take another nap?"

Gil had the head of the bed elevated, and Michael leaned over him until their faces were inches apart. "Gilbert, I'm not going to leave you here alone. Am I being overly cautious? Maybe." He ran his index finger over Gil's full lips, and they parted slightly. "The only thing worse than watching you fall would have been losing you, right when I figured my shit out. If I'm a little overprotective for a while—I'm afraid you're just going to have to live with it." He closed the distance between them and kissed Gil, planning for it to be a short, sweet kiss, but Gil apparently had other plans. He lifted one of his hands to the back of Michael's head, and circled his shoulders with his other arm. He slipped his tongue along Michael's lips, not demanding but requesting, and with a soft sigh Michael opened to him.

Michael's hand moved to Gil's cheek, barely touching, his thumb stroking beneath his chin. He angled his head slightly, deepening the seal between their lips. Gil's fingers slid into Michael's hair, and he sucked on his tongue, trapping it against the roof of his mouth.

"Whoops!"

Michael jerked back and looked over his shoulder into the very red face of the woman who'd been lining up the hospital bills with Gil's insurance carrier.

"I can come back," she offered apologetically.

"No, that's okay." Michael sat back, knowing his face must be as red as hers. Gil took the whole thing in stride, signing the forms she gave him and giving her a sweet smile when she gathered her things to leave. Michael thought she had a bit of a crush on Gil; walking in on that must've been an education.

"Well, there's one thing I found out from that little exercise," Gil muttered, "before she interrupted it."

"What's that?"

Gil caught Michael's hand, pulling it beneath the blanket over his lap. When his hand reached Gil's groin, he encountered the tangible proof of his arousal. His big cock was half-hard.

Gil's grin was impish. "Everything still works."

Michael curled his fingers around the thick shaft just as a nurse bustled in, and he snatched his hand back, feeling the tips of his ears burning. If he wasn't careful, he was going to turn into David.

Gil chuckled, obviously pleased with himself.

JACKSON ARRIVED at the hospital to sit with Gil while Michael was gone, and he walked out into the bright sunlight. It was after three, and the sun had yet to set, the best indication spring was finally there in earnest. He hadn't left the hospital before dark in days, and he slipped on sunglasses before he backed out of his parking place. It took him twenty minutes to drive downtown to the main police office connected to the courthouse and the county jail. He parked in front, taking a deep breath before entering through the double doors. There was an officer sitting at the reception desk, and Michael went up to him.

"I'm here to see Detective Mitchell?" he said when the man looked up at him. "He's expecting me."

"Your name, sir?"

"Michael Crane."

"One moment."

The officer picked up a phone, and Michael walked away slightly, looking through the window at the view of the Gothic courthouse. More than anything it resembled a Scottish castle with its round towers and turrets, and while Michael appreciated the architecture, he bet being taken in there in the back of a squad car was frightening. He turned away, his hands slipping into his jacket pockets.

A door opened to the right of the desk and Detective Mitchell entered. His dark suit was wrinkled and his patterned tie had a small stain on it. He gave Michael a weary smile.

"Michael, come on back."

He held the door open, allowing Michael to pass, then walked ahead. Michael followed him through what felt like a rabbit warren of desks and ringing telephones. "Leo, Carell." Mitchell gestured with his head, and two of the busy people stood, one a woman in a pencil skirt and a boxy jacket and the other a middle-aged man with bright red hair. Mitchell led them into an office and closed the door.

"Mike Leo, Clare Carell, this is Michael Crane. He's here for the lineup, including a perp from the tagging last night." He opened a file on the beat-up wooden desk. "His name is Brent Wiley. He's not in the system, but I get the feeling he's responsible for some of the more creative art left around town."

"Where did they finally catch him?" Detective Carell asked.

Mitchell leaned his hip on the desk and picked up the phone. He hit several buttons and then waited. "He got picked up tagging the bridge across from the Methodist church next to the McDonald's."

The woman officer laughed. "Gotta give him credit for balls."

"Well, yeah," Mitchell agreed, "except they're suing for damages. This poor bastard is up to his neck in it. Yeah," he said into the phone. "Get the lineup ready, please. Thank you." He looked at Michael. "They'll call when they're ready."

Michael felt twitchy under Detective Leo's steady regard.

"You were at David Snyder's the night of the vandalism, so you've actually seen this guy, haven't you?"

Michael shrugged self-consciously. "Well, as much as you can see when a man is wearing a ski mask."

"But you thought there was something distinctive about him?"

"He has a mark on his eyelid," Michael answered, nervously rubbing his fingers on the side seams of his jeans. "I think I'd recognize it if I saw it again. I just wish there was a way to connect him to the vandalism that almost killed Gil Chandler."

"The scaffolding collapse?"

The phone rang and Mitchell answered it, listened, and grunted in response. "Good. We'll be right there." He hung up the phone. "Okay, folks. Let's do this thing."

A man in an expensive suit waited for them outside the door. He sneered at Mitchell. "Detective."

"Counselor. What are you doing here?"

"I believe you plan to have a lineup including my client."

"And how did you find that out?"

The lawyer gave him an oily smile. "Now, that would be telling."

Mitchell scowled and turned away. "This way, Michael."

They entered the lineup room. It was small and they were crowded once the door was closed behind them. A large one-way window offered anonymity as they looked into an adjacent area. Mitchell pushed a button and six men walked through a door, lining up against the far wall.

"They can't see or hear you, so don't be afraid to step closer."

The men were all relatively young, dark-haired, and when they stopped and turned forward, Michael could see they all had dark eyes. The lighting wasn't great, and it was almost impossible for Michael to tell if the one who'd terrorized him was there.

"I don't know. I can't be sure."

"Take your time, Michael," Mitchell said. "We aren't in a hurry."

He did take his time, studying each face. After several minutes, the lawyer made an exasperated noise. "He can't pick him out. Are we done here?"

"Wait." Michael zeroed in on one face, the man on the end to the right. "Can number six come closer?"

Mitchell pushed the button again. "Number six, step closer, please."

He clearly didn't want to, but he took a couple of shuffling steps.

"More?" Mitchell asked. Michael nodded.

"More," Mitchell ordered. And then it was close enough. Cold slipped down Michael's spine.

"It's number six," he announced, taking a step back. At this distance there was no mistaking the rage and the small liver spot on the lid of his right eye.

Mitchell pushed the button again. "Thank you, gentlemen." He turned to the lawyer with a smile. "Looks like your client will be hanging around for a bit after all, counselor."

The others walked toward the exit, but Michael hesitated. Most of the men in the other room filed out, but the one on the end, the one Michael had identified, hadn't moved. He stared, almost as if he could see right through the glass. Michael backed up another step.

"You're sure he can't see me?"

"Absolutely." Mitchell saw him standing at the glass and pushed the button. "You can go."

Still, Wiley didn't move. Just stared, the black eyes filled with rage. Michael took another step and felt the wall at his back. A uniformed officer came in. He handed Mitchell a note, and spared Michael a slight smile and a nod as he left again.

"Michael."

Michael tore his eyes away from the man on the other side of the glass. Mitchell gave him a grim smile.

"They found his car parked in a lot downtown. There was a hacksaw in the back seat."

Michael blinked, his heart beginning to thump hard. He looked back at the angry man in the other room in time to see the black eyes snap with barely leashed fury. As Wiley stared into the two way mirror, the corner of his lips curled up in a sardonic, almost vulpine smile that sent a chill the length of Michael's spine. Another uniformed officer came in behind him and touched his elbow. Shaking him off, Wiley turned away.

"He could hear us." Michael looked at Mitchell. "For that last part, about the hacksaw. Did you see his face?"

For the first time since Michael had met him, he saw a genuine, satisfied expression on Mitchell's careworn face.

"Yeah. I sure did."

CHAPTER FOURTEEN

GIL WAS released from the hospital on the sixth day after the accident. He'd been up and down the hallway on crutches, and the swelling had gone down on his face a lot, allowing him to open his right eye. It was still a Technicolor wonder of bruising. Michael drove him home in his little car, which was almost impossible. They had to scoot the front bucket seat almost into the back seat, but they were finally able to give him enough leg room. Michael bought him sweats to wear, but they had to cut off the right leg at the knee in order to get them on over his cast. Gil didn't care. He was more than ready to be out of the hospital, and Michael was anxious to get him home.

When they pulled into the driveway, the front door to Gil's house opened and their friends spilled out onto the porch. Even Shirley and Beverley were there. Michael was reminded of the weekend they'd painted David's house. There was a full meal of chicken and all the fixings, and three different kinds of pie, no doubt courtesy of the moms. The beer was obviously the result of the guys, but Michael decided if Gil wanted one, that was okay. Any more than that wasn't happening. Nearly every one of the four medications that came home with him read "Do not take with alcohol" on the label.

But Gil drank iced tea with his pain pills, and once a raucous meal in front of the local broadcast of the hometown basketball team was over, the guys headed out. Shirley and Beverley lingered, cleaning up the kitchen, while Gil dozed on the couch.

Michael hadn't really had an opportunity to speak to Gil much while their friends were there, and he approached him now, studying the still-bruised face, taking advantage of the fact his mouth was open to lean in and kiss him.

"Hmm." Gil's eyes opened, and he gave Michael a sleepy smile. "Hey, handsome."

"You're not so bad yourself."

Gil snorted. "I look like Van Gogh's *Starry Night*. All those blues and greens."

Michael touched his face. "It's not that bad."

"It scares me, you know. How good of a liar you are."

"Pfft. You ready for your bed?"

"Oh God, so ready."

"Okay, let me get your crutches." Michael went to get them from the corner as the moms came out of the kitchen.

"We're going on home, Gil." Beverley came to him. "Now, you listen to your doctors and Michael; they've only got your best interests at heart."

"Yes, ma'am." He gave her a lazy salute, and she pressed a kiss to his very discolored forehead.

Shirley grabbed his chin and peered into his eyes. "You take good care of yourself, Gilbert Chandler. I knew your momma, and she'd have kicked your ass if you don't. I might not be able to do it"—he leaned and touched his nose with hers, closing his eyes—"but Bev here can."

Bev laughed. "What she said."

Gil grinned and kissed Shirley gently, and Michael walked them out to their car. He waited until they were locked inside with the ignition started before he backed away, waving as they left the house. He went inside and armed the burglar alarm Jackson had installed, then went to Gil, who was pushing up with his crutches. He'd gotten really good at getting around on them, but he was tired and Michael stayed right behind or beside him, stepping under his arm for the three steps up into the dining room.

Gil was leaning on him pretty heavily, so Michael stayed under his arm as they passed the painting of the old man. "Is that your grandfather?" he asked, gesturing toward the portrait.

"Yeah. My dad's dad. What a character. He was a rumrunner during prohibition, then drove race cars in the thirties and forties. Never met a curse word he didn't love. Taught all us kids to shoot a gun and tune up a car."

Michael smiled. "My mother's dad was a forest ranger, not that you'd ever hear her admit it."

They were in the bedroom now, and Michael helped Gil as far as the edge of the bed. He sat heavily with a deep sigh.

"What do you sleep in, big boy?" Michael asked.

Gil gave him a lazy grin. "Usually just my skivvies."

"That's easy."

Michael helped him pull off his sweats and sweatshirt.

"You staying?" Gil asked, catching Michael's wrist when he would have walked away.

"Until I know for sure Wiley is put away in a big cement cell for a very long time. Attempted murder is typically fifteen to twenty, according to Mitchell." Michael was sure Wiley would be convicted, but he didn't want to tempt fate.

"Why just until then?"

"What?" Michael helped Gil stand long enough to pull back the bedding, then helped him sit and took his crutches to lean on the wall by the bed.

"Why are you only staying until he's convicted?"

Michael looked away as he folded Gil's shirt. "I have a place, Gil. And a lease."

"Don't you like my house?" Michael looked back at him, his mouth slightly open. "I know it's not for everybody," Gil went on.

"Are you nuts? I love midcentury modern, and I love your house."

Gil smiled. "Oh, good. I'm glad." He lay back against his pillows.

"And we'll discuss anything else when you're well." Michael covered him to his chest, tucking the blankets under his arms.

"Killjoy. Will you at least sleep with me? I know I can't do anything for a while. The doctor told me, between my leg and my head, we can't have sex. We can, however, just hold each other. We can do that, Michael. Can't we?"

Michael was embarrassed at how easily he caved. "We can do that. I'll go change in the other room and then come back."

While he was in the guest room, he called David and told him he was staying. Then he threw on sweats and a T-shirt and went to join Gil.

By the time he got there, Pixie, who had made himself scarce for most of the evening while the noisy crowd was there, was stretched out next to Gil, who was idly petting his head.

Michael put his hands on his hips and looked down at the giant cat, who looked right back at him. "You're in my spot," he told him mildly.

Gil opened his eyes. "Down," he ordered firmly, and Pixie gave him a dirty look, then jumped to the floor.

"Great, now he's going to want to eat me." Michael slipped in beside Gil, reaching over his head to turn off the light.

"Naw. You're too stringy."

"Gee thanks, pal."

Gil made a soft, sleepy sound as Michael laid his head carefully on his shoulder.

"But I like you stringy. All those long, lean lines are sexy." Gil caught his hand, pulling it onto his chest and then linking their fingers.

"Okay, I'll allow you to live." Michael was fighting a smile as he snuggled closer. Within moments he was asleep.

THEIR DAYS followed a pretty regular pattern. Michael got up first and made breakfast; Gil was big on scrambled eggs and bacon, and Michael made killer scrambled eggs and bacon, so that worked out well. If Gil had physical therapy, Michael helped him pull on bike shorts and a T-shirt. While Gil was with his therapist, Michael checked work notes and pictures David sent him of the progress on the mansion. It was moving along nicely, and Richard and Lyle had decided on the linens they wanted for the wedding venue. Michael ordered them with a few clicks of the keyboard, then sent an e-mail off to David. By then Gil was done.

The morning Gil went to the neurologist to have the staples removed, he wanted Michael to go in with him.

"I'm having some headaches," Gil confessed to the doctor. "And occasionally my balance is still off."

"Be patient, Gilbert. Your test results look good. It's all resolving faster than even I would have expected." He gave Gil a hand mirror. Gil held it up to look at the scars, and he grimaced.

"I look like I had a zipper in my head."

"Well, for all practical purposes, you did. This too shall fade, my friend. Keep telling yourself 'patience is a virtue.' It won't be long before they're just thin white scars."

Gil turned to Michael. "What do you think?"

Michael came over and looked at the two spots, then impulsively leaned forward and kissed each of them. "It looks to me like it saved your life."

"Okay." Gil gave Dr. Pillai a slight smile. "That's the seal of approval."

After they left, Michael drove south past the children's hospital, and he recalled something he'd meant to share with Gil long before.

"I've seen your murals, you know. The ones in the children's oncology unit. After Richard talked about them, I needed to see for myself." He glanced over at Gil, who was looking at him, an enigmatic expression on his face. "They're stunning. So is the peacock. And the portraits at your house. You're so good, Gil. Have you ever considered doing a show?"

Gil looked away, his ears pink. "When I was a kid, I thought about it. Then I found out you can't make any money at it."

"So, do it for the pleasure. Don't you enjoy it?"

"I love it. It's just finding the time."

"Baby." He waited for Gil to look at him again. "Right now? You have the time."

Gil turned to look thoughtfully out through the window.

DAVID CALLED Michael one morning and asked him to stop by the mansion. Gil happened to have an appointment with the neurologist at the same time, so he took him to Sacred Heart, and since Gil was doing so well on the crutches, Michael stood back and watched him make his way into the elevator. Gil grinned and winked at him as the doors slid shut. Michael went back to his car to drive up the hill to the O'Banyon house. He pulled in the driveway and stared at the old place in wonder.

It looked so clean, so elegant. He got out of his car, trying to take in all of the changes. The river rock foundation and the same stones that created the porch arches were beautiful. He didn't know if the previous old faded paint had hidden their glory, but the pearlized gray, dark gray, and black on the house brought out every color in the granite. It made the hundred-year-old house look like a wonderful combination of timeless charm and modern lines. Michael thought it looked amazing.

He knew the guys were there—all their vehicles were parked on or around the property—but he didn't see any of them. He climbed up to the front door and rang the bell.

It took a few minutes, but Richard answered. When he saw Michael, he opened his arms and pulled him into a hug.

"Oh, Michael." He eased back to look at him. "We haven't seen you since Gil was hurt. I understand he's doing well?"

"He's at the neurologist right now. And he's doing really well. But he's got another three months in the cast, then more than that in PT. It's driving him nuts, but I'm not sure how soon he'll be back to work."

Richard waved that away. "I just want him to be all right. And anything his insurance won't cover, our homeowners' will. I don't want him having to worry about money right now."

"Thank you. That's really nice of you."

"And what about you?" Richard's gaze was ardent but cautious, as if he didn't want to overstep, and Michael felt him searching his face. "I know you left your last job. Are you doing all right financially?"

"I'm fine," Michael assured him. "But thank you for asking. I really do appreciate it."

"All right. I believe David and Jackson are waiting for you out back."

"Thank you." He turned and went through the massive ballroom. Vern and his guys were in the process of repairing the plaster on the walls, and he stopped long enough to say hi before continuing through to one of the glass doors that led outside. David was seated at a patio table with design books open around him, and Jackson appeared to be repairing the gazebo that sat on the back corner of the property.

"Hey." Michael walked to David, who looked up, his face breaking into a smile.

"Michael!" He stood and pulled him into a tight embrace, then called over his shoulder. "Jackson! Michael's here."

Jackson turned, then set down the new cornice piece he'd been working on and headed toward them across the lawn. "How are you?" Jackson hugged him too.

"I'm okay. Gil's at the doctor down at Sacred Heart, so I don't have long."

"Understood. Take a seat."

Michael pulled out the chair next to David, briefly studying the sample books of wallpaper and drapery swatches. "Ballroom?"

David nodded. "Hopefully you'll be back before we start hanging the new silk wall covering."

"Oh joy." Michael grimaced. David grinned.

"Listen, there's a reason we asked you to come by." Jackson pulled out another chair, and David's grin faded.

"Okay." Michael looked between them, suddenly nervous. "Is it bad?"

"Not at all. We just wanted you to have a heads-up." He looked to David, who sat back down in his chair with a short sigh.

"We heard from Detective Mitchell last night," David said. "The man they caught, the one you identified in the lineup, his name is Brent Wiley."

"Yeah, Mitchell told me."

"The DA has decided they have enough for an indictment. He's being charged with the damage to the house and with sabotaging the scaffolding too. He's also being held because he can't make bail."

"Good." Michael felt a moment of fierce satisfaction.

"Yeah," Jackson agreed. He paused, his expression serious. "We want you to know because you're probably going to have to testify at his trial."

"Oh." Michael let that sink in, frowning slightly.

David touched his hand. "Are you okay?"

"Yeah." Michael sighed. "I mean, I think I always knew that I would have to testify, because I was there. It only makes sense. I'm just so glad they caught him."

"So are we." Jackson's voice was calm and measured. "And they feel certain the case against him for what he did at David's place is solid. Their problem is making the case involving the scaffolding."

"Wait. They found the hacksaw in his fucking car." Michael looked between them, flabbergasted.

"His lawyer is saying it was a coincidence."

"Oh, for fuck's sakes."

Jackson shook his head. "I know, man. But the case is still circumstantial, and Mitchell thinks we should make sure the stronger case involving the vandalism puts him away."

"Isn't attempted murder the one they should try to prosecute?" Michael was so angry. The son of a bitch had tried to kill Gil; how could he get away with that?

"They've got attempted murder, Michael." Jackson studied him as if watching for his reaction.

The truth finally dawned on Michael, and he felt like he'd been doused in ice water. By coming after him with the shovel, Brent Wiley had tried to kill him. Michael's hands were cold and trembling. "Oh, right. Well. Okay, then."

"The DA is going to want to sit with you and discuss your testimony," David said. "It'll probably be late summer before that happens. Wiley has been charged, and his bail was set at two hundred and fifty thousand. There's no way for him to come up with twenty-five grand."

"Yeah, okay." Michael's voice sounded faint even to his own ears. "Is Mitchell sure he's the only one involved?"

A line formed between Jackson's dark brows. "Why? Do you have a reason to think there's more than one?"

Michael wished he hadn't said anything about what nagged at him when he couldn't sleep in the wee hours of the morning.

"Michael?" Jackson pressed.

Michael shook his head and slipped his cold hands into his armpits. "No. I don't."

"Michael?" David persisted. His green eyes looked stormy behind the lenses of his glasses.

"I don't. Not really. It's just… a feeling. Probably stupid."

"Sweetheart, you had a really scary experience." David leaned closer, putting his hand on Michael's arm. "I freaked out, and all he did was break my car window."

"And all those months, when you thought someone was watching the house? Do you think it was just Wiley doing it? Didn't the guy have a job?"

"He delivered pizza—for the Domino's on Sixteenth." Which was less than a mile from David's house.

"Oh. That would give him the opportunity, wouldn't it? But—why? I mean, clearly he hates the gay, but why us specifically?"

David gently rubbed Michael's arm. "They think he delivered the pizza the day we moved Gil's furniture into my house."

That was back before Thanksgiving. And almost every vehicle in the driveway and parked out front had some sort of rainbow sticker on it. It was startling that the suspect might've been the same guy who delivered pizza to a house with six gay men in it.

"Oh God. It fits, doesn't it?"

Jackson nodded.

"Do they know why he hates gay people so much?" Michael leaned forward intently.

David sighed. "Honey, why does anyone?"

It was a question without an answer, but one Michael knew would haunt him, maybe always. He pushed back his chair and stood. "I need to go get Gil."

Jackson stood too. "You okay to drive?"

"I'm fine."

David didn't look convinced.

Michael bent and kissed him on the cheek. "I am. Don't worry, Mama Bear. I'm tough."

David's smile was weak, and his eyes looked suspiciously bright. Michael needed to get out of there before they all ended up having a big group cry.

Of course, when he picked Gil up, it took him all of five seconds to know something was wrong. He'd looked so jubilant when he came out too.

"It's nothing," Michael said. "Give me your news instead."

Gil stared at his profile for so long Michael wondered if he was memorizing his features.

"Let's try this. You tell me what's going on, or I'm calling Jackson."

"What makes you think Jackson knows?"

"Jackson knows everything."

Michael hated how true that was. He sighed but told Gil what he'd learned. About how they were making a case for all of the incidents, from Jackson's truck clear through to the scaffolding.

"But that's good, isn't it?"

"It is," Michael agreed. "I'll just have to testify against him, because I'm the only one who's seen him."

"Okay." Gil didn't seem to understand why it was a problem.

"He's fucking scary, okay? I mean, I think he's nuts, and what if… what if he gets off and I was the one who tried to put him away?"

"Baby. You're hyperventilating. Take a deep breath. Here"—he gestured to a fast-food restaurant—"pull into Sonic and park."

Michael did, pulling into the drive-in and immediately taking the car out of gear. He shoved his trembling hands under his arms, his brow furrowed. "I wasn't hyperventilating." Although he was very afraid.

"It doesn't matter. Now, look at me."

Michael took a deep breath, just to prove he could, then turned to him.

"Babe, come here." Gil held out his arms.

Michael looked at him as if he'd lost his mind. "Come there, how?"

"Unfasten your damned seat belt, lift across the console, and sit on my lap."

Michael was horrified. "I am not going to sit on your lap!"

"Can I have your order, please?"

Michael glared at the speaker on the order menu, aghast someone had been listening.

"Give us a few seconds, okay?" Gil reached over Michael and unfastened his seat belt, then pulled on his arm.

"Order whenever you're ready."

"Gilbert." Michael resisted him, but not in any significant way, and Gil was much stronger than he was. He lifted him, then sat him sidesaddle against the passenger door. Michael held himself stiffly, afraid of hurting Gil's leg. Gil was undeterred and put his arms around him.

"Okay, first of all, everything you've told me is a good thing. They've got the guy, Michael. He's in police custody. You were able to identify him. He can't hurt any of us anymore."

Michael, still stiff with his legs stretched into the driver's seat, gave him a dark look. "What if he gets out, Gil? What if somehow he gets off? It happens."

"If it happens, we'll deal with it when the time comes. But you have to remember something, babe." He ran his hands up Michael's back, pulling him in until he had no choice but to lean against the big chest. Defeated, he laid his head on the broad shoulder. "You aren't alone this time. You won't be alone."

Michael sighed. "Gilbert, you can't be with me every minute of every day."

Gil's embrace tightened. "Care to take a bet?"

"Gil."

"Michael."

Michael closed his eyes, inhaling the scent of the man, allowing himself to luxuriate in being held again in the strong arms. "I'm not worried about me," he admitted finally.

"So, Jackson is with David all the time, Vern and Manny are together, at least temporarily, although if Manny doesn't kill him it will be a goddamned miracle. And I've got you. We're good."

Michael turned his face into Gil's neck. "I'm still scared," he whispered.

"Of what, sweetheart?"

Michael closed his eyes. "How would I take care of you, if someone tried to get at you again? I don't think I could take it, Gil. The day you fell—" A shudder moved over his body from his head to his toes. "—I don't think I could live through something like that again."

"Ah, babe."

"Have you decided on your order?" the tinny voice asked.

"Seriously?" Gil growled. "We'll let you fucking know."

There was a static-laced click as the speaker shut off.

"Well, that must've entertained the kitchen."

Michael couldn't help it; he giggled. And as he giggled, Gil began to laugh, and within moments they were laughing together for the first time in… well, it felt like months. Michael finally relaxed fully against the wall of Gil's chest.

"I won't be able to help being worried, Gil." He ran his hands up Gil's sides, then kissed his neck.

"That's okay, as long as you don't let it take over. Take a deep breath and just be proud of the fact that you got him."

"I didn't get him," Michael scoffed. "He was on the other side of a two-way mirror, and I about shit my pants."

"And yet you still identified him, right?" Gil persisted.

Michael exhaled loudly. "Yeah, I did."

"Okay, then. Be proud of that. He's where he can't hurt anyone else. That's a good thing. And when you have to testify against him, I will be right there in the front row. Now, lean back and look at me."

Michael met Gil's steady gaze.

"Michael, I love you."

A slow, sweet warmth stole through Michael's chest. "I love you too."

"And it's taken us a damned long time to get here."

"Yeah, it has. Also my fault."

"Doesn't matter. We're here. And personally, I'm just really glad we've arrived. Can we just enjoy it now? Please?"

Michael stared into the large hazel eyes with the long lashes he loved, and slowly, he nodded.

"Thank Christ." Gil kissed him gently, then pulled back. "Now, let's go eat. I'm starving, and I'd just as soon not have to look at whoever finally comes out here to take our order."

Michael laughed. "How about Shari's?"

"Excellent. Their pie rocks, and I feel like celebrating."

Carefully, Michael climbed over the console and back into the driver's seat. When he turned to fasten his seat belt, he realized four girls in the next parking place in a convertible VW Bug were staring at him. Impulsively, he gave them a cheery wave before putting the car into gear. He was delighted when the girls watched them go, giggling and waving back.

CHAPTER FIFTEEN

THEY WALKED in the door as long shadows grew across the lawn and softened light filtered through the house's windows. Gil managed to make it all the way into his bedroom on his own, even taking the stairs with little difficulty, and Michael marveled again at how strong he was, how fit in spite of the weeks spent without the physical activity he was used to. When they got as far as the bedroom, Michael went to the bureau to take out sweats and a T-shirt so Gil could change out of the khaki board shorts and the green polo he was wearing.

Gil sat on the edge of the bed, taking off his loafers. "Hey, I never told you my news."

Michael came back to him, laid the comfortable clothes beside him, then took the polo and folded it after Gil pulled it off over his head. "No, you didn't."

Gil stood, leaning on Michael's shoulder as he unbuttoned his fly with his other hand. The shorts slipped over his hips and down his legs, and he sat, pulling them off over his feet. He was left in just his Jockeys, and Michael admired the beautiful big body even as he took the shorts from his hand. He folded them, then took the shirt and shorts to put them away.

"Dr. Pillai gave me a clean bill of health."

Michael came back, standing beside him, waiting to see if he was going to need help. He'd been more and more able to do for himself, but clothes still occasionally got hung up on the cast. "That's wonderful," he said, meaning it.

"Yeah, I haven't had any headaches in a few days, and my latest CT scan looked good, so... he said I can start a more active form of physical therapy. He also said I don't need to curtail... certain activities anymore."

"Okay." Michael smiled at him. "So...." He was still sort of confused as to what Gil meant.

Slowly, Gil turned and lifted his legs onto the bed, leaning back on his elbows with a slow-spreading smile on his face. "So...."

Michael stared at him for another moment, admiring the long, fit body, and then it hit him. "Oh!"

"Now he gets it," Gil teased, shaking his head.

"Oh, shut up."

Michael pulled off his jacket and threw it on the floor, then sat on the bed next to Gil's hip and leaned forward until they were inches apart.

"Hello." He smiled into Gil's face.

"Hello, there." Gil's answering grin was slow, and so sexy it made Michael's toes curl.

"So, did Dr. Pillai clarify which 'certain activities' he was referring to?"

Gil pretended to ponder, looking toward the ceiling. "Let me see if I can recall his actual wording." He cleared his throat. "Intercourse might be too strenuous at this juncture, but other sexual activities, including orgasm, should be acceptable."

"Thank Christ." Michael's dick started to react to just the idea of an orgasm.

"No shit," Gil retorted. "Now, I do believe one of us is overdressed."

"Is that right?" Michael looked down at himself. "Must be me."

"I would say."

Michael started to stand, then noticed the thick bulge of Gil's cock distending the front of his white Jockeys.

"My goodness, Gilbert. Is this for me?" He gave him a flirtatious smile before tracing the thick length through the soft cotton. The tip was peeking above the elastic waistband, and he rubbed the reddened tip with his index finger. Gil caught his breath.

"I haven't had a hard-on in a year that wasn't for you, Michael."

Michael felt the words to his core, and his teasing expression softened. "You say the sweetest things."

"I try."

"You're good."

Michael eased the waistband over Gil's erection, pushing the snug pants to the middle of Gil's thighs. "I think the least I can do is be good right back. And I may question some of my skills, but this isn't one of them." With that he lowered his head, licking a long stripe from the base of Gil's prick to the very tip before circling it with his tongue.

Gil gasped. "Clothes, Michael. Get rid of the clothes."

"You don't like me staying dressed while you're naked?" Michael lifted and nuzzled Gil's heavy balls.

"Maybe at some point. Right now I want access to as much skin as I can get my hands on."

"Yes, sir." Michael stood, and knowing how Gil loved his body, he took his time divesting himself of his clothes. He unbuttoned the blue button-down, pulled it from his waistband, and eased it off his shoulders, allowing it to fall to the floor. Then he unbuttoned his fly and pushed down his snug jeans and briefs at the same time, remembering at the last moment that he hadn't taken off his shoes.

"How sexy is this?" he laughed, unzipping his boots and then hopping from foot to foot to take them off. He was half-hard, so his dick bounced as he did it. "So sexy."

"Oh, I don't know." Gil had eased his Jockeys off and threw them aside, then lay back, his dick in his hand. He stroked it as he watched Michael. "That little dance you're doing there is pretty arousing."

Michael stripped off his socks, then bent and stripped off Gil's. "You're weird." He climbed on the bed and straddled Gil's knees. "Fortunately for you, I like weird. I also—" He lifted Gil's thick cock from where it lay, heavy with swollen veins, against his thigh. "—like this."

He opened his mouth, and took Gil in slowly, relaxing his throat until the tip of his nose brushed Gil's dark brown pubic hair.

Gil grew larger as Michael worked him with his mouth, so much so that he needed to wrap his hand around the wide base, using his saliva to ease the movement of his fingers as he worked the head with his mouth and tongue. Gil made some lovely, needy sounds above him, which just made Michael determined to wring more from him. He went down on the hard cock as far as he could, using his throat muscles around the head, working it as he pumped with his hand. The bittersweet, salty taste of precome filled his mouth and he hummed around the mouthful. It wasn't long before Gil gripped the back of his neck, moving his hips restlessly.

"Michael," he said in warning. "Baby, it's been too long. I can't hold off."

Michael rubbed his hand over Gil's thick, lightly furred thigh and smiled up at him around the hardness. Instead of pulling away, he went down again, swallowing around the head and working the length more firmly. Gil made a startled sound and arched, and Michael watched him as he moved his fist up and down and his tongue worked the crown. Gil's eyes were clinched closed but his mouth was open, and he made a startled sound as he stiffened, pumping bursts of thick, salty semen in to Michael's throat. He swallowed it down, lips and tongue working him until Gil made a protesting noise, grabbing Michael's shoulder. Understanding that his skin had attained the sharp sensitivity of postorgasm, Michael pulled off and rested his head on Gil's thigh, studying the slick sheen of sweat on his skin and the rise and fall of his massive chest. After a few minutes, Gil raised his head and looked down at him.

"Come here."

Michael climbed slowly up his body, coming to rest with his arms on Gil's chest and his chin resting on them.

Gil wiped his hand over his face, then looked into Michael's eyes. "I knew you had hidden talents." He reached down and pushed dark hair back with a gentle touch. "That was… amazing. Thank you."

Michael's smile was slow but genuine. "You're welcome."

"Are you going to allow me to return the favor?"

Michael shrugged negligently. "It's not really necessary."

Gil angled his head to one side. "The hell." Gil scowled. "Get your ass up here." Slowly, Michael pushed up. Gil patted his chest. "Straddle my neck with your knees." Michael gave him a dubious look but pushed up until his knees were on either side of Gil's head. His dick, which had come down quite a bit while he'd been blowing Gil, perked up at the vicinity of Gil's mouth. Gil stroked him several times.

Michael angled his hips forward with a pleased sound. "Nice."

"Yeah? Okay, up."

"Huh?"

"Get up onto your knees, lean on the headboard, and put your dick in my mouth."

"Pushy," Michael complained. Gil grabbed one asscheek and pulled him forward until he was in the position Gil wanted.

"Now, grab the headboard."

"What, you think you're going to rock my world that much?" Michael teased wryly.

"Just do it." Gil smacked his ass lightly. "And shut up."

"Hey!" Michael started to complain but stopped when Gil wrapped his hands around his hips and pulled him closer, opened his mouth, and took him into the sweet, hot suction. "Oh God," Michael moaned when Gil pulled back, grabbing on to the headboard. Gil mapped the delicate skin with his tongue, then slipped a finger in his mouth along with Michael's cock, sucking both until they were sloppy wet. It felt amazing, and it was all Michael could do to not fuck his mouth.

He stiffened when Gil ran the wet finger from his balls over his taint to the beginning of the crease in his ass. Slipping his fingers into Michael's crack, he instantly found the sensitive furled opening. The tip of his finger pressed against him, and Gil pulled off his cock.

"Bear down," he ordered. Michael looked into his upturned face. "Bear down, Michael. I know for a fact you've done this."

"Shut up," Michael grumbled. But the next time Gil pressed against the ring of tight muscle, he pushed and it was much easier for Gil's wide finger to slip inside. Michael bit down hard on his lower lip at the sensation of his entrance stretching in combination with the warm, wet suction of Gil's mouth.

"Oh yeah," he murmured, unable to fight the need to thrust, even if just shallowly. Then Gil pushed in farther, found Michael's prostate, and Michael gasped, muscles stiffening.

"Oh, he likes that," Gil pulled off long enough to say. Gil began to massage the spongy gland with the tip of his curled finger, and Michael pushed back into his touch with a whimper. He'd known he had a hypersensitive prostate since he was fourteen and he'd accidentally found it while beating off in bed. His ass to his dick lit up like a Christmas tree. He'd come so hard he'd shouted and then had to scramble back into his pajama bottoms when the housekeeper had come to find out what was wrong.

Gil hollowed his cheeks, bobbing on Michael's cock while he pressed more firmly against his gland, and Michael's arms and legs began to shake.

"I'm going to come," he gasped, looking down at Gil. Gil nodded, his other hand slipping around to grab an asscheek, and he pulled Michael in as far as he could go. Moments later a final caress against his prostate sent him over the edge, and all Michael's muscles locked. He shook as he spilled himself down Gil's throat in hot spurts. Finally, after hanging, gripping the headboard, and shuddering for several seconds, Michael's muscles went limp and he collapsed slowly onto his side. Gil caught him, easily pulling him down until they were lying face-to-face.

"Okay there?" Gil tenderly pushed Michael's hair out of his eyes.

"Mmfl."

Gil smiled, caressing the side of his face. "So, is that an admission that your world was well and truly rocked?"

It took a few seconds, but Michael was finally able to answer somewhat coherently. "Your ego, dude. And I'm fine." His voice softened. "Just, I can't brain."

"It's okay." Gil wrapped his arms around Michael's waist and pulled him in. "You sucked my brains out through my dick a few minutes ago. I get it."

They shifted around enough that Gil was finally able to pull the thick comforter up over their shoulders, and he dropped his arm easily around Michael's slender waist.

"I love you, baby," he murmured and dropped a soft kiss onto the tip of his nose.

Michael didn't know why, but the gesture flooded him with tenderness. He gently brushed his fingers over the dark pink scars on Gil's head. "I love you too, Gilbert."

Gil yawned. "I know you have a thing about muscles, Michael. Have you got a scar kink too?"

Michael snorted softly. "Only yours."

"Good to know."

Gil snuggled farther down under the comforter, pressing the side of his face into his pillow. He pulled Michael closer, resting his chin on the top of his head. Michael luxuriated in being surrounded by all the strength, the leashed power in Gil's body.

"Gonna rest for a few," Gil muttered.

"I'll be here when you wake up," Michael promised.

"Mmm, good."

Michael listened as Gil's breathing slowed, his chest rising and falling with quiet, soft sounds. He rubbed his hand over the smooth, warm skin under his cheek and found the solid heartbeat under his palm.

"I'll be here, Gilbert," he whispered, making a solemn vow to the man who slept in his arms.

And he would be. No matter what happened with the trial, no matter what the future brought.

He'd be there.

DIANA COPLAND began writing in the seventh grade, when she shamelessly combined elements of *Jane Eyre* and *Dark Shadows* to produce an overwrought Gothic tale that earned her an A- in creative writing, thanks entirely to the generosity of her teacher.

She wrote for pure enjoyment for the next three decades before discovering LiveJournal and a wonderful group of supportive writers, who encouraged her to try her hand at original gay fiction.

Born and raised in southern California, Diana moved to the Pacific Northwest after losing a beloved spouse to AIDS in 1995.

She lives in eastern Washington with three obnoxious cats, near her two wonderful adult children.

David,
Renewed

DIANA COPLAND

Delta Restorations: Novel One

When interior designer David Snyder buys a beautiful century-old house in eastern Washington, he is reeling with heartbreak and looking for somewhere to put down roots. Unfortunately his new home comes with a laundry list of problems: electrical, plumbing, heating… things David knows nothing about. When his mother offers him the business card of a local handyman, David pictures an overweight, balding man in his fifties. But Jackson Henry couldn't be further from that stereotype.

Dark-haired, muscular, and handsome, Jackson left a large construction firm in Seattle to take care of his sick mother. However, his hometown still has an active "good old boy" network, and finding employment in construction is almost impossible for an openly gay man. Determined to persevere, Jackson takes odd jobs as a handyman. He's exactly what David needs—in more ways than one.

David isn't ready for his attraction to Jackson, not considering the way his last relationship ended. But as the two men get to know each other, it becomes clear that the heart often knows best, and it rewards those willing to listen.

www.dreamspinnerpress.com

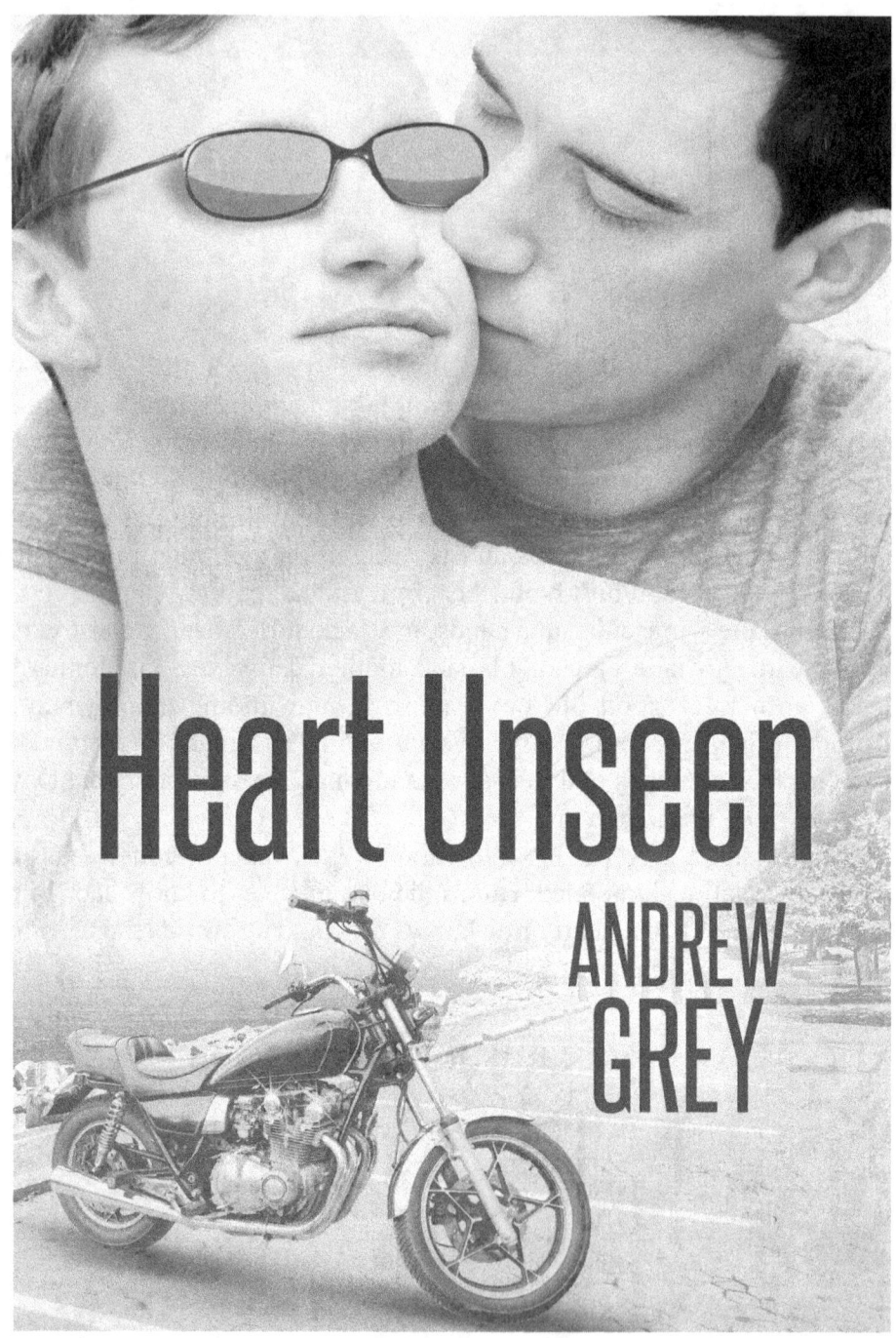

Heart Unseen

ANDREW
GREY

Also from Dreamspinner Press

www.dreamspinnerpress.com

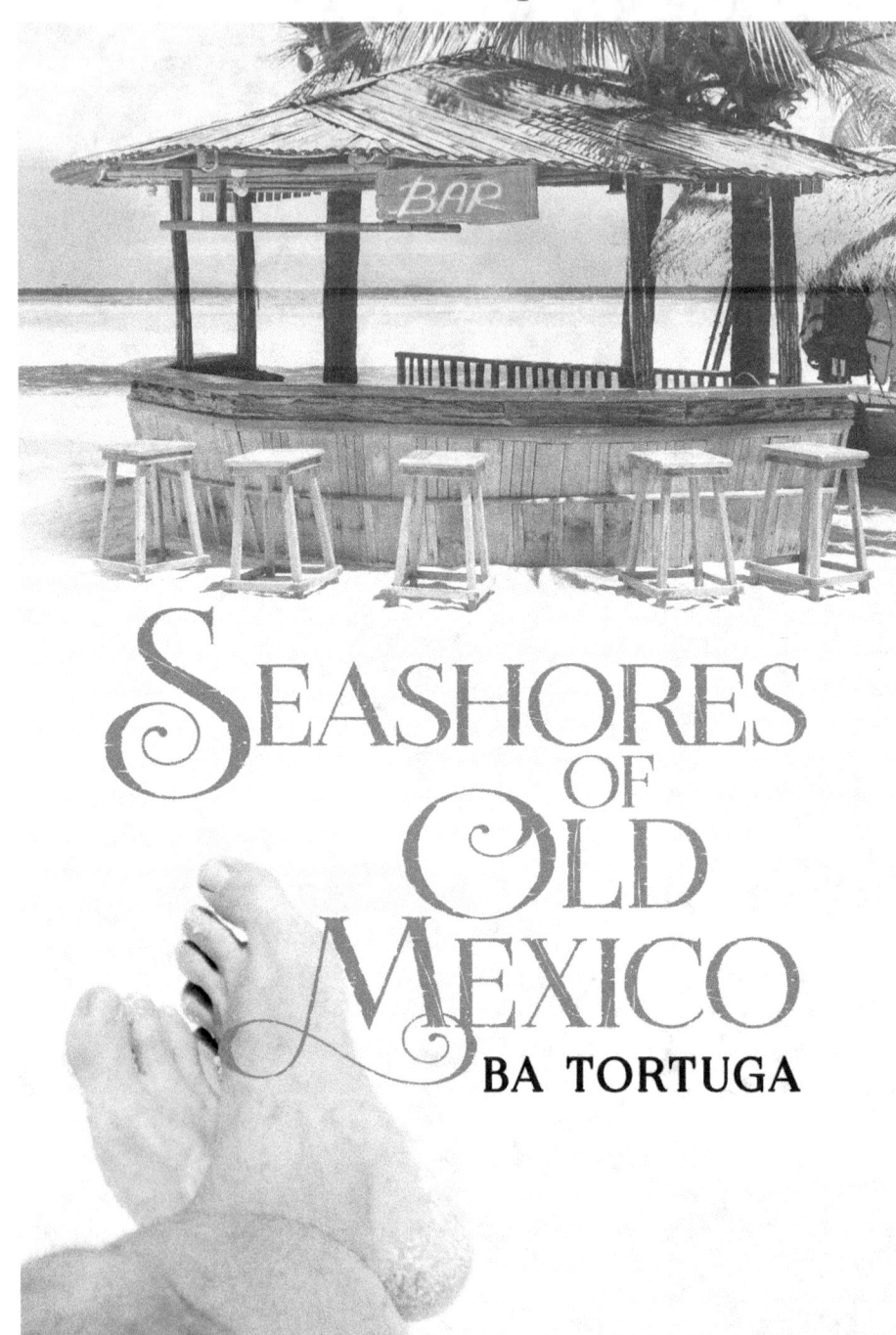

Also from Dreamspinner Press

DREAMSPUN DESIRES

TALL, DARK, AND DEPORTED

Bru Baker

Crossing the border into love.

www.dreamspinnerpress.com